JUNKER BLUES

CHRIS KELSEY

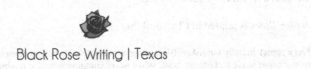

Black Rose Writing | Texas

First printing

This is a work of fiction. Names, characters, businesses, places, events, and incidents are either the products of the author's imagination or used in a fictitious manner. Any resemblance to actual persons, living or dead, or actual events is purely coincidental.

ISBN: 978-1-68433-954-9
PUBLISHED BY BLACK ROSE WRITING
www.blackrosewriting.com

Printed in the United States of America
Suggested Retail Price (SRP) $19.95

Junker Blues is printed in Chaparral Pro

*As a planet-friendly publisher, Black Rose Writing does its best to eliminate unnecessary waste to reduce paper usage and energy costs, while never compromising the reading experience. As a result, the final word count vs. page count may not meet common expectations.

To the good ones. You know who you are.

*Special thanks to Lisa and Judy Kelsey
for their long attention spans.*

JUNKER BLUES

PROLOGUE

The times, they are a-changin'.

I first heard Bob Dylan sing those words on a public television show a few years back. I do not recall being impressed. In fact, if you want to know the truth, I remember being fairly *un*impressed.

Back then I thought young Bob was just a pale imitation of my fellow-Okie, Woody Guthrie, although I expect I was being extra judgmental, since Woody's one of my all-time heroes.

To my eyes and ears, Dylan tried everything short of plastic surgery to be as much like Woody as he possibly could. He wore his hair stuck straight up from his head, just like Woody. He dressed in a work shirt and jeans, same as Woody. Dylan even affected Woody's sunken-cheeked, half-starved countenance—the difference being, with Woody it wasn't a pose, but the toll taken by a life of riding the rails, living in hobo camps, and being poorly recompensed for his music and other labors. I reckoned young Mr. Dylan had traveled an easier path, but even if he hadn't, he was still too young and baby-faced and well-fed to be mistaken for a down-at-the-heels Dust Bowl refugee like Woody Guthrie. I'll be honest. I changed the channel before the song was halfway done.

It was only later, after I started hearing it everywhere, that I appreciated how relevant that song was. The world just about spun off its axis in the 1960s. Give credit where it's due: Bob Dylan saw it and sang about it in a way that touched people where they live.

(I still don't think he has much of a voice, but Woody kind of sang through his nose, too, if I'm to be honest.)

The place I live is called Burr, Oklahoma, in Tilghman County, snug up against the border of the Texas panhandle. I'm the town's police chief and have been for a good number of years.

Lately I've had ample reason to think about Mr. Dylan's song. Judging by the lyrics, he seems to think change is a good thing. I guess it is when it comes to some matters. Given the nature of my job and my pessimistic temperament, however, I hope you'll forgive me for dwelling on the negative side.

If you've had your head in the sand these last few years and need to be convinced the pace of change on this planet is moving faster than is healthy, I'd advise you to watch the nightly news, where accounts of humankind's ever-growing capacity for venality and corruption are on regular view. I remember when I was a kid hearing our president Franklin Delano Roosevelt say on the radio: "The only thing we have to fear is fear itself." That guy we got in the White House now appeared on TV not long ago just to tell everyone he wasn't a crook. You wouldn't think a President of the United States would feel the need to say that, but Nixon did, because he is a crook, and everyone knows it. In FDR's time, we fought wars to save the world. These days, we fight them to help politicians get reelected. We thought we had finished with Vietnam, yet here it is heating up again, two years later. Some people say Nixon plans to get us back into it as part of some bassackward way to save his hide. All I can say is, I hope to hell they're wrong.

The boys and girls in Washington aren't the only culprits. This past July, some maniac set off a bunch of bombs in Los Angeles; one of them exploded at the LA Airport and killed three people. That's a special brand of crazy, right there. It reminded me of the slaughter of those Israeli athletes at the '72 Olympics. The newspapers have a name for attacks like that. They call it terrorism. Whatever you want to call it, I reckon it's something we're going to have to live with for a while.

The most recent world event to have affected us here in western Oklahoma is the Middle East oil embargo. It's been going on for about a year now. "Affected" probably isn't the right word. "Transformed" might be more to the point.

If you follow the news, you know all about it, so I won't bother to explain in much depth. Suffice to say, some of the Muslim countries over there got fed up with the United States' support of Israel and decided to teach us a lesson by refusing to sell us their black gold. In the old days, we would've just flipped them the bird and drilled our own. Oil's something we've always had a lot of. Somewhere along the line, however, we calculated it was cheaper to buy it from a country like Saudi Arabia than drill for it ourselves. That's how they were able to stomp on our necks with this oil embargo. As soon as they cut us off, gas prices went through the roof.

For most of the country, it was a mess. For Oklahomans, it was a chance to harvest a good deal of cash.

If someone from New York or California knows anything about our state, it's typically one of three things. First, our state university has the best football team this side of the NFL. Second, every inch of land within our borders once belonged to the Indians, until it didn't anymore. Third, we've done all our football-playing and land-stealing on top of an ocean of oil.

That third thing is the biggest reason the second thing came to pass. The Indians had the land and the oil. The white folks wanted it. In this country, what white folks want, they get. That's what happened here. We wanted it, we got it. Now we've come to depend on it. Oklahoma's economy lives and dies with the petroleum industry. When gas prices are high, we're driving Cadillacs and eating rib-eye steaks; when they're low, it's broken-down trucks and store-brand headcheese.

That embargo hit, and it seemed like overnight everyone around here was in the oil and gas business. New companies sprang up out of nowhere. Old companies stepped up their drilling. In Burr we had hundreds of oil field workers move in. New motels rose out of the red clay and became more-or-less-permanent homes for many. Farmers rented camping space for workers to pitch their tents. Real estate speculators built fancy houses. Residents began taking in boarders.

We also got more places for people to shop. A strip mall opened on the main north-south thoroughfare. We used to have just one sit-down restaurant and a couple of drive-ins. Now we've got two new diners and a

McDonalds, meaning you can finally buy breakfast in this town on your way to work. Instead of that old dump of a Piggly Wiggly downtown, we've got a big new Safeway and a 7-11. If you need new underwear, or a toy for your child, or a twelve-gauge shotgun, or pretty much anything, really, TG&Y opened a huge new store on the outskirts that will accommodate your spending needs.

Burr is still not much more than a wide spot in the road, but the spot's a lot wider than it used to be.

Drilling's not the only thing that's booming. For example, we've got a brand-new air-conditioned livestock auctioning facility the size of the Houston Astrodome. It's transformed the local agriculture business. What were once small family farms are turning into huge corporate feed lots, some of them so smelly, folks sell their houses just to get upwind of them. It's led to an increase in jobs, though. The Cudahy company recognized the advantage of having so much product close at hand and opened a meatpacking plant in Butcherville, a small town north of Burr, putting more people to work. That's a good thing.

Of course, with the good comes the bad.

Or, depending on your point of view, you might say: With the bad comes more bad.

At one time, folks here in America's outback never thought we'd have to deal with the same troubles as Chicago or Los Angeles or Kansas City. I'll bet those folks still write yearly letters to Santa. You've probably heard the saying, "Shit rolls downhill." We're living proof.

In the first ten years I was chief, we had a couple of murders. In the seven-plus years since 1966, we've had almost a dozen. That's one-half of one percent of our current population. An equivalent number of homicides in a city like New York would come out to something like 40,000. Think about that.

In fact, crime has increased across the board. Burr has had more rapes, robberies, and assaults in the last few years than in the entire history of the town before 1970. I don't expect that trend to change any time soon.

Worst of all are the drugs. When I was a kid, we had our share of bootlegging, but illegal drugs? They were never a problem. Now?

Oh yeh, they're a problem.

The times, they are a-changin'.

I doubt Mr. Dylan was thinking of towns like ours when he wrote that. He doesn't know us any better than we know him. I'll tell you what, though. Over the years, that song of his had an impact on at least one small-town police chief.

It's a pretty good song, but more than that, it's one hell of a warning.

CHAPTER 1

It was one of those days—and I've had many like it—when I'm tempted to exchange my current job for one hauling nitroglycerin over the Andes on a unicycle or scrubbing the undercarriage of a moving freight train with a toothbrush. In other words, something less stressful than being police chief of a town that, until recently, was so small it didn't even have its own zip code.

I'd stuck it out until almost quitting time, and still the outer office of our little cinderblock police station was crowded with people—most of them hot and sweaty and irritated to no end.

My dispatcher Cindy Bartlett had it worse than any of us, trying to answer the phone and simultaneously deal with a line of folks waiting to buy passes to the town dump.

It used to be, anyone could use our dump, until the local citizenry got outraged by the monumental injustice of having their taxes pay for the disposal of foreigners' trash.

Suddenly, they decided they didn't like that their empty Hi-C cans and leftover green bean casseroles were being forced to cohabitate with morally suspect garbage from nearby communities. Burr's Dump for Burr's Trash, that was their motto. The town council succumbed and passed an ordinance requiring a dumping permit available only to citizens of Burr and our northern neighbor, Butcherville. For some reason, they thought it a good idea to issue all the permits on a single day at a single place: Friday, August

9, 1974, at the police station. I got mine by coming in early, but by the time we started selling them at 8:30, there was a line. For the rest of the day, we did almost nothing but sell dump permits.

Well, mostly Cindy sold them, but we all chipped in.

Presently, a skinny shirtless fella with eyes as red as a baboon's rear end was acting out a fantastical story to my deputy chief, about how black widow spiders had crawled into his ears and taken up residence in his cerebral cortex. Angel dust can have strange effects on people, or so I've been told.

I was trying with no success to calm an elderly woman who insisted my dog had been getting into her trash. Ten years ago she might've been right, but my dog's been deceased for quite some time. I tried to explain, but that just got her back up. She said she'd had enough of my lies and intended to complain to the town council. I told her to have at it, albeit in a more polite way, whereupon she turned on one orthopedic heel and waddled out the door like an arthritic penguin.

I closed the door to my closet-sized office, only to have it swing open again, courtesy of my auburn-haired deputy chief. She had extricated herself from the guy with the spiders on the brain and now had important news to impart. I asked her to close the door behind her, as I couldn't understand what she had to say through the noise. She did, lowering the racket by two-thirds.

"I don't appreciate you slamming the door in my face, buddy," she said with a pretend scowl.

Even though I'm her boss, I have to let her talk to me that way, since she's also my wife.

"Didn't mean to," I said. "Sorry, Red."

She has to let me call her that for essentially the same reason. I am the only one afforded that honor. Everyone else calls her Karen. Her last name used to be Dean. Now it's Hardy.

"I didn't see you there," I said. "What's on your mind?"

She gave me a once-over. "You're not wearing your new shirt," she said.

Last spring, we ordered short-sleeved uniform shirts for the department. Shipment was delayed repeatedly, and we didn't get them until about a week ago. Too late, in my book.

"What's the point?" I asked. "Fall's just around the corner."

"That's not what the thermometer says. It got over 100 degrees today."

I shrugged. "I can roll 'em up just as easy. Short sleeves make me look like a high school English teacher." I hoped she wouldn't ask what I meant by that because I wasn't sure myself.

"Well, you're not the only one who's not wearing them," she replied. "Lester hasn't picked his up, either. Anyway, as I was about to say, you need to hang around until Bernard gets here."

Lester is Lester Filer, the newest addition to the Burr Police Department. Bernard is Bernard Cousins, current Tilghman County Deputy, and the man Lester replaced. For years Bernard was my deputy chief, until the county sheriff, Keith Belcher, hired him away about a year ago.

It's not like Keith stole him from us; he did it as a favor to me. We needed another officer. My town council said we couldn't afford one. I griped to Keith about it. He had money in his budget, so he volunteered to hire Bernard as a deputy and assign him to Burr more-or-less full-time. We figured the council couldn't expect us to function with only three full-time officers (including me), so they'd have to let us replace him. Our underhanded scheme worked to perfection. Keith hired Bernard. I promoted Karen, and the council let me hire Lester. The net result was, I gained an additional officer on the county's dime.

"Why do I need to wait for Bernard?" I usually do anyway, but I had reason to get out of there quick.

"You need to tell him about the graffiti. Pete Deskin over at the tag agency says someone spray-painted a swastika on their dumpster."

"Silver paint?"

She nodded.

"Probably the same guy," I said. In recent weeks, silver swastikas had popped up all over town.

Karen said, "I hope it's just some stupid kid who doesn't understand what it means."

"Whoever it is, I'm going to give him an ass-kicking when we catch him."

"You can use my foot, if that'll help."

"I'll give you first kick," I said. "Anything else Bernard needs to know?"

"He should keep an eye on our future home," she said, meaning the new police station under construction a couple of blocks away. "Kenny was over there this morning. He said it smelled like someone'd been smoking marijuana in your new office."

"Any idea when they're going to put in some doors and windows?"

"The contractor said this week, but I'll believe it when I see it."

We've gotten a lot of rain this summer, which has slowed construction considerably.

"Who's on duty tonight?" I asked.

"Lester."

I took down the fedora I wear instead of a cowboy hat from the nail it hangs on and retrieved my service weapon from the locked drawer in my desk. "Red, how 'bout telling Bernard and Lester what you just told me so I can get a jump on things and get some supplies?" We'd planned a cookout for the two of us, to celebrate the impending resignation that night of Richard Milhous Nixon, the 37th President of the United States.

Cindy stuck her head in before Karen could answer. "Deputy Cousins is here," she said.

"Speak of the devil," I said. "I'll tell him myself."

The line of permit-buyers had evaporated, leaving only Cindy and now Bernard. Cindy should've already signed out for the day, but her relief was late. I asked if she'd heard from him. She said he'd called to say he'd be there shortly. His name is George Longabaugh. George was a state trooper for 25 years until retiring a few years ago. He's gained so much weight since his Highway Patrol days, I doubt he'd be able to fit behind the wheel of a cruiser, much less pass the department physical. You don't need to be an athlete to do what he does for us, however, which is sit on his butt from 5:00 to 12:00. After that, our calls get automatically forwarded to the county sheriff's dispatcher. George is never on time, but he always shows up eventually, and anyway, I'm too lazy to find a replacement. I work days, so we seldom cross paths. I have a sneaking suspicion that always being late is his way of avoiding me.

I turned my attention to Bernard, standing on the other side of the Formica counter—the model of politeness, as always, his Smokey the Bear hat in hand.

I mentioned the swastika painter and asked him when he intended to catch him. Or her. But probably him.

"I'll get him if he's out tonight," he said.

"Be gentle if you do," I said.

He gave a shy smile. Sometimes Bernard doesn't know his own strength.

Karen asked him if he had any idea who was responsible.

"I don't know, Mrs. Hardy." Years ago, Red tried to get him to call her Karen, but he never would. She's given up. "I can't keep up with who's who anymore." he added. "Town's getting too big."

"You got that right," she said.

Karen told him about the pot smoking in my soon-to-be office and a few other odds and ends. Bernard said he'd be on the lookout.

I asked Red if she was ready to go.

"I guess," she said. She squeezed behind Cindy to retrieve her purse. Cindy had to stand up and flatten herself against the wall.

"I swear, I can't wait until we move into the new place," Cindy said.

"You and me both, hon," said Karen.

I asked the assembled if they were going to watch Nixon's speech. Reports his resignation was imminent had been on the radio all afternoon.

"I am," said Cindy.

"What's the point?" said Bernard, wearing a hang dog expression.

"What's the point?" I said. "It's history."

He frowned. "It's sad, is what it is."

Bernard likes Nixon. He's too young to know what a weasel that five-o'clock-shadowed SOB has always been.

"Well, Gerry Ford's a good man," I said, hoping a mention of the new guy might cheer him up. He nodded glumly.

Red and I bid the others goodbye. I was halfway out the door when I remembered something.

"Hey Bernard, did you hear about how the OSBI thinks those murders in Idabel and Kingfisher are related?"

Recently, the body of a white male was found on the side of a highway near Idabel. It seemed like the fella was a drifter using his thumb to get from place to place. It's sad that he got killed, but sad things happen in this world, and nobody thought it seemed that out of the ordinary. However, when an entire family was found shot to death in their Kingfisher home a couple of weeks later, rumors started circulating among law enforcement types that the two crimes were connected. I'd heard on the radio that the Oklahoma State Bureau of Investigation confirmed it earlier in the day.

"Yeh, the sheriff told me about it," said Bernard.

"What's he think?"

"He thinks it's strange, since the two places are so far apart."

Kingfisher is in the central part of the state, while Idabel's clear down in the southeast corner.

"No inside info, though?" I had hoped Keith might've heard something. He shook his head. "Not that he told me," said Bernard.

"Ok," I said. "You take care of yourself tonight."

"Will do, Chief. You two have a nice evening."

Karen walked to one of the department's cruisers parked on the street in front of the station. Last spring, the town council appropriated funds to purchase a pair of '71 AMC Javelins from the Alabama highway patrol. They were in rough shape when we got them, but Wes Harmon, the mechanic we use, rebuilt the engines, replaced the transmissions and the brakes, and added upgrades wherever he could. Now they run like bats out of hell. Wes even did some body work, including a first-rate paint job: black and white, like a cop car ought to be. I exercised the prerogatives of command and had him install cassette tape players in both, something we haven't had in the past. I figured that so long as we don't jack up the volume too much, we should be able to hear any calls we get. Unlike my last car—an old Galaxie Police Interceptor like Andy Griffith used to drive—those Javelins look fast sitting still. We donated that old Galaxie to the local high school Pep Club. They charged people a dollar apiece to take a whack at it with a sledgehammer.

"Let's take my truck," I said to Karen. "Leave the cruiser in case it's needed."

"Lester's the only one on tonight."

"Yeh, but you never know. George might need to call in someone else. Anyway, I think the air conditioning is going out."

She let go of the door handle like it was radioactive. "Say no more," she said and got in my truck.

In late summer, the sun doesn't set around here until about 8:30, so it was still plenty hot. The time and temperature sign at the bank read 89 degrees at 5:13. That's better than 103, which it had been earlier. The air conditioner in my new Ford F-150 could make a polar bear's teeth chatter, so I kept the windows rolled up, sparing ourselves the stench of oil and chemicals that's pervaded the community in recent months—another negative side-effect from the expanded drilling activity.

"Are you stopping by Safeway?" Red asked.

"I thought I'd take you home first," I said. "You've had a long day."

"No longer than yours," she said. "I don't mind going with you."

"No, you go home and get the grill started, so it's ready when I get home."

She yawned. "I think I will if you don't mind. I wouldn't mind taking a shower and getting out of this uniform."

I tried to think of some flirty remark about her getting out of her uniform, but I couldn't, so I just smiled and raised my eyebrows.

We pulled into our driveway a couple of minutes later. "I think I'll drive to the Safeway in Watie Junction," I said matter-of-factly. "They've got a better meat selection than the one here in town."

"That'll take more than an hour, there and back."

"I don't mind. It's not every day Tricky Dick walks the plank."

She started to get out, then stopped. "Don't do it for me," she said.

One half of my mind said, "She knows." The other half answered, "Of course she doesn't."

I winked. "Well, naturally, I'm doing it for you. I need you to conserve your energy, if you know what I mean."

She rolled her eyes and smiled faintly. "Yeh, right, Romeo," she said, then leaned over and gave me a kiss. "You'd best make it quick or I'm liable to be asleep."

I drove away feeling more than a little ashamed of myself. I hadn't outright lied to her, but I hadn't been 100% honest, either. The Safeway in Watie Junction sells better cuts of meat than the one here in town, but there was another reason I wanted to drive all that way.

I needed to buy some booze.

CHAPTER 2

I used to have a drinking problem. I'm not proud of it, but I'm not going to paper over it, either.

When was a kid, getting my hands on a bottle of sour mash and staying a few steps ahead of the authorities was a rite of passage. After football games, my friends in the marching band and I would procure a bottle and drive out to Burr Lake. We'd play our saxophones and trumpets and drums and listen to the music echo over the water, our way of howling at the moon. Folks didn't consider drunk driving such a big a deal back then—it was, I suppose, but it was more laughed at than worried about. We'd creep home at 35 miles per hour, sneak into our houses on our tiptoes, and hope our parents were fast asleep.

Somewhere along the line, I stopped drinking for fun and started doing it to blot out the world. What caused me to drink too much also inspired me to join the Marines, who sent me on an all-expenses-paid trip to Korea. There I watched people be killed, killed a few myself, and did what I could to keep from freezing to death.

I survived the war, but almost didn't survive the booze. In 1966, I had what you might call a nervous breakdown. Ultimately, faced with either losing everything or getting my ass in gear, I chose the latter. I gave up the hooch and stayed off. In fact, until my dad died last year, I hadn't touched a drop in seven years.

But after laying my father to rest, the urge became too great to resist. The day of his funeral, I drove to a small liquor store outside Watie Junction and bought myself a bottle. They didn't have the kind I used to drink, so I bought Jack Daniel's instead. It could've been anything, so long as it contained alcohol. I told Karen I was going over to my father's house to sort out his things and that I'd probably spend the night. She offered to help, but I said I preferred to be alone. I locked myself in his house, watched an old Alan Ladd movie on TV, and drank until I passed out.

I used to be immune to hangovers. Apparently, my immunity had a shelf life. The morning after my binge, my brain felt like it had a sunburn, my breath smelled like I'd been chewing compost, and my stomach had mounted an armed response. I promised myself it was a onetime thing, that I wouldn't make a habit of it. I kept the vow for a couple of days until I forgot how lousy I'd felt and did it again.

Since then, I've been drinking on the sly. Not too often. Let's just say I drink less than Elmer Gantry, but more than Billy Graham. Unlike the old days, I'm handling it well. I switched to vodka and started using mouthwash and chewing Doublemint so nobody can smell it on my breath. Nobody's noticed that I know of.

The clerk at the liquor store doesn't know anything about me except that I come in once a week and buy a bottle of Smirnoff. I don't know his name and he doesn't know mine. So far, I've limited my purchases to one bottle a week, although this time it'd only been four or five days since the last one. I reckon I should slow down.

It took me a little over half an hour to get there, time I spent listening to music. My new pickup came with a cassette player, which is how I got the idea to put them in the Javelins. I keep a box of tapes on the seat next to me and pop one in when I'm riding alone. My preferences run to instrumental music, especially jazz, but one of my officers, Kenny Harjo, has gotten me interested in old country bluesmen like Robert Johnson, Skip James, and Charlie Patton. Kenny's got an enormous record collection and a home stereo that makes it sound like you're right there in the room with the musicians. He copies the records onto a cassette and gives them to me. Kenny's latest contribution to my musical education is an album by a fella named Champion Jack Dupree. Mr. Dupree is younger than those others I mentioned, and he plays piano, not guitar. The album's name is *Blues from the Gutter*. It sounds like the name would lead you to expect. There's saxophone on it, which is maybe why I like it so much.

Before I got too close to Watie Junction, I picked up over to the side of the road and took off my uniform shirt so I'd look like just another fella in a t-shirt and jeans. The parking lot was empty when I got to the liquor store. The clerk and I did our business the same as usual. From there, I drove to Safeway and bought the fixins for dinner. On the way home, I stopped at a Tastee Freeze in Watie Junction and bought myself a Coke. I looked around to see if the coast was clear, then poured about a third of it out the window and topped it off with Smirnoff. Once I'd left the city limits, I pulled over again, put my uniform shirt back on, then hit the road back to Burr.

When I first recommenced drinking, it only took a few swallows before the world started swimming. I guess I've built up a tolerance after these past several months. I've always been a pretty good judge of what I can and can't do when I'm under the influence. This time, I estimated 85 percent of my faculties were intact, which I reckoned was enough to make it home unscathed. Just to be safe, though, I took an alternate route. After the rain we'd gotten earlier, the going was a little treacherous on those dirt roads, but I managed.

I finished my redneck cocktail right before I got to Burr. I dumped out the ice and chewed half a pack of gum to hide any telltale signs. When I got home, I tossed the paper cup in the garbage on my way into the house. Did I forget anything? I don't think so.

The perfect crime.

***

Gloating over Nixon's fall from grace may not be noble. Ask me if I give a damn. I'm as fond of Dick Nixon as I would be if a colony of fire ants took up residence in my jockey shorts.

Karen had showered and changed into cutoffs, a long gold-colored short-sleeved cotton top, and a pair of brown sandals. She asked me what had taken so long. I told her I'd gotten into a conversation with the butcher, which was true, as far as it went.

She'd gotten the charcoal ready to go. I seasoned the meat and tossed it on the grill along with two ears of corn. I do most of the cooking at our house. I've gotten pretty good at it, as long as there's a grill involved.

We sat and ate at our backyard picnic table. The vodka had kicked in. I had quite a buzz on and had to use most of my brain power trying not to slur my speech, so I don't exactly recall what we talked about. It was still hot, and I was sweating like a pig, which often happens when I drink. I tried my best to act normal, but when the whine of a lawnmower a couple of houses down started irritating me to where I wanted to go over there and use it to give the fella a manicure, I reckoned it was time to go inside.

I did the dishes myself, to put some distance between us, and give me time to get myself together. Red went out to the living room and turned on the TV. Walter Cronkite and some other fellas were sitting around a table setting the stage for the night's main event. I finished the dishes and made myself some instant coffee, hoping it'd clear my head.

I took my coffee and joined Red on the couch. Nixon came on around 8:00 and put on his usual aggrieved, woe-is-me act. Since no one gets my goat like Dick Nixon, I started talking back at the television. Even without the booze, I'd have had a hard time keeping quiet. Given the state I was in, I reckon I was lucky I didn't put my foot through the screen.

Karen kept elbowing me, trying to get me to shut up, but I just kept talking. When Nixon got the point and I let out a mighty whoop, she looked at me like I had an extra nose.

"Was I bein' loud?" I asked.

"Happy now?"

"Aren't you?"

"I don't love him, but he is our president."

"*Was* our president."

"Ok, *was*. I guess I'm kind of like Bernard. I can't find joy in someone else's pain."

Karen voted for Nixon twice, in '60 and '68, although by '72 she'd seen the light. Nixon won in a landslide, of course, but Red pulling the lever for McGovern felt like a victory to me.

We switched channels and watched David Brinkley and some other news fellas talk about what it all meant. When it became clear the news coverage was going to spill over into Johnny Carson's time slot, I suggested we go to bed.

"You don't have to ask me twice," Karen said. "I'm beat."

As we tucked ourselves in, I said, "You're a better person than I am."

"Faint praise," she said and turned over.

I reckon she thought I was being a smartass, but I meant it. It's probably because of her being a Christian and all. I'd like to have faith in a higher power, but I can't bring myself to. I usually try to keep any doubts to myself, especially around her, although occasionally I'll let loose a blasphemous comment. Sometimes when I do, I feel like peeking up at the sky, in case God decides to unleash a lightning bolt with my name on it.

Unfortunately, the one that gets you is the one you don't see coming.

CHAPTER 3

The telephone on my nightstand rang at 12:17. A ringing phone in the middle of the night is scary enough, but when you're trying to sleep off a drunken binge, it's like a cattle prod being applied directly to your brain.

I knocked over a glass of water, trying to pick it up. "Hello," I said, contorting myself to avoid getting wet.

"Chief, this is Lester. There's been a shooting."

Karen propped herself up on an elbow and switched on the lamp.

"Alright," I said. "Where?"

"The 89er." The 89er is a drive-in movie theater about a half mile out of town on State Highway 43, one of two main roads crisscrossing through Burr. "Young adult Caucasian male. Shot in the back of the head. I was doing my rounds when I discovered him."

"Is Bernard there?"

"He is. We're securing the scene. He had me call you. He called the highway patrol."

"You got an ID for the victim?"

"Not yet. We've begun a preliminary search, but we don't want to disturb anything."

"Call the sheriff, if you haven't already, and try to raise the OSBI." I paused. "Never mind about the OSBI. The sheriff's department will call them in."

"Will do, Chief."

I hung up.

"What's going on?" said Karen.

"Lester's got a shooting out at the 89er. One dead."

"The drive-in?"

"Yeh."

I hauled myself out of bed, put on a fresh pair of underwear and the pair of jeans and uniform shirt I'd just taken off. Karen asked if Bernard was there. I said he was, and she suggested I let him handle it. I said I intended to, but I was going out there, anyway.

Truth be told, there wouldn't be much for me to do. The sheriff's department and state agencies—Highway Patrol and Oklahoma State Bureau of Investigation—handle homicides. Probably no one would squawk if I just stayed in bed. But I've always figured the day someone gets shot to death in my town and I'm too lazy or indifferent to attend to it, it's time to find another job.

She asked if I wanted her to come. I said no, but suggested she stay close to the telephone. She said she wouldn't be able to sleep anyway and got out of bed. She put on her robe and slippers and shuffled off to the kitchen to make coffee. "You want some?" she asked. I said, "I'll grab a can of Tab on the way out the door." I've recently taken to getting my doses of caffeine from soft drinks: first Coca-Cola, then Tab, when I started having trouble buttoning my Levi's. I expect the vodka's not helping in that area, either.

I strapped on my gun belt and retrieved my .45 Colt semi-auto from my nightstand drawer. I thought I'd tossed my keys on the dresser, but they weren't there. Karen found them on the hook next to the front door where they're supposed to be.

I took a cold Tab from the refrigerator and told her I'd be back when I was back.

I could feel the beads of sweat pop out as soon as I stepped onto the porch. I had to shoo away a cloud of moths and a few June bugs on my way to my truck. The effects of the booze had faded except for a slight headache. I got in and I pulled out a package of BC Powder from the glove box. I emptied it into the Tab and drank as much as I could in one swallow. I thought about how I'd almost for sure have to pee before I got home.

Few people were out-and-about that time of night. The sign over Edna's Eats was still lit up. I could hear *Okie From Muskogee* blaring from the jukebox as I drove by. I put on some Champion Jack Dupree to drown it out. The song that came up was about a guy named Billy who loses everything while gambling with a gangster named Stack-O-Lee. First, he loses his money, then his hat and finally his life. It ends with Billy falling to his knees begging for mercy and Stack-O-Lee shooting him dead.

Champion Jack wasn't kidding when he named that album *Blues from the Gutter*.

I wondered if I was about to encounter something like that. I hoped not. Murders hardly ever used to happen around here. Now we get them fairly often and bunched closer together. I'm almost ashamed to say I've gotten a little numb to it. Not that they've become matter-of-fact, but let's face it: Worrying about having to pee on my way to a murder scene is a sign they're becoming more routine than they ought to be.

I've always had a soft spot for drive-ins. For a while back in the '50s, we had one called The Camelot. It was built out of bricks and masonry and designed to look like a castle from the times of King Arthur. The tall, round turrets on each side of the enormous screen had gargoyles mounted on top looking down. On the back of the screen, "The Camelot" was written in huge gothic lettering. Even the kids' playground in front had a medieval style. I didn't go as often as I would've liked, but I loved that place.

Unfortunately, The Camelot went out of business. It cost too much to build and the owner never made his money back. That's a common tale in this town. I expect a lot of the new businesses that've sprung up recently will meet the same fate. The fella eventually tore down the screen with the intention of building a shopping center, but the financing fell through. All that's left are the posts that used to hold the speakers, sticking up out of the ground like giant porcupine quills.

In contrast, The 89er was built on the cheap. The postage-stamp-sized screen looks like it was built with an erector set. The box office looks like a porta-potty. The marquee is tiny and so dimly lit, it's hard to read what feature's playing until you're right up on it. They don't make 'em like they used to.

I could see Lester and Bernard's emergency lights flashing from a distance. I turned onto the gravel driveway. The box office gate was pulled shut and padlocked. There were no obstructions on either side, so I just drove around it.

Lester's car was the Plymouth Fury cruiser Bernard used to drive when he worked for us. It's ten years old, but Wes Harmon's kept it in tip-top running condition. Bernard treated it like his first-born child. I doubt he feels similar affection for the lime-green Ford Fairlane cruiser he's driving these days.

Both cars were parked on the gravel path that circled the property, approximately 10 yards behind the last row of speakers. On the other side of the path was a 20-foot strip of mowed grass. Past that was where the tall weeds start. There was no fence.

The two cars' searchlights lit up the scene. I pulled up next to the Fury, cut my engine and got out of the car. Bernard and Lester stood side by side on the grass, a few feet away from a body lying face-down on the gravel road. Bernard walked over to me. Les stayed put, hands on hips, staring down at the victim.

"What's the story, Bernard?"

"White male, in his teens or early twenties, I expect," he said quietly. "Shot execution-style in the back of the head." He nodded toward Lester. "The kid's shook up."

"He the one who discovered the body?"

"That's right. Says he was driving through the parking lot after the movie got out, checking for stragglers, like he always does."

"That makes sense. Let's take a look."

We walked over to where Les stood. The night was hot and still and smelled like an oil field. I missed the aroma of alfalfa and cow manure we used to have before the oil boom. About the only sounds came from passing cars on the highway beyond the front gate. Even the crickets had the decency to keep quiet. Lester's face was pale and expressionless.

"You ok, Les?" I asked.

He nodded slightly. "Yeh, I'm fine."

I gave him a pat on the shoulder. I noticed he was wearing long sleeves, the same as me, only his weren't rolled up like mine were. I thought to ask if Karen had given him grief about it but decided it wasn't a good time.

I asked him to fill me in.

"Well, you know," he started then stopped. He wiped his forehead with his sleeve. His voice was strained. "I mean, I usually drive through here a couple of times a shift. Sometimes I end up chasing off teenagers." He paused. "They come here to smoke pot sometimes." He paused again. "Or drink beer. You remember last week? I brought a couple in and called their folks?"

"Yeh, I remember. Was this boy one of them?"

"No. At least, I don't think so. I can't be sure until I see his face."

I turned to Bernard. "Did you call the medical examiner?"

"They're on their way. Also Sheriff Belcher and the forensic team."

I turned back to Lester. "Any witnesses?" I asked.

"Not that I know of," he said, his voice breaking. Tears formed in the corners of his eyes.

"How 'bout you go sit in your unit until the OSBI gets here. They'll want to talk to you."

He nodded and sleepwalked back to the Fury.

The Oklahoma State Bureau of Investigation agent I've worked most often with, Special Agent Ovell Jones, retired last year. His former partner, Agent Isabel Cruickshank, is now the resident agent in charge of Tilghman County. Isabel's not as easy to know as Ovell, but she's a top-notch detective. As soon she and the state troopers arrived, the case would be out of my hands. Of course, I always take an active role in any investigation of serious crime in my town, regardless of what any higher-ups in the field of law enforcement have to say. I live here. They don't.

In a few seconds, a small caravan of state and county cars would enter the property. I kneeled to examine the body. I still had a minute or two before my betters arrived. Until then, I was still in charge.

CHAPTER 4

I shined my flashlight on the victim. He lay face down with his nose and forehead buried in the road. His arms were splayed at his sides and his legs stretched out straight. I couldn't estimate his age because I couldn't see his face, but he was definitely adult-sized.

The legs of his blue jeans ended several inches rose above his ankles, so his socks were visible. One was white with yellow stripes, the other was white with blue stripes. A brown patch on the back pants pocket said "Toughskins." His white high-top sneakers were dime store knockoffs of name-brand shoes. They had holes in the canvas and were stained red with dirt. His t-shirt was brown with alternating red, white, and yellow stripes.

I hoped to hell it wasn't some teenager. Investigating the death of a young boy is part of what sent me to the funny farm. That and the drinking. I used to think the only thing that'd drive me back to boozing would be investigating another child murder.

Of course I was wrong about that.

His hair was a medium shade of brown. It appeared not to have been cut or even washed in a while. I would have preferred not to look at the red crater in the back of his head, but that wasn't an option. The dirt underneath his head was moist with blood. White-ish-pink specks of what appeared to be brain matter spread out in front of him. When I got close, I could smell burned hair and flesh.

I'd have liked to have seen his face, but I couldn't roll him over until the detectives arrived. Ten years ago, I'd probably have known who it was if he was local. Nowadays, it's possible I'd never seen him.

The caravan of official vehicles parked in a line beside my pickup. Isabel Cruickshank got out of one of the cars.

Oklahoma State Bureau of Investigation Agent Isabel Cruickshank is a fair-skinned woman of medium height and build, with long, straw-blond hair she ties into a thick braid hanging down her back. She tends not to wear a lot of makeup; up close you can see a smattering of light-brown freckles across her nose. She's partial to black or gray pantsuits and crisply ironed white cotton blouses. I've always thought she was an attractive gal, although I get the feeling she does what she can to downplay her looks. Given her occupation, I reckon there are plenty of reasons why she'd do that.

In terms of style, Isabel is one of those Joe Friday, just-the-facts-ma'am types of police. I'm not, but that's okay. We get along fine. I don't know much about her life except that she's married and doesn't have any kids. That latter fact appeared about to change, judging by the basketball-sized bump she was carrying under her blouse.

She and a tall young fella in a black-felt cowboy hat approached. I stood and stepped away from the body onto the grass.

I nodded. "Agent Cruickshank. It's been a month of Sundays."

She gave me a faint smile. "Yes it has," she said.

"When did this happen?" I said, nodding at her belly.

"About eight-and-a-half months ago, or so the doctor tells me."

She wore a maternity version of her usual pantsuit—charcoal-gray, with a white blouse and a small gold crucifix around her neck.

"So it's one of those 'any day now' deals, huh?" I said.

"I should have a couple of weeks." She yawned and arched her back with her hands, the way pregnant women do. She introduced the man in the hat as Probationary Agent Raksin. We shook hands and exchanged brief pleasantries.

A technician from the medical examiner's office began tending to the body. Two men from the Tilghman County Sheriff Department's forensic team had started setting up flood lights so they could inspect the scene.

Agent Cruickshank asked me some questions. I answered the best I could. I told her Lester and Bernard were who she probably wanted to talk to since they'd been first to arrive. She thanked me and went over to them, with Agent Raksin in tow.

My bladder felt like it had swelled to the size of a pumpkin, as I knew it would when I drank that Tab. I walked the 50 yards to the restroom, only to find it padlocked shut. I slunk away in the dark and tried to find a suitable place to do my business. I had to walk quite a distance to evade notice and avoid contaminating the crime scene.

The weeds and brush surrounding the parking area formed a wall of foliage three or four feet high. I walked along it until I was sure I couldn't be seen and did my business.

After I'd relieved myself, I clicked on my flashlight and searched through the weeds leading up to where the body lay. The area was littered with discarded paper cups, empty candy wrappers, and those little red-and-white-striped popcorn boxes. I'd covered about 30 feet when I found something: a wallet, wedged into the brush a couple of feet off the ground.

I looked at it for a few seconds without touching it. It was a kid's cowboy-style wallet made of brown tooled letter with dark brown lacing. My curiosity got the best of me. I made sure I wasn't being watched, then picked it up by the edges and opened it. In the little plastic ID window was a Foreman Scotty Circle 4 Wranglers membership card.

Foreman Scotty is (or was—I don't know if he's still around) the title character on a kids' show produced by an Oklahoma City TV station. I've never had kids, so I'm not too familiar with it, but I expect his target audience is considerably younger than our victim. The card was green and yellow with a drawing of Foreman Scotty and the words: "This card certifies that_____is an official member of Foreman Scotty's Circle 4 Wranglers." The name "Frankie Gately" was scrawled with enough strength to have almost pierced the card. At the bottom there was an ID number: 44444. I wondered if all the cards had the same number, or if this guy had just gotten lucky.

If so, his luck had surely run out.

I carefully put the wallet back as I'd found it and called out to Agent Cruickshank. "You're going to want to have a look at this," I said. She hurried over, with Agent Raksin right behind.

I pointed out the wallet. She called over a member of the forensic team. A photographer came over and took pictures. I walked over to where Bernard stood next to his ugly lime-green Fairlane.

"What'd you find?" he asked.

"A kid's wallet."

"Any ID?"

"I didn't look."

He smirked. "Like heck you didn't."

"Alright, I did, but don't tell anybody,"

"I won't. Did it belong to our victim?"

"Maybe. The only thing in it was a Foreman Scotty club membership card."

He gave me a skeptical look. "Is it the victim's?"

"Who knows? I guess we'll find out."

A small circle of people surrounded the medical examiner. A collective moan went up as he turned over the body.

Lester got out of the Fury and started to walk over.

I stepped between him and the body. "I wouldn't look too close if I were you, Les," I said.

"Bad?" His face was as blank as a sheet of paper.

I nodded and followed as he walked back to the car.

Lester Filer is about as handsome a young man as there is in this town. Karen thinks he looks like a young Marlon Brando. I think he favors the actor who played Captain Kirk on *Star Trek*. Maybe we're both right. That Captain Kirk fella seems basically like a made-for-TV Brando, anyway.

Lester's dark brown eyes, pouty lips, and head of wavy golden hair (which seems to fall naturally into place; I've never seen him use a comb) make him a romantic target for many unattached—and not a few attached—women in town. If, for some reason, they were ever to make a movie about him, I reckon those Hollywood types could do worse than to cast Lester Filer as himself.

He came to us after graduating from a Christian college in Kansas City. He'd originally studied to be a minister but had a crisis in faith and decided preaching wasn't for him. He changed his major to criminal justice and became a cop. This was his first job in law enforcement.

He's done a fair job for us. He makes mistakes, but we all do at that age. He gets down in the dumps a lot, which I reckon comes from being separated from his fiancé, who stayed behind in Kansas. I give him weekends off when I can, so he can go visit. Still, I reckon he'll feel a lot better after they get married and he can be with her all the time.

Finding that body sure hadn't done anything to cheer him up. He didn't even try to put on a tough guy act. That's to his credit as a man, I suppose, but as a police officer, it bothered me, at least somewhat. I almost hadn't hired him in the first place. I was afraid his religiosity might make him soft. This was his first murder. His unsteady response made me think I might've been right.

I wasn't going to fire him, but I'd be a lousy boss if I didn't at least talk to him about it.

He sat back down in the Fury's driver's seat. I stood next to the car and leaned on the open door.

"You're not looking too good, son."

"I'm sorry, Chief," he said, seemingly in a daze. "This whole thing's been hard to deal with."

"Don't worry, son. I'm not going to rake you over the coals. I just want to make sure you're ok."

He looked away from the people surrounding body and instead focused on the show put on by the red and blue emergency lights dancing across the giant movie screen.

"I'll be ok," he said, so softly I had to strain to hear him.

"It's part of the job," I said. "I assume you told your story to Agent Cruickshank."

He nodded and said, "I hope you're not going to ask me to tell it again."

I clapped him on his shoulder. "That's not necessary," I said. "I've got a clear-enough picture for now."

We stayed quiet for a moment, listening to the sparse overlapping sounds of traffic and voices.

I asked how his fiancé was doing.

"She's fine," he said.

"Set a date?"

"Not yet."

"June weddings are nice," I said. "Women seem to think so, anyway."

"Yeh," he said. "The original date was June 6th, but it got postponed."

"June 6th? That's D-Day."

"What's D-Day?"

"You never heard of D-Day?" I could hardly believe my ears. "June 6th, 1944. The day the allied armies stormed the beaches in France during World War II." I've never had trouble remembering D-day. The anniversary falls the day after my birthday.

He looked up at me. "Were you part of that?"

"No, I'm not that old. Korea was my war. It was bad enough."

There was an awkward silence.

"You must miss her," I said.

"Yeh, I do."

More silence.

"Any chance of getting her to move here?" I asked.

He sighed and kind of laughed. "No, not really."

I'd said all I could think of to say and reckoned I'd best stop when I was ahead. I clapped him on the shoulder one more time and told him to hang in there.

"Hey Chief," he said as I started to walk away. "You mind if I ask you a question?"

I turned back. "Sure," I said. "What about?"

"It's about Korea," he said hesitantly. He opened his mouth, then closed it. "Never mind," he said. "Another time."

"Let me know if you change your mind. My life's an open book."

He gave me a sad smile. "Ok, thanks."

The scene had gotten more crowded. Sheriff Belcher was on the scene, helping coordinate with the Highway Patrol watch commander. We exchanged nods from a distance but didn't get to talk. Before long everybody seemed busy except me. I asked Agent Cruickshank if she'd mind if I headed home. She said I could go, but Lester and Bernard would need to stick around.

On the way home I bought another Tab at the 7-11. I half-listened as the pimple-faced clerk droned on about how he'd just joined the Army and was set to leave for basic training in a couple of days. He got my attention when he said he was sorry we'd withdrawn from Vietnam because now he wouldn't get a chance to kill any "gooks."

I thought of the pain I'd seen on Lester's face and the dead man I'd just left, not to mention the friends I'd lost while serving in Korea. I imparted some hard truths to the kid and stomped out to my car.

The parking lot was empty. I didn't have to be especially careful as I spiked my Tab.

Karen was awake when I got home. She'd been monitoring the police scanner and had a reasonably clear idea of what happened. I filled in a few details, careful not to get too close so she couldn't smell my breath. They say vodka doesn't have an odor, but that's not entirely true. I promised to tell her more in the morning, but I was out on my feet and had to go to bed that very second.

She didn't argue.

CHAPTER 5

When your first thought upon opening your eyes in the morning is about how the world is a sewer of evil and the human race is a blight on the planet, chances are the rest of the day's not going to be a carnival of wonderfulness.

I get a little sick hearing people my age—I'm in my 40s—talk in longing tones about the old days and how things were so much better back then than they are now.

Things were every bit as bad back then. We remember them being better because our memories are so selective. If we told ourselves the truth—hope is a sucker's bet, life is a nightmare, and no one gets out alive—we'd give up and ... oh, I don't know. Drink ourselves to death?

I'll raise my spiked Tab to that.

At least I woke up in decent physical shape. As always, Karen was up before me. She'd showered, gotten dressed, and made breakfast before I could wipe the overnight drool from my face.

I only had to pull on a pair of pants since I'd slept in my uniform shirt. Karen was dressed in a chambray shirt and blue jeans.

"You're not working today?" I asked.

"It's my day off," she said, sipping her coffee. "You're on your own."

"What are your plans?"

She looked at me over her half-moon reading glasses. "My plans are to not go to work," she said. "Other than that, I'm open to suggestions."

"I'd love to join you, but one of us has to be there to run the show," I said. "I'm curious about the fella we found last night." I described what had happened in more detail.

"Carrying a Foreman Scotty card?" she said with a sigh. "My Lord."

"It might not've been the victim's wallet," I said and took a sip of the coffee she'd sat in front of me. "I'm sure Isabel will follow it up."

"That's her job," she said. "What do you think about her?"

"You know what I think. She knows her stuff. I liked Ovell Jones, but Isabel's a better detective. She doesn't have much in the way of a personality, but that's not what they pay her for."

"Don't confuse the way she acts around men with not having a personality. A woman in that job has to watch herself."

"Yeh, I reckon so."

"You treat her well, I hope."

"I treat her like I would a man doing the same job."

"I expect you mean you give her the same respect you would a man."

"Correct," I said, feeling a little smug. Temporarily.

"But she's not a man, so you don't need to treat her like one."

I feel like throwing my hands in the air when Red talks about women's lib stuff. I'm sympathetic to the raw deal women have in this world and in favor of evening things out. Somehow, however, no matter what I say, it's always wrong. I expect I'm not smart enough. When I find myself backed into a corner like that, I tend to nod in agreement and excuse myself. Which is what I did. Anyway, I needed to get ready for work.

By the time I'd gotten dressed, she was at the washing machine sorting whites from colors. I gave her a peck on the cheek on my way out.

The sun was low in the sky, but it was already hotter than the devil. Like every other day, I still half expected my dog Dizzy to jump into my truck alongside me, even though she's been dead for over a year. She lived to a ripe old age, but I still miss her. Thinking of her added to the day's gloomy start.

When I got to the station, Lester was sitting in a chair tilted against the wall, drinking coffee with Cindy.

I asked if he'd been home. He had not.

"Any major discoveries after I left?"

He shrugged. "If there were, they didn't tell me. They made me go through the story a couple more times, then let me go. Fortunately we didn't get any more calls."

We tend not to get tons of overnight calls, but when we do, they're routed through the sheriff's office in Temple City. Lester claims to like the late shift. No one else does, so he gets it most of the time.

"No ID on the victim?"

He shook his head.

"Did they find anything else? A spent shell? There were footprints 'cause I saw them myself."

"I couldn't say, Chief. They were taking plaster casts and stuff, but they didn't include me in their conversations." He took a sip of coffee. "I thought they were acting kind of uppity, to be honest."

"Agent Cruickshank can seem a little stuck-up until you get to know her."

He shook his head. "Nah, it was more like the way they were all whispering to each other." One of his legs kept bouncing like he couldn't control it. Sometimes I'll fidget like that when I'm running on fumes. "I don't know, Chief. I heard someone mention Idabel and Kingfisher, like maybe they thought they could connect this to those two killings."

"You sure one of them wasn't saying 'Isabel' instead of Idabel?" I said. "Agent Cruickshank's first name is Isabel."

"Nah, it was definitely Idabel."

Bringing up Kingfisher and Idabel in the same sentence made me think Agent Cruickshank might suspect a connection between this and those other killings—which would be stunning, considering the OSBI had just admitted the first two were connected. The notion that we might have a multiple murderer on our doorstep started my heart beating a little faster.

"Do you think Bernard might know what they were talking about?" I asked.

He shrugged. "Possibly. They talked to him more than they did me."

I asked if he'd written a report. He said he had. Cindy handed it to me. I told him to go home and get some sleep.

He stood up and stretched. "I'll do that. See you tonight," he said and walked slowly out the door.

I said to Cindy, "I reckon it hit him kind of hard."

"This is his first, isn't it?" she asked. I nodded.

"You don't think the boy last night was shot by the same person who killed those people in Idabel and Kingfisher?" she asked.

"Your guess is as good as mine, Miss Bartlett." I retreated to my office.

I went back to my office and read Lester's report. It was clear and straightforward and told me what I already knew. Kenny Harjo reported in at the stroke of 7:00 and came straight back to see me. Since Bernard left, Kenny's my best officer, along with Karen, of course. He started with us part-time almost ten years ago. I made him full time as soon as I could. He'll have his own department to run one of these days.

He pulled up a chair. I filled him in on what had happened overnight.

"No ID on the victim?"

"I found a kid's billfold near the scene. The only thing in it was a Foreman Scotty membership card."

He tensed up. "Was there a name on the card?"

"Yeh, there was," I said. "Frankie Gately. Why? You think you know who it might be?"

His face went white. "Oh Lord, I hope not," he said.

"What's the matter, son? Did you know him?"

He laced his fingers together behind his head and looked up at the ceiling. "Frankie Gately's my little brother."

CHAPTER 6

"I didn't know you had a brother."

Kenny shook his head. "We're not related. I work with an organization called Big Brothers of America. The match up men with boys who don't have a father or another good male role model in their lives. Frankie's been my little brother since he was 13 or 14."

"You never mentioned him."

He sighed. "I don't mention a lot of things, Chief."

It bothered me he'd say that. I'd always thought we were close.

"This couldn't have been him," I said. "This person must've been close to six-feet tall."

He shook his head. "Frankie's not a boy. Not age-wise, at least. He's 23, but he's got the mind of a 10-year-old."

"Well, let's not get ahead of ourselves. Finding that wallet could just be a coincidence. When did you see him last?"

"A couple of days ago. We're supposed to meet today after I get off work."

"Where does he live?"

"With his older sister south of town. She's a mess. He's on his own most of the time. She might not even notice he's gone." He stood in a rush. "I'm going out there and check on him."

"I'll go with you."

We took one of the Javelins. I let him drive.

"Frankie's had a hard time," Kenny said when we were underway. "His father left his mother before he was born. His sister told me their mom tried to have Frankie aborted, but she lies so much, who knows if it's true. Their mother must not have wanted him, though. She left him with his sister and disappeared when he was eight. He and his sister—Shannon's her name— were living with some fella working on the rigs, but he got fired and cleared out. Now it's just her and Frankie." He took a deep breath. "Really just him. She's loves him, but she's a mess."

The Gatelys lived in a pair of decrepit house trailers off a county road. The larger of the two was yellow and white, about thirty feet long, and eight feet wide. The little blue-and-white camper behind it was half as large. The paint on both was faded, the sides were dented, cracks in the windows had been repaired with duct tape. Neither strictly fit the definition of "mobile home." Both sat on cinder blocks, the wheels having been removed. If Kenny hadn't assured me this was where Frankie and his sister lived, I'd have thought both trailers were abandoned.

We parked and got out.

"Looks like their car's gone," I said

Kenny said tightly, "They don't have one."

He trotted to the smaller trailer and tried the door. It was locked. He pushed his face to the side window and looked inside. "This is Frankie's," he said. "No one's home." He hurried to the other trailer and knocked on the door.

"Shannon! It's Kenny Harjo. Open up!"

The door cracked open. A woman's face peeked out. It was pudgy and wore last week's makeup.

"Frankie ain't here, Kenny," she said.

"Where is he?"

"I don't know. Check his trailer."

"We did. He's not there.

"Then I have no idea where he is. He comes and goes as he pleases. I got to go back to bed." She started to shut the door. Kenny stuck his foot in the opening. "Leave me alone," she groaned. "I'm so tired."

"Shannon, this is important. When was the last time you saw him?"

"Last night," she said, sulking. "A pickup came and picked him up after dark."

"You know who it was?"

She shook her head.

"Can you describe it?" I said. "Color? Make? Anything?"

"No!" she said with a pouty frown. "It was dark. What's this about, anyway?"

I left it to Kenny to decide how much to tell her. "I just wanted to talk to him," he said. "That's all. I haven't seen him in a few days, and I was wondering how he was."

"Well, I ain't seen him."

"You mind if I look inside?"

"He ain't here, Kenny."

"C'mon, just a peek and I'll leave you alone."

She stomped her feet like a bratty child. "Fine!" She held the door to let Kenny in. I stayed outside and inhaled the pot-pourri of cigarette smoke and stale beer and rancid cooking oil and what I thought were rotten bananas wafting out the door.

Kenny shook his head at me when he came out. He asked Shannon if it would be ok if he looked in the smaller trailer.

"Fine," she said with a shrug. "Here's the key."

I followed Kenny to the other trailer. He unlocked the door and went in. It was too small for more than one person, so I stood in the doorway. It was a single small room with a closet-sized bathroom. It smelled a little like sour milk, but compared to Shannon's, it was spotless.

We found nothing suspicious and walked back to where Shannon was standing outside her front door. She was wearing knee-length cut-off jeans and a long, ratty men's T-shirt that reached below her waist but fit tight over her belly. I hoped it was because she was a hearty eater and not in the family way.

"You sure you don't know who he went with?" asked Kenny.

She scowled. "It might've been Randy Braley," she said. "He comes out here sometimes. Him and Frankie are friends."

"Do me a favor and call me when he turns up."

"You know I don't have a phone."

He sighed. "Try to get word to me some way. I'll come back out later and check if he's gotten home."

"Ok, I'm going back to bed," she grumped and went back inside.

We got back in the Javelin. "If that's who's looking after that young man," I said, "he's got problems."

"Tell me about it."

"Did you notice she didn't even ask why we were looking for him?" I asked.

He put the car in gear and backed onto the road. "Yeh, well, that's Shannon. At least we got a name."

"Braley?"

"Yeh."

"You know him?"

"I do," he said. "I wish I didn't."

"You see how big she is, right?" He nodded. "Think she's pregnant?"

"No. She just eats like a horse."

I turned on the radio. Dolly Parton was singing about a young lady named Jolene. I knew what our next step should be, but I wanted Kenny to suggest it.

He spoke up after a minute or so. "I know what I need to do," he said, like it was something that pained him to consider.

"What's that?"

"Check the body. Make sure one way or the other."

I said I thought that was a good idea.

***

The Tilghman County morgue is in the Temple City Municipal Hospital. The medical examiner wasn't around. He seldom is. He's got a private practice that takes him all over the western part of the state. I told the attending nurse we needed to see the young man whose body we found the night before, that my colleague might be able to identify him.

She led us to a cold, dark room and hit the light switch. The room was stark and mostly bare, except for the table in the middle where they lay out bodies for autopsies. Along one wall was a metal sink and some cabinets containing bottles of different chemicals and fluids. The room was painted as white as the inside of a milk carton. To the right of us as we came in was a gurney. A sheet revealed the outline of a body.

"Are you related to the boy?" she asked Kenny.

"If it's who we're afraid it is, I'm his big brother."

She looked at him funny, possibly because Kenny's a Creek Indian and the dead boy was white. "Are you ready?" she asked.

He nodded.

She pulled down the sheet.

Kenny groaned and turned away. "It's him," he said.

CHAPTER 7

Cops don't cry on the job, although I've learned from experience tears are sometimes shed behind closed doors. Kenny's tough, but he cares about people. People care for him back.

"Who would do this, Chief?" he said in a pained voice. "They might as well shoot a puppy. Frankie's the best kid. He didn't have a mean bone in his body." He sat and buried his face in his hands.

"I'll give you a minute," I said. He nodded.

I called Karen from the phone at the nurse's station and explained that we'd identified the boy as Frankie Gately. I told her about Kenny's relationship with the boy and how it devastated him. I asked her to cover Kenny's shift. She said of course she would.

Next, I called Sheriff Belcher and told him we had an ID on the victim. He said he'd get in touch with Agent Cruickshank, but by the time I got off the phone she was standing 20 feet away from me at the end of the hall, having a serious conversation with her partner, Probationary Agent Raksin. As I walked to meet them, he exited through the revolving emergency room doors.

My expression gave me away. "What is it?" she asked.

"You remember Kenny Harjo, one of my officers?"

"Sure."

"He ID'd the victim," I said. "Frankie Gately."

She nodded. "So it was his wallet."

"I guess so. Whoever killed him must've gone through it and tossed it aside. Could've been a simple mugging gone wrong, although if it was, I doubt he got away with much. I saw where Frankie lives. I'd be surprised if he had two nickels to rub together."

"It wasn't a mugging," she said. "Or if it was, it wasn't simple."

"How do you know?"

"I'll get to that in a minute," she said. "First, I need to sit down." She gestured toward a couple of chairs by the elevator across from the nurse's station. I didn't think they were much of an improvement on standing, but then again, I wasn't eight-and-a-half months pregnant.

She asked about Kenny's relationship with Frankie Gately. I explained.

"I'll need to talk to him," she said.

"Sure," I said. "He's in there with him now. He should be out soon."

The hard chair only added to Isabel's discomfort. I flagged down a nurse and asked her to bring a pillow. It seemed to help a little.

Isabel took out a notebook and pencil. "Frankie Gately was from Burr?" she asked.

"He is. He and his big sister live in a couple of junked trailer houses outside town. Kenny and I went out there first thing this morning. His sister's name is Shannon. She said Frankie went out last night with someone driving a pickup. She couldn't give us a solid ID on the driver, but she said it might've been a local high-school punk named Randy Braley."

"Is Braley known to you?"

"Not to me. Kenny knows him. He doesn't hold the kid in high esteem, although he didn't go into any details. He told me he'd had a couple of run-ins with him and that he's bad news."

She wrote down my answer. "I called the TV station about that ID card," she said. "They have no way of tracing down members of that club. Not that it matters now."

"I guess not," I said. "So how do you know this wasn't a simple mugging?"

She put an index finger to her mouth. "You need to keep this to yourself," she whispered, "but I got a call this morning from the agent who's handling the investigation into the killing of that family in Kingfisher. He thinks this could be related to those and that hitchhiker's murder in Idabel."

"Why's that?"

"Certain similarities between this one and those two, including a few details we hold back from the press."

"And local yokels like myself?"

She looked at me sideways. "You know me better than that, Chief."

I shrugged. "Sorry. I've never been able to rid myself of chip I have on my shoulder whenever you folks get involved."

"I don't mind telling you what I know. I trust you to keep it to yourself."

"So what are we talking about, then?"

"One thing we held back was the fact that they were all killed by an unusual type of gun, a 7.62-millimeter Russian Nagant revolver."

"Really?" I said. "How can they be that specific?"

"Number one, this particular cartridge is unique. The bullet is placed inside the casing. It has something to do with the way the cylinder moves forward when the gun is cocked, allowing it to seal tightly against the barrel so no gases escape. That also makes it possible to use a silencer on it, unlike with most revolvers."

Ballistics are a mystery to me. "I guess your people know their stuff."

"They do," she said. "Not only that, but they also know the exact gun, or at least they think they do. A gun dealer in Broken Bow had his store broken into a few days before the Idabel murder. Guess what was stolen?"

"A Nagant 7.62 mm revolver?"

"And a box of shells for it, which are pretty hard to find, or so I'm told."

"A silencer?"

She shook her head. "It's easy to construct a homemade silencer, though."

I nodded. "Broken Bow is close to Idabel."

"12 miles. The store owner says he bought both the gun and shells from a World War II vet. Supposedly he took it off a dead German soldier."

"Gun dealers like to attach colorful stories to their inventory."

"I suppose, but in this case it's probably true."

"What do you think about it?"

"I believe our lab techs when they say the same gun was used in the Kingfisher and Idabel slayings."

"But not this one?"

"Perhaps this one, too. We recovered the slug. It was jacketed, like those used in the other two killings. I haven't been involved with those other investigations, so I haven't seen those bullets, but the lab is confident they're the same type as the one from last night."

"When will they know for sure?"

"They're doing a full ballistic test and comparison, but they think it's almost a sure thing."

I looked down the hall. No sign of Kenny.

"Y'all find anything else at the scene last night?" I asked.

Isabel frowned. "Nothing of much use. There were tire tracks, but the place has cars driving in and out all the time, so I doubt they'll be of any use."

The whole thing seemed incredible, even to me, and I've become so cynical over the years, you could tell me Walt Disney was a Nazi and I'd probably believe you. "You're telling me some spree killer is responsible for murders in Idabel, Kingfisher, and now Burr?"

"I'm not ready to say that for sure, but the only evidence we have points at that, yes."

I tried to think of other possibilities. "Execution-style killings aren't especially uncommon," I said.

"True," she said, "but we can only go where the evidence leads us. If the ballistics confirm it was from the same gun, then ..."

"... then we're more than likely looking for a single suspect for all three."

"Exactly."

"I still don't think we should ignore the possibility that Frankie's killer might be from around here."

She thought for a second. "Well, I suppose it's possible that whoever did all three killings lives here in Burr, but I'd say the odds are against it."

I shrugged. "I suppose, but while you and your team are tracking it from one direction, I can track it from another."

She shifted in the chair and grimaced. The pillow wasn't doing it for her anymore. "To be honest," she said, "I can use all the help I can get. The only reason they're letting me lead this investigation is because it's on my patch—plus, virtually every other agent in the state is working on the Kingfisher and Idabel murders. I fully expect them to either cut me out of the loop or fold this case into the other two."

"They can't do that, can they?"

She scoffed. "Are you kidding? In a heartbeat. I guess what I'm saying is, if you want to work the local angle, feel free."

"I expect I'll start by trying to track down this Braley kid."

"How sure is the sister it was Braley who picked up her brother?"

"She didn't sound too sure, but she's the kind who doesn't seem too sure about anything."

"I take it there are no parents?"

"Nah, according to Kenny, she's raised Frankie since he was a little kid."

"How old is Frankie now?"

"Kenny says about 23."

"Let's see how things evolve on my end. If they refuse to tell me things or end up putting someone else in charge, I might ride with you."

"Suits me."

She closed her eyes. At least I'd gotten a few hours of sleep. I doubt she had.

"You know, Emmett," she said, "I'd almost rather it be one of the boy's friends than some crazy person shooting folks at random."

"Uh huh," I said. "There needs to be a reason. Even a stupid reason is better than no reason at all."

"It could be it's the work of some psycho killing folks for the fun of it. If that's the case ..."

She didn't need to finish. I knew what she meant. It's hard to catch someone who kills at random.

Kenny came out. He looked around, saw us sitting there, and walked over. His eyes were red. He nodded at Isabel and addressed me. "I'm sorry I lost control like that. Not very professional, I know."

"I wouldn't call what you did losing control."

He shook his head. "Yeh, ok," he said.

"Don't worry about it, son."

He sat down in a chair next to us.

"The Chief here told me about how you got matched up with Frankie through the Big Brothers program," Isabel said. "I used to be a Big Sister."

Kenny nodded. "Then you understand what kinds of kids get involved. Some of them have normal home lives, only they're being raised by a single parent and lack a male—or female—role model."

"On the other hand," she said, "some of their home lives are anything but normal."

"Yup," said Kenny. "Frankie was one of those. His father ran off. Later, his mother got herself a boyfriend and ran off herself. She left Frankie with his older sister, who I think loves him in her way, but can't give him what he needs."

"Did you ever notify the Department of Institutions, Social and Rehabilitative Services?" she asked, using the long-winded name for Oklahoma's child welfare service.

Kenny laughed without humor. "I did, back when he was underage. The best they could do was put him in reform school, which was ridiculous. I reckoned I'd be better off looking in on him myself whenever I could."

"What kind of kid was he?" I asked.

Kenny leaned back and let his head bounce hard off the wall. "Frankie wasn't a prize winner in school. I'll tell you that much. He should've been in a special education program, but Burr didn't have one, so they put him in with all the other kids and left him to fail. He got in trouble from time to time when he was in high school, mostly because of the kids he hung out with. Frankie'd follow along with whoever and do whatever. He was just happy when people paid attention to him."

I asked if he thought one of that crowd might've had something to do with this.

"Since he got out of school, he hasn't had many friends. Somewhere along the line, he met Randy Braley, who's five or six years younger than him. Braley's a punk, but for whatever reason, he lets Frankie pal around with him. Frankie likes him." He paused for a second. "Liked, that is."

"Think Braley would hurt him?" I asked.

He shook his head. "I don't think so, but you never know."

I asked Isabel if it was alright for me to tell Kenny what she'd told me.

She hesitated then nodded. "Only him. This needs to be kept quiet."

I turned back to Kenny. "Agent Cruickshank thinks there might be a connection between Frankie's killing and those in Kingfisher and Idabel."

His eyes opened wider. "You're kidding," he said.

She explained why.

"So you're saying we might be looking for a multiple murderer?" he said.

"Looks like it," she said, "but I told your chief to feel free to investigate other possibilities."

"We'll do as much as we can," I said.

Isabel said she needed to get back to work. We all got up and started walking toward the door.

"Oh, you know, I almost forgot," Kenny said. "I noticed something strange when I was in there with Frankie. He had this little plastic police badge he wore everywhere. It wasn't on him just now."

"Someone could've taken it off him when they were moving him," I said.

"We found nothing like that at the scene last night," said Isabel, "although we're not done looking."

I asked them to wait a second and approached the head nurse. I asked if they'd retrieved any other possessions from Frankie. She shrugged. "The clothes on his back."

"Maybe he forgot to put it on," Isabel said.

"Unlikely," said Kenny. "He wore that thing everywhere. He wore it to bed. It said, 'Deputy Sheriff.'" He wiped his eyes. "I told him I was just a regular officer, so I guess that meant he was my boss. Lord, how he loved that." He gave a bittersweet smile. "He'd ride along with me on my shift and pretend to order me around."

"Ok," Isabel said gently. "We'll check that out."

We went out through the revolving door and walked toward our respective vehicles.

Before we split up, I said to Isabel: "I'm always happy to work with you, Agent Cruickshank, but the farther I am from the highway patrol, the better I'll like it."

It took a moment for my meaning to register.

"Oh, that's right," she said, "you have a history with them, don't you?"

"You might put it that way," I said. Seven years ago, I was abducted and nearly killed by a rogue trooper. I ended up getting the last laugh in that I shot him before he could shoot me, but still.

"I wouldn't worry," she said. "It's doubtful you'll have to deal with them any more than usual."

"Even that's too much," I said. "On the bright side, they've never asked me for help. I don't expect they will now. We'll do what we do and try to keep out of everyone else's way."

"Then it shouldn't be a problem."

CHAPTER 8

Over the years my department has developed a better relationship with the OSBI agents assigned to our county—formerly Ovell Jones, now Isabel Cruickshank—than is typical of the other small-town forces in the area. That's not to say they rely on us to help them to any significant extent when a serious investigation arises, but they tend not to object when we conduct our own separate inquiries, so long as we stay out of their way.

I intended to do just that. Perhaps it's true this was the work of a crazed mass killer, but I was content to nibble around the edges and look at other possibilities.

That meant checking out Frankie Gately's friends and acquaintances, trying to get some idea of who'd want to do him harm. From what Kenny told me, I reckoned that wouldn't take long. He and this Randy Braley character were Frankie's only friends, just as Shannon was his only family. The Braley kid sounded like a bad seed. If he was, in fact, the one who picked up Frankie that night, we'd need to look at him closely.

We also had to consider that, with all the changes this town has undergone in the last several years, there are more places for kids to cross paths with criminally inclined adults. And by all accounts, Frankie was still a kid, despite his age.

The consumption of recreational drugs is one such intersection.

Back in the '40s when I was in high school, we got our thrills from drinking. Lord knows I'm not excusing it. It's done me enough damage, although I've taken it up again on the sly. But I never knew anyone back then who died from drinking too much. The stories you hear these days, about people taking certain drugs and going insane, or taking something that's been mixed with a poison like strychnine and dying—those are scary, even if most of them are exaggerated or downright false. I'm no doctor, but I would think ingesting any kind of chemical that affects your brain is probably a bad idea.

Of course, booze affects the hell out of your brain. I've drunk it most of my life, though, and I'm still here. Sometimes I have trouble believing it myself.

About a year ago, we hauled in an honor student at Burr High for growing pot in his bedroom and selling it to his friends. His parents thought it was parsley, though why they'd think a 16-year-old boy would grow parsley on his windowsill is beyond me. We didn't charge him. He might've been convicted of distribution and gotten sent away for a long time. Anyway, from what I've read, marijuana is less harmful than alcohol, and booze is legal (or quasi-legal; this is Oklahoma, after all). We reckoned he was a good kid who just made a mistake. He about messed his pants when I told him he could go to jail. He promised not to do it again. I check in on him from time to time. So far he's walked the straight-and-narrow.

Unfortunately, not all drug dealers are high school honor students. There's a business behind it. We see all manner of dangerous pills and powders and can't pin down where they're coming from. Kids are taking them, and that's a problem. Between the sheriff's department and us, we've made a few arrests for possession. But that hasn't stopped the flow.

I didn't have any specific reason to believe this case was related to such activity, but as long as Agent Cruickshank and her people were following the mass murder lead, it was worth looking into as an alternative theory.

**

I offered to drive out to Frankie's sister's place and give her the bad news, but Kenny insisted on doing it himself. He said no when I asked if he wanted me to come along. I had him drop me off at the station.

As I walked in, the air-conditioner over the front door drooled on my head. The water seeped through a hole in my hat. I took it off and cursed.

"You need to get a new hat," said Karen. "Over this hat's dead body," was my reply.

She and Cindy were working on some project that involved a mountain of paper. Back when Red had Cindy's job, she handled all the paperwork. She thought she'd left all that behind after we made her a full-time officer. No chance. All of us have to do it, although to be fair, she and Cindy do the lion's share. Every year the State of Oklahoma comes up with more forms for us to fill out, and more rules and regulations we've got to follow. They've even raised the qualifications for becoming a cop. Before you know it, someone like me without a college degree won't be able to get a job in law enforcement. That might actually be a good thing.

We currently have four full-time officers: Lester, Kenny, Karen, and me, plus a part-timer we use in emergencies. That might sound like a lot of cops for a town this size, but we're kept plenty busy. Even with the help of Bernard Cousins, we're stretched thin.

I asked Red how things were going.

"We've been getting calls about the killing last night. People are nervous."

I thanked her for coming in on her day off.

"Of course," she said. "I feel so bad for Kenny. I'm sure he's just torn up about this."

"He's upset," I said, "but he's tough. He'll do what needs to be done. He's going out there right now to break the news to Frankie's sister."

"Why on earth didn't you go with him?"

"I offered. He wanted to do it himself."

Judging by the look she gave me, I reckon she thought I should've gone with him anyway.

I told her I was on my way out to the drive-in, and that she was in charge until I got back.

Like a nightclub or saloon, by the light of day a drive-in movie theater loses whatever charm it has. That morning the 89er looked like a cemetery, with its long gravel paths interspersed by sections of grass and speakers on metal poles in place of gravestones.

The area where the victim had been found was marked off with crime scene tape. There was a chalk outline where Frankie had lain. A couple of cars were parked nearby, one of them an OHP cruiser. Agent

Cruickshank's partner was walking around the perimeter, hands in back pockets and head down, presumably searching for clues.

I parked my truck in the middle of the lot next to the small building housing the restrooms and concession stand, a few dozen yards from where the body was found. A tall, skinny man in his early 20s with shoulder-length jet-black hair leaned against the door and watched me get out of the car. His skin had that fish-belly-white pallor you see in folks who work nights and sleep days. He had on black jeans and a black T-shirt with a pack of Marlboros rolled up in one short sleeve. A large black wallet stuck out of a rear pocket, attached to a belt loop by a chrome chain. To one side of the building stood a large black Harley-Davidson motorcycle.

He started yelling at me before I was halfway out of the car. "Why don't you a—holes leave me alone? I already told those other guys; nobody got shot last night while I was here. If it happened, it was after I left, and if you want to know where I was until 2:00 this morning, just ask the bartender at Edna's." Up close, he was even taller than I'd thought. Six-six, at least. His face was long and his cheeks were hollow. An ugly scar ran from his left eyebrow to the corner of his mouth. The edges didn't quite match, like when you skip a button when you're buttoning your shirt. He didn't look stupid, though, I'll say that. Something about his eyes. I suspected he was smarter than his motorcycle attire might suggest.

I held out my hand and introduced myself. He looked at it like he'd rather spit on it, but ended up shaking it, after all. "Sam Carter," he said in a hoarse growl.

I asked if he was the manager.

He nodded. "And the owner."

"I apologize for making you answer these questions all over again, Mr. Carter, but sometimes that happens in situations like this."

His face softened a bit. "Ok, I get it. It's just that I didn't get much sleep last night. My phone was ringing as soon as I got home. I had to turn around and come back here."

"When was that, exactly?"

"I don't know. I wasn't looking at a clock. Around 2:30, I guess. They kicked me out of Edna's when it closed around 2:00."

"Who called?"

"Some guy from the Highway Patrol."

"What time did you leave work?"

"After the movie got out. 10:30, 10:45."

"Was anybody working with you?

"No, I run the place myself on weeknights."

"Where'd you go afterward?"

"I went to make a night deposit at the bank, then home. I changed clothes and went to Edna's."

"About what time was that?"

"Around 12:00."

"So you were home between 11:00 and 12:00?"

"Yeh, and before you ask if someone can vouch for that, no. No one can. I live alone."

"Lots of people do," I said. "One of my officers tells me you've had some trouble with kids coming out here after closing time."

"Was it Lester who told you that?"

"Yes it was."

"Yeh, well, it's a recurring problem. As you can see, my gate isn't exactly a formidable obstacle. If someone wants to trespass after hours, all they got to do is drive around it. I've called you guys about it a few times. Lester's been pretty good lately about driving through after we're closed."

It was strange hearing words like "recurring" and "formidable" coming from someone dressed like a Hell's Angel.

"Have any of them been violent?"

"They know better than to hang around when I'm here, so I really couldn't tell you. For all I know, they're all beating the hell out of each other. I come in the next morning and have to deal with the mess they've made. Our customers make messes, too, but at least they don't treat the place like a garbage dump."

I heard gravel crunching beneath car tires. Agent Cruickshank's slicktop cruiser crept through the front gate on its way to where the body had been found.

I asked Carter if he knew the name Frankie Gately.

"Is that the guy who got killed?"

"I can't give out that information."

He smirked. "Of course you can't. Listen, I don't know the names of these punks. Maybe if I saw him, I'd recognize him."

"Who would know, do you think?"

"Lester might. Ask him."

"I'll do that."

I asked for his phone number. He led me into the concession stand, reached under the counter, and pulled out a small notebook. He grabbed the nearest piece of paper, which happened to be one of the bags they sell pickles in. On the front was a drawing of a smiling pickle wearing a red top hat. Above it was a thought bubble that said, "Delicious Pickle," like he wanted to be eaten. I guess movie theater pickles are complicit in their own demise.

I thanked him. He followed me to my truck. "One last question," I said. "Does the name Randy Braley mean anything to you?"

For a second, I thought I saw a glint of recognition in his eyes, but he shook his head. "Nah. Like I said, I'm not good with names."

CHAPTER 9

I left Sam Carter to do whatever the Sam Carters of the world do. We'd be speaking again, and probably soon. I got in my truck and moved it to the back of the lot near the crime scene. Agent Cruickshank was standing by the white chalk outline where the body had been found, conferring with her partner, Probationary Agent Raksin. I was proud of myself for remembering his name.

I told Isabel what Carter had told me. None of it was news to her. "I've got someone trying to track down the bartender at Edna's last night to confirm that Carter was there from 12:00 to 2:30, like he said."

"What about from 11:00 to midnight?" I said.

"We'll try his neighbors. Maybe someone saw his car. Also, the bank might have him on their surveillance camera, so we'll check that."

A call came in on her radio. "Don't worry about it, Emmett," she said as she walked to her car. "We'll deal with Carter." She answered her call, and I tried to make small talk with her partner. It was tough sledding. I remember thinking it might be quite some time before he lost the word "probationary" in his title.

Isabel finished her call and yelled, "Raksin!" He rushed to her side like a puppy that'd gotten caught diddling on the rug. She handed him a sealed evidence bag. They spoke for a few seconds, then he got in his car and left.

I asked what the call was about.

"Headquarters in Oklahoma City got an anonymous phone call from someone claiming to know who did this."

"Think there's anything to it?"

She shrugged. "You never know. They gave me a couple of names."

"From around here?"

"Looks like it. Cottrell. Sound familiar?"

"Not really."

"They gave me the address of some apartment complex here in Burr."

"Where'd your partner go?"

"We found a disposable cigarette lighter in the weeds. I had him take it to the lab to check for prints."

"Isn't the lab in Oklahoma City?"

"It is."

"That's a long drive, there and back."

"Should take most of the day," she said with a twinkle in her eye.

I grinned. "Trying to get rid of him, huh?"

"He's getting in the way. I'd rather not have to train a rookie in the middle of a murder investigation."

"You're not going to check out that address on your own, are you?"

"Why? You want to come along?"

"Got nothing better to do."

She had a few things to square away, so we made plans to meet at the station. By the time I got back, Kenny had returned from talking to Frankie Gately's sister. Cindy and Karen were there as well.

"How'd it go?" I asked Kenny.

"Bad," Kenny said. "She didn't believe me at first, then she lost it."

"Did she have any idea who might've done it?" Karen asked.

"Nah, she wasn't making any sense, she was so upset. I got a picture, though." He handed me a smudged school photograph of Frankie. "That's about five years old, but he still looks pretty much the same. By the way, it wouldn't hurt if we could send someone out there to sit with her."

"Cindy, would you mind going out and sitting with Shannon?" I asked.

"Sure, if y'all don't mind answering any calls that come in."

I gave her directions. She left. The rest of us went back to my office.

Kenny heaved a sigh. "Shannon might not have taken the best care of Frankie, but she loved him. I didn't realize how much until now."

"Was she able to tell you anything useful?" asked Karen.

"Only one thing, that she was sure it was Randy Braley who picked Frankie up last night."

"Finding out her brother died sharpened her memory, I guess," I said.

"Someone needs to hunt down Randy Braley," said Karen

"I assume Isabel's on it," I said. "I wouldn't mind talking to him myself."

"I know where his mama lives," said Kenny.

"Let me talk to Isabel about it first, see if she's been there already. It might not matter." I told them about the anonymous tip to the OSBI. "Isabel wants me to help her run it down."

"Did she say who it was?" asked Karen.

"Cottrell. Sound familiar?"

They both shook their heads.

Karen asked Kenny, "What do you know about Randy Braley?"

He scowled. "That one's going to wind up in jail one of these days—if he doesn't turn up dead first. He's a bully who I suspect is selling marijuana to grade schoolers. As far as I know he hasn't killed anyone. He might someday, but he hasn't yet."

Agent Cruickshank walked in the door, looking overheated. She asked if I was ready to go.

I said I was, then added, "We were wondering if you'd had any luck tracking down Randy Braley."

"Not yet," she said. "We've talked to his mother, but she hasn't seen him since yesterday morning. Or so she says."

"You two want to try tracking him down?" I asked Karen and Kenny.

"Someone has to stay here to answer phones," said Karen.

"Kenny, you could use a break. How 'bout you tend the store while Red talks to Mrs. Braley?"

He looked a little surprised. "Well, uh, sure. I guess." I expect he thought I'd have him go and ask Red to stay.

Karen reached for the phone book.

"If you're looking for the address," said Kenny, "it'll be under Wishon, not Braley. Randy's mom's been divorced twice. Her first name is Delia. Delia Wishon."

Karen thumbed through the directory. "Here we go. Delia Wishon. 113 Oakview Drive."

"Go ahead and check," I said. "If he's there and gives you any sign of trouble, call Kenny or me."

She marched out with an annoyed look on her face. She doesn't like that I worry about her.

Isabel and were next out the door. She wanted to take her car. In her condition, getting behind the wheel wasn't a simple matter.

"You want me to drive?" I asked.

"Why would I?"

"No reason," I said. "Have any trouble getting me permission to ride along?"

"No, because I didn't ask." she said. "I'm sure it wouldn't be a problem. You've got a pretty good reputation at the bureau."

"I reckon I can thank you for that."

"Not me so much," she said. "Mostly Ovell." Agent Ovell Jones was the one who showed her the ropes. The two of them partnered for years before his retirement. "I've put in a good word for you here and there."

"How's Ovell doing?" I said.

"Can't go anywhere without an oxygen tank," she said as she lit up a Marlboro.

I told myself it was none of my business.

"We're looking for a Dwight and Amanda Cottrell," she said. "They're brother- and sister-in-law. Amanda's married to Dwight's brother Billy Wayne."

I cracked my window. "I guess there's something to be said for keepin' it in the family."

The Cottrells lived in the Sooner Arms, one of the new poorly built apartment complexes that have sprung up in recent years. It comprises a pair of two-story buildings about as long as the distance between the pitcher's mound and home plate. The concrete courtyard looked like they originally meant it to be a street, until someone realized it was too narrow and blocked the ends off with a chain-link fence. Looking at the place from the road, you might be fooled into thinking the buildings are made of brick. Up close, you can see flimsy vinyl siding covers the outer walls. The corners were pulled away, revealing cheap plywood underneath.

"Oh, this place," I said.

"Been here before?"

"I haven't," I said, "but I think Karen and Kenny answered a wife-beating call here a while back."

"We're calling it 'domestic-violence' these days, Emmett."

"Oops, sorry."

"It didn't by any chance involve the Cottrells, did it?"

"I couldn't tell you."

Isabel said, "The tipster didn't give us an apartment number."

"No 'Manager' sign that I can see."

She opened her door and got out. "Let's check the mailboxes."

I followed her to a line of aluminum mailboxes built into the wall of one building. Some had a typed label. Most didn't. At best, they had a name scrawled in magic marker on the metal.

"Looks like we're going to have to knock on some doors," I said.

"Let's split up. You take one building, I'll take the other."

"You sure we shouldn't go together?"

"If either of us needs back-up, we're only a few feet away."

I thought about trying to formulate a diplomatic way to point out her condition but decided against it. This was her show.

I asked if she was carrying a gun. She opened her jacket to reveal a shoulder holster containing what looked like Smith & Wesson .38 Special. "Does this meet your approval?" she asked. "Just making sure," I said.

We split up and made our way down the line of apartments. Nobody answered the first four doors on my side. Isabel had similar luck, or lack thereof. A gentleman in the end apartment finally answered my knock. I'd obviously woken him up and he wasn't too happy about it. He did, however, point out the first apartment on the upper level on Isabel's side as a place where a trio of shady customers had been coming and going.

I turned to look. Suddenly I heard Isabel holler and saw a yellow kitchen chair somersault down the staircase opposite. Following close behind was a short, skinny fella wearing a Jesus Loves You t-shirt and a pair of saggy BVDs. Isabel stood at the top of the stairs, one hand supporting her back, the other holding the .38. "Stop! Police!" she shouted, then: "Heads up, Emmett!" I rushed over to block his egress.

Unfortunately for the skinny fella, the chair got stuck several steps before it reached bottom. He tried to jeté over it, but his foot got caught on one of the legs and he fell head over heels to the bottom. He lay stunned at my feet, a small puddle of blood blossoming on the concrete beneath his head. He gawked up at me, evidently confused at the current state of affairs.

I leaned over and said, "Mr. Cottrell, I presume?"

CHAPTER 10

He lay on his back with his head resting on the asphalt and his feet slanting upward on the steps at a 45-degree angle. His greasy dark hair nicely complemented his greasy five o'clock shadow. He looked like Bluto after Popeye'd kicked the hell out of him, except he was as skinny as Olive Oyl. His lips were bloody and two of his front teeth had broken off. Maybe they'd always been that way. I kind of hoped so.

I rephrased my question. "Your name wouldn't be Cottrell, would it?"

He looked up stupidly and mumbled something I couldn't understand. I looked up and saw Isabel coming down the stairs. She un-wedged the chair, carried it to the bottom and sat down, resting her .38 on top of her big belly.

"I definitely did not need that," she said, taking deep breaths and arching her back. "I knocked," she said. "This genius opened the door." Another deep breath. "I identified myself. He pushed me away and took off. This thing—" she pointed at the chair "—was sitting by the door. I tossed it down the steps past him to block his escape." She gave me a look halfway between a grimace and a smile. "It appears to have worked."

"It did," I said with a chuckle. "One of us should call an ambulance, though."

"I'll do it," she said, rising painfully and holstering her weapon. "We should probably get him a pair of pants to put on, while we're at it." I tried to beat her to it, but before I could, she was halfway up the stairs to Dwight's apartment.

"You ok, Mr. Cottrell?" I asked. He moved his head in something like a nod and stretched his arms and legs trying to sit up, so I knew he hadn't broken his neck. I gave him a hand. He sat on the bottom step with his head in his hands. The gash on the back of his head looked plenty ugly, and his jockey shorts were revealing too much of what the good Lord gave him, but other than that, he looked pretty good, considering the tumble he took.

"Yeh, I'm ok," he said dully.

"You're Dwight, correct? Billy Wayne Cottrell's brother?" I asked.

He nodded.

Isabel tossed a pair of raggedy jeans and carpet slippers at Dwight on her way down the steps. "Put these on," she said. "I just ate lunch."

I asked her if Amanda was up there. Dwight answered instead.

"Nah, I don't notice where she is," he said as he pulled on the jeans. Isabel shook her head as if to confirm.

"How 'bout Billy Wayne?" I asked.

He shook his head. "Ain't seen him."

"Where were you last night, Dwight?" asked Isabel.

"Here."

"Alone?"

"Yeh."

"What about Amanda?" I asked.

"I told you, I don't know where she is."

"What do you know about that shooting last night?" Isabel asked.

He looked at her like she was speaking Chinese.

"What shooting?"

Isabel handcuffed him and we got him to his feet. His legs were wobbly. The slippers were too big. I had to help him to the car. I stashed him in the back seat and left the door open. Pretty soon, the ambulance arrived. The medics declared him healthy enough to go to jail.

***

Rather than drive the suspect to her office in Temple City, we put him in the little holding cell in my office. Cindy was still at Shannon Gately's and Red hadn't returned from searching for Randy Braley, so Kenny was still holding down the fort. I asked him if he'd heard from Karen. She'd called in and said

Braley still hadn't come home, and his mom was getting worried. I thanked him and told him to go home and take it easy the rest of the day. He said he'd take me up on that, but I should call him if I needed him.

Isabel wanted to question Dwight Cottrell there in my office, but when she called her boss and told him we'd arrested Cottrell, he insisted on doing the interrogation himself. I'd have argued with him, but she took it calmly. She arranged for the highway patrol to drive Dwight to Oklahoma City, while I sat outside the cell chatting with him.

"Used to be I knew everyone in this town," I said trying to be friendly. "These days I see a new face every day."

Dwight sat slumped on the pull-down cot in the holding cell. One eye looked a little to the right, the other a bit to the left. I tried to position myself somewhere in the middle.

"I ain't been here long," he said.

"How long?"

"About three or four months, I guess."

"What's your line of work?"

"I was working out at Cudahy, but I got fired."

"What for?"

"Stealin' meat."

"Did you do it?"

He hung his head. "Yeh, I done it."

I pictured him walking out the door with raw chitlins in his pockets.

"Where y'all from, then?" I asked.

"Oh, all over, I guess."

"Did you kill that boy last night?"

His already bugged-out eyes bugged out a few millimeters more. "What boy?" he said, a note of panic in his voice. "Why y'all asking me that? I ain't never killed no one! Hell, I just thought y'all were after me for that warrant out of Duncan for passing bad checks."

I gave him my disappointed schoolteacher look. "You been passing bad checks, Dwight?"

He opened and closed his mouth like a catfish out of water. "What I mean to say is ... yeh, I passed some bad checks, but I ain't killed no one. Why y'all think I did?"

It wasn't my place to answer, so I didn't.

"Who you been living with, Dwight?"

"My brother and his wife. Amanda. Now just her. She got tired of him beatin' on her and kicked him out. Her and me's fixin' to get married as soon as she gets a divorce. We're in love."

I'll bet you are.

"What's your brother think of that?"

"Not much, but he don't get to say."

Isabel came in and crooked a finger at me. I followed her into the outer office and shut the door to avoid Dwight's prying ears.

"The highway patrol should be here any minute," she said.

"Doesn't it bother you that your boss is taking over?"

She sighed. "I'm used to it. God forbid I get any credit."

"Even so, I don't get the point of driving him all the way to the city."

"I guess they want to parade him in front of the cameras in case he's the killer."

"He's not."

"How do you know?"

"I can just tell. He's too stupid and too scared to lie. He thought this was about some bad checks he passed in Duncan."

"Huh," she said. "No one said anything about outstanding warrants."

"I'll bet you anything this just a case of Billy Wayne being jealous and getting revenge."

"Probably, in which case I'll have wasted most of the day."

"Let the boys in Oklahoma City question this idiot while you get some real work done."

She nodded. "Yeh, I think I will."

A pair of state troopers arrived. Isabel conferred with them. They handcuffed Dwight and frog-marched him out the front door.

Isabel said, "I'm still on the hook for finding Amanda Cottrell."

I looked out the front window. "I think we just found her," I said.

Outside, a heavy-set woman with long bleached blonde hair and coke-bottle eyeglasses was scuffling with the troopers, trying to pull Dwight out of the car. Dwight was laughing and enjoying the show. Isabel and I rushed out to lend a hand.

One of the troopers had the woman's arms pinned behind her and was holding on for dear life. Isabel confronted the woman, hands on hips, her pregnant belly sticking out like a balloon. "Are you Amanda Cottrell?" she asked. The woman screeched an invitation to perform a physically impossible feat. "Yup, that's Amanda," whooped Dwight. The trooper holding her managed to cuff her and push her into the back seat next to her brother-in-law/fiancé, who watched with a goofy smile. Isabel confiscated the woman's purse and looked at her driver's license. "Amanda Cottrell," she said, "You are under arrest."

"For what?" Amanda Cottrell screamed, then elaborated upon her prior suggestion that we all engage in a peculiar act of self-love.

"Right now we'll stick to interfering with a police officer in the performance of his lawful duties," said Isabel, and slammed the car door. "Two for the price of one," she said to the troopers.

The troopers drove off. Isabel dusted herself off and held her belly for a few seconds. She looked concerned, then relieved. "There we go," she said, smiling faintly. "Just felt him kick."

We went inside the station.

"It's nice when they fall in your lap like that, isn't it?" I said.

"Is that what that's called?" she said. "'Falling into my lap'?"

We talked for a couple of minutes, then Karen came through the door.

"About time," I said. "What's the story?"

"Hold on, let me catch my breath," Karen said, then noticed Isabel. "Agent Cruickshank," she said, "I do believe you are with child!"

"You noticed," she said. Karen laughed and congratulated her.

"I tried talking to Randy Braley's mother. She said she hadn't seen him since yesterday. Although she doesn't seem like an especially trustworthy type. After I left her, I rode over to the high school and cornered Principal Jeff."

For several years, Jeff Starns was a part-time officer with us and an assistant football coach at Burr High School. He stopped moonlighting with us when he got promoted to head coach, then principal. We threw ourselves a little party on the day he resigned.

"Why'd you do that?" I asked.

"Because Randy's mama said he was going out for football this year. She thought he might've shown up for practice."

"Isn't it a little early for football?" asked Isabel

"This is the first week of pre-season practice," I said.

"Those poor kids," said Karen. She took off her police hat and mopped her brow. "It's hot as the devil out there. Let's go into your office. I need to sit down. I'm not as young as I used to be."

Isabel sat on the cot in the holding cell. I sat in a folding chair. Karen commandeered my desk—it's more hers than mine, anyway—took a brush out of my desk drawer and got to work on her hair. It only took a couple of strokes to get her back to looking like Susan Hayward.

"So did Braley show up to practice?" I asked.

"He did not," said Karen, "but Jeff saw him last night while he was picking up his girls at Chrisler's around 9:30. Frankie was with him."

A while back, a fella by the name of Jim Chrisler (rhymes with 'chiseler') built a pre-fab metal building on US 14, put in a snack bar and a bunch of foosball tables, pool tables, pinball machines, and this new game that looks like a black-and-white TV only you play table tennis on the screen by twisting a couple of knobs. Apparently it's the latest thing. I don't get the attraction, but then again, I'm teetering on the verge of geezer territory. Chrisler calls it Family Fun Center. Most everyone else calls it Chrisler's.

I call it a casino for kids.

"It looked to Jeff like they were having an argument while they were sitting in Braley's truck. Frankie got out, and Braley drove off."

"That's interesting," said Isabel.

"There's one more thing," Karen said, leaning forward and talking low, like she was about to reveal a state secret. "Mrs. Wishon says Randy used to work for Jim Chrisler. Maybe still does."

"That's very interesting," said Isabel.

"We need to go over there and talk to Mr. Chrisler," I said. "See if he knows anything."

"I hope you don't mind if I allow you the pleasure," said Karen. "That guy gives me the creeps. Anyway, someone has to man the dispatch until Cindy gets back."

"I'll go," I said, "although I'd rather not do it alone." I'd never officially met him, but Chrisler had a reputation of being someone you shouldn't turn your back on. "I guess I'll call Kenny and take him with me."

Isabel said, "Don't do that, Emmett. I'll go," then stood up too fast and had to sit back down.

I said, "Isabel, I expect you've dealt with enough sleaze-bags for one day."

She patted her stomach. "I hate to admit it, but I think the little person in here is telling me the same thing."

CHAPTER 11

Karen Hardy is good at hands-on police work, but when it comes to running a police station, she's Willie Mays and Johnny Unitas and Jerry West all rolled into one. That's the main reason I try to steer her toward desk work—that, and I worry about her going head-to-head with bad guys. She thinks it's because I'm a male chauvinist. Maybe I am a little, although I try not to be. I subscribe to the philosophy, "from each according to his ability; to each according to his needs." The person who said that was a communist. In fact, he invented communism, if what our local librarian Kate Hennessey told me is correct. Maybe that makes me a commie, too. I don't give a rat's behind. All I know is, we're required do a lot more administrating than we used to. Of all the people on our payroll, no one does it as well as her.

That includes yours truly. If it was me who had to balance the books, I'd end up locked up in my own jail. I can't add a row of numbers to save my life.

When we got married back in '67, she'd just been hired as a full-time uniformed officer after having been our dispatcher for several years. She started slow those first months, mostly because she got pregnant and had to take time off. She had a miscarriage, the first of three. After the third, we went to a specialist, who told us we could keep trying but would likely continue to have the same result. Something about the structure of her uterus, I don't know. Karen reckoned she couldn't bear going through it again, nor could I, so we started being more careful. Our string of bad luck continued with the death of my dog, Dizzy, and then my dad, Everett Hardy.

Red threw herself into her work. I threw myself into taking up drinking again. Now, she's the brains of the outfit, and I'm doing whatever I can to keep my secret under wraps.

***

I called Kenny. He arrived within five minutes. "I didn't even take off my uniform," he said. "I had a feeling you'd need me." Isabel left to connect with her OSBI colleagues. Kenny and I took off in one of the Javelins. He drove. First, we stopped by the Gatelys' to see how Shannon was doing. Cindy was still there and met us in the yard. Shannon had cried herself to sleep. I thanked Cindy and sent her back to the station, then peeked in on Shannon. Her face was tear- and mascara-streaked. She was out like a light. Kenny and I headed to Chrisler's.

Chrisler's clientele for the most part comprises kids, 12 and up. The only time you'll see mom or dad go in there is to pick up a son or daughter who's too young to drive, like Jeff Starns did the other night. A fair number of the Coca Colas and Seven Ups sold at the snack bar are taken out to the parking lot and spiked with liquor from underage customers' illicit stock.

"Haven't you had some run-ins with this guy?" I asked Kenny as he negotiated traffic on Main Street.

"That's right, you've never met him, huh?"

"I haven't had the pleasure."

"Then you're in for a treat." He chuckled. "Yeh, we've all had to go out there. Bernard's been out there a bunch of times."

"What for? Kids drinking?"

"Yeh. I've also smelled pot a few times, but never nailed down who was smoking it. We're always confiscating beer from some kid."

"Chrisler ever give you a hard time?"

He thought about it. "I guess. He complains we're bad for business, but he always does it with a big shit-eating grin on his face. I know Bernard's cited him for a few things. Just to let him know we're paying attention."

Kids need someplace they can go to have fun. I just wish they'd do it without the help of alcohol. Do as I say, youngsters. Not as I do.

Kenny added: "Bernard told me the sheriff and OSBI suspect he's selling something besides hotdogs and Cokes."

"Drugs?"

"That's what Bernard says, but they don't have any proof. He's got a record, but not for drugs."

"What's it for?"

"He owned a pool hall in Lawton a few years back," Kenny said. "I guess he got into it with a soldier from Ft. Sill. Hurt the guy pretty bad."

"He go to jail?"

"A little while, but most of his sentence was suspended. I guess there was some question whether he was provoked."

"I reckon if we jailed every fella involved in a poolroom brawl, we'd have to build us a lot more prisons."

"Yeh, but that ain't all. He's been arrested several times for various things."

"Like what?"

"A couple of domestic disturbances, although he wasn't convicted. He also got caught selling cigarettes without the tax stamp."

"That's an organized crime trick," I said.

"I guess he convinced the judge it was a onetime thing and got off with a fine."

"He's never been busted for drugs, though, huh?"

Kenny shook his head. "Maybe there's nothing to the drug thing. He's been clean since he moved here, as far as I know, if you don't count all the times we've been out there to confiscate beer from kids. We've never charged him with anything."

"Maybe we should."

It started storming just as we arrived at Chrisler's. Lightning flashed and thunder boomed like distant artillery. We had to wait and let an orange Pontiac Trans-Am drive out of the parking lot before we could pull in. I tried to get a look at who was driving, but the rain was too heavy to see. "Nice car," I said. "Real nice car," replied Kenny.

We put on our hats and ran for the door, somehow staying fairly dry.

Family Fun Center is basically nothing more than a big windowless barn. Chrisler had drywall and insulation and an HVAC unit put in, so it's inhabitable year-round. At night it gets busy, but this time of day it was practically empty. I could hardly hear the juke box over the pounding of rain on the roof. A girl of about 16 stood behind the snack bar looking extravagantly bored. I asked for her boss. She pointed to a door at the back of the room.

Chrisler's office was only slightly larger than my own. It was made to seem smaller by a mountain of clutter on all sides and on all surfaces. Little red and blue plastic men from a disassembled foosball table were scattered across his desk. The metal rods were stacked like pickup sticks on the floor. The table itself was jammed in a corner. A can of lubricating spray sat on an oily paper towel in the middle of the playing area. Chrisler was a scruffy looking man in his early 40s. He sat in an elderly Naugahyde office chair that had tufts of fluffy white stuffing poking from the seat cushion. A cigarette was burning itself out in a plaid beanbag ashtray while another, newly lit, hung from his lips. His sweaty face was darkened by the beginnings of a beard, black with specks of gray. A half-empty hard pack of Pall Malls stuck out from a pocket in his dirty t-shirt. The shirt didn't cover his belly and his dingy gray work pants didn't quite cover his backside. The wild thatch of greasy black hair attached to his skull made him look like a malevolent Buddy Hackett.

This was my first encounter with him. I disliked him on sight.

He smirked when he saw us. "Hey there, Officer Geronimo," he said to Kenny.

"That's a hell of a way to talk to an officer of the law," I said, "especially from someone who's been letting underage kids drink in his parking lot."

He smiled like a game-show host who'd given up brushing his teeth. "Oh, come on, Kenny, tell your boss here we're buddies." He mashed out one Pall Mall and took a long puff on the other. "You're Chief Hardy, aren't you?" He wiped his right hand on his pants and held it out. "Pleased to meet you." I held my breath and shook his hand. "Officer Harjo, you know I ain't selling kids alcohol," he added. "I can't help it if they drink before they come in."

I could feel Kenny trying to hold his temper, so I reckoned it'd be best if I did the talking.

"We're not here for that," I said, "although I'll remind you that if underage persons are caught drinking on your property, you're liable for prosecution." He grunted. "We want to know if you're acquainted with a young man named Frankie Gateley, and whether he was here last night."

"If he's a kid, he probably was," he said. "No place else in this town for 'em to go. I see 'em all, but I don't know none of them by name."

I showed him the picture Kenny had gotten from Frankie's sister. He glanced at it. "Oh, the retard. He's the one got killed last night, ain't he?"

"He's a young man, and he was killed last night," I said.

Chrisler picked up one of the chrome rods lying on the floor. "Yeh, he was here."

"You see who he was with?"

"I didn't notice."

"Did you talk to him?"

He ground out his cigarette and let out an exaggerated sigh.

"Okay," he said. "I expect you'll find this out anyway, so I might as well tell you. I kicked him out."

"Why?"

Chrisler grabbed one of the blue plastic men and used it to tap a disjointed rhythm on the desktop. "He was giving the girl that works for me a hard time. Glenda. Glenda Osgood. The retard assaulted her."

"His name was Frankie," I said.

"Yeh, whatever. He assaulted her in the parking lot as she was coming in. She told me about it, so I kicked his ass out."

"There's no way in the world Frankie would assault anyone," said Kenny. "Especially a girl."

Chrisler spat something brown and soggy into a dirty Dixie cup. "Ah, you'd be surprised," he said. He jammed his dirty index finger into his mouth and fished around, pulling out something still browner and soggier—snuff, I reckoned. He looked at it for longer than I thought was warranted, then shook it off his hand into the garbage can beside him. He wiped his top teeth with the neck of his t-shirt, leaving a brownish stain. "Just 'cause he's a dummy don't mean he don't like girls," he said.

"Liking them and assaulting them are two different things," said Kenny.

He shrugged and started attaching the plastic man to the chrome rod.

"How'd you kick him out?" asked Kenny.

"What do you mean, 'how'? I told him to get out."

"How?" I said. "Draw us a picture."

He finished fiddling with the plastic man. "Alright," he said, lighting up another Pall Mall with a red disposable lighter. "Guess this makes me look bad since he turned up dead, but I went out there and said to get the hell off my property. I didn't lay a hand on him. All I done was pretend like I was going to kick him. He ran off crying and that's the last I saw him."

"Did he get in a car or truck with anyone?"

"I couldn't tell you. It was dark. He just disappeared."

"What did you do then?"

"I came back inside and made sure Glenda was ok, then I came back here and worked on what I'm workin' on now."

"Anyone else witness the incident?" asked Kenny.

"Glenda. There were a lot of customers, too, but I couldn't tell you their names."

"So if I go out there now and asked her about this," I said, "she'll give us the same story?"

"She will if she's telling the truth."

"What time would you say this happened?" I asked.

"I wasn't exactly keeping track," he said, the orange tip of the cigarette bouncing up and down as he spoke. "Sometime between 10 and 11."

"Let's go ask her," I said. Chrisler got up as if to come along. I lightly pushed him back into his chair. "That's ok. We can handle it."

Kenny and I walked over to the snack bar. Glenda was waiting on the only customer in the house. She was little-girl cute; I could see where she might inspire lust in a thirteen-year-old, but in a grown man? Maybe, if the grown man has the mind of a thirteen-year-old.

"Is your name Glenda?" I asked when she'd finished. She nodded. I showed her the picture of Frankie. "You know this person? His name is Frankie Gately."

She blinked and nodded. "I know Frankie. I know he's dead. I heard it at school this morning."

"Aren't you still on summer vacation?"

"Summer band. We're getting ready for football season."

"What instrument do you play?"

"I don't play anything," she said. "I'm a twirler."

She looked like a twirler.

"So the kids were talking about it this morning?"

"Oh yeh. It's so sad." She pronounced 'sad' with an extra syllable: 'Say-id.'

"I understand he was giving you a hard time last night."

She nodded. "Kind of. But that don't mean I wisht he'd died."

"What did he do to you,?" asked Kenny.

"Well ..." she paused. "He ran up to me real fast when my daddy dropped me off. I didn't see him comin' and it scared me. I reckon I screamed."

"He just ran up to you?"

"Uh-huh, he came up behind me and said 'Hi, Glenda,' real loud. It scared me, and I screamed."

"Did he touch you?"

"He might've brushed up against me a little."

"But did he hurt you?"

"No, he didn't hurt me. Just scared me, is all."

"Mr. Chrisler says he attacked you."

"He did?" she said. "Well, I guess he kind of did. I mean, he scared me and made me scream and all." A customer approached the snack bar, a boy about ten years-old, clutching a dollar. Glenda gave him a smile and said, "I got to get back to work y'all, ok?"

"Just a second," I said. "Did anyone else see what Frankie did?"

"I don't think so. There were cars driving by, but me and him were the only ones in the parking lot."

"Did you tell Mr. Chrisler what happened when you came inside?"

"Yeh, I think I was laughing when I told him. After it was over, it seemed kind of funny."

"What did Mr. Chrisler do when you told him?" asked Kenny.

"He looked pretty mad and went outside. I reckon he went to chase Frankie off."

"How long was he out there?"

She frowned. "I don't know. I was busy."

"Did he come back?"

"Well, of course he came back."

"But you don't know how long he was gone?" said Kenny.

The little boy with the dollar was still waiting patiently. Glenda said, "Listen, I need to help this guy."

The little guy said, "That's ok. I can wait."

Glenda gave him a dirty look. "Listen," she said to us, exasperated, "I don't know. I was busy." She looked back at Chrisler's office, so I looked over my shoulder and saw him pull his head back. "It wasn't very long. I know he was back by 12:00, when we close."

I didn't see how badgering her any further would help. I handed her my business card, told her she wasn't in trouble and to call me if she thought of anything else.

She gave me an uncertain grin. "I don't think I will, but ok."

Kenny and I went back to Chrisler's office.

"What did she say?" Chrisler asked.

"Pretty much what you said," I lied. "You told us you came back inside after you got rid of Frankie, right?

"I had to. I can't leave these kids to run the place by themselves."

"You didn't go back outside for any reason?"

He squinted at me through a cloud of blue smoke. "Listen, Chief Hardy. I don't know what you think you know, but all I did was go outside and tell him to get lost. I watched him run off until I couldn't see him anymore, then I came back inside. That's it." He paused. "Maybe I took the trash out at some point."

"That didn't take very long, I reckon?"

"A minute or two."

"But other than that, you were in your office for the rest of the night?"

"Until closing. Then I went home."

"What time was that?"

"We close the door at 12:00. I count the money and I'm out of here by 12:30."

"Do you run this place by yourself?" I asked. "I mean, besides the kids you got working for you."

He leaned back in his chair and folded his hands over his expansive gut. "Well, I got me what you might call a silent partner."

"Mind telling us his name?"

"See, that's part of being a silent partner," he said with a smile. "Not lettin' people know your name."

I let that go for the moment. "One more thing," I said. "Do you know a young man by the name of Randy Braley?"

He shrugged. "Yeh, he comes in sometimes."

"His mama says he used to work for you."

Chrisler scoffed. "I wouldn't say he worked for me. I paid him to do a couple of deliveries for me. I needed someone with a pickup."

"What kind of deliveries?" I asked.

"As I recall, I had him take some stuff to the dump."

"When was the last time you saw him?"

"I couldn't tell you. It's been some time."

"Was he in last night?"

He shrugged. "I don't know. He might've been. If he was, I didn't see him."

"We have a witness who saw him drop-off Frankie Gately in your parking lot."

"Maybe he did. I didn't see it."

He got back to work screwing little plastic men onto the chrome rods. I dropped my business card on his desk. "We'll leave it there, for now. You have a good day, Mr. Chrisler. If you think of anything else, I'd appreciate it if you gave us a call."

"Be glad to," he said. His tone suggested the opposite.

Kenny's and I went outside. The rain had stopped, but the air felt like a hot wet blanket hanging over everything.

"I don't trust that SOB as far as I could throw him," I said.

"He's a shifty son of a gun," said Kenny. "Although he could just be downplaying what he did because he's afraid it makes him look bad."

"He practically admitted he was the last person to see Frankie alive. I'd say that makes him look bad enough."

"Yeh, I guess it does," said Kenny. He started the engine and cranked up the air conditioner. "That girl couldn't pin a time on when he came back. If all this happened between 10:00 and 11:00, he'd have plenty of time to kill Frankie and get back in time to close."

"Why would he kill him, though?" I said. "Just because he spooked his employee? That's got to be up there with some of the all-time ridiculous motives, don't you think?"

"Folks have been killed for less," he said, a dismal look on his face. "Hey, do you think we should've asked him about the Kingfisher and Idabel murders?"

"Maybe," I said. "I thought about it, but I decided I'd best leave that to Isabel, at least for now. I'd rather focus on what's right in front of us."

"Yeh, that makes sense," said Kenny. "You know, I'm kind of wondering if whoever was driving that Trans-Am might be Chrisler's silent partner."

"That's a thought," I said.

Kenny waited for a truck hauling a trailer loaded with drilling gear to pass, then pulled onto the highway. "You ever have time to listen to that Champion Jack Dupree tape?" he asked.

"I did."

"What'd you think?"

"Pretty bleak," I said. "But I like it."

Kenny chuckled. "He wasn't kidding when he named it *Blues from the Gutter*."

On the way back, I tried to think of reasons Jim Chrisler would want to pull a Stack-O-Lee on Frankie Gately. I couldn't come up with even one.

CHAPTER 12

Kenny dropped me at the station. I felt bad about first giving him the day off, then calling him back in to work, so I asked him if he wanted to punch out early. He said he wanted to finish his shift. I didn't argue and sent him out on patrol.

Karen was out of the office. I assumed she'd absconded with my pickup, since it wasn't where I'd left it. It was getting close to quitting time, anyway. I gave Cindy some instructions to pass on to Lester—who was working a double for the second night in a row—and made the short walk home.

I used to let my dog Dizzy have the run of the town. She'd catch up with me when I'd walk home, and we'd travel the rest of the way together. I miss her and was more than a little perturbed when that woman made me have to explain she was dead. It's not something I enjoy recalling. I came home from work one late-summer day a couple of years ago and found her motionless at my front door, foam on her muzzle, and her eyes open and unblinking. The worst part was that I wasn't there for her when she passed.

My father Everett Hardy died not long after Dizzy. As hard as it was to lose Diz, losing him was even worse.

***

I'd gone over to his place for one of my daily visits. I knocked and nobody answered, but it was Dad's nurse's day off, so I didn't think much of it. I let myself in and found him in the recliner I'd bought for him. Unlike my old beat-up La-Z-Boy, which I bought for next to nothing 20 years ago, Dad's was the best money could buy. I reckoned if he was going to sleep sitting up, I might as well find him something better than the ratty old armchair he'd been using.

It was the least I could do. I couldn't even cook for him anymore. Our afternoon lunches were one of the last things binding us together. Now we didn't even have those. The dementia that made us strangers to one another had robbed him of his appetite. It seemed to bother me more than it did him.

His eyes were closed. I assumed he was asleep. He had on the same dark yellow Carhartt coveralls he wore most days of his adult life and a green Army blanket draped over his lap. His head was thrown back and his mouth open like he was snoring, except he didn't make a sound. I tried to shake him awake. I couldn't. His forehead was cold. He was gone.

I wasn't exactly shocked. He'd been declining for years: fast at first, then gradual enough that you didn't notice any change from one day to the next. Maybe it was because of that slowness that his death hit me so hard. I was a grown man with a wife and a good job and money in the bank, but I cried like a baby.

I called out to him and tried to open his eyes with my fingers, but they wouldn't stay open. I don't know what I was expecting.

I guess people do strange things in situations like that.

The chair was not reclined. Dad sat upright, his slippered feet flat on the floor. Between them was a worn black satchel—the kind doctors used to carry when they made house calls. This one was bigger, though. More like a suitcase. In one hand, he held a small, black, leather-bound book. I didn't remember having seen either the book or satchel before.

I opened the satchel. Inside were bundles of what looked like five-dollar bills. Each bundle was held together by a paper ring labeled "$100." I shuffled a stack like a deck of cards. There was something odd about the bills. The engraving seemed fancier, and instead of having Abraham Lincoln on the front, there was a picture of an Indian chief in a headdress. On the back was a big "V" where the Lincoln Memorial was supposed to be. In various places on the front and back were the words "silver certificate."

I knew what a silver certificate was. I'd even seen a few, although none like this.

The inside of the satchel smelled like an old storage trunk. I kneeled and dumped the contents onto the rug. Sure enough, four or five mothballs fell out with dozens of bundles of the strange currency. I counted over 100. I've never been good at math, but even I can multiply 100 by 100. It came out to more than $10,000.

I got up off the floor and called Pate's Funeral Home, with whom I'd made prior arrangements, knowing this day would come eventually. I returned to the living room and sat down at my father's feet.

"What is this, Dad?" I said. I was embarrassed by the strange high-pitched voice that came out of my mouth, even though there was no one around to hear it. I removed the little black book from my father's hand. It appeared to be at least as old as the satchel. I opened it.

On the inside front cover in faded black ink was written, "Emmett's Rainy Day Fund." Underneath it read, "June 5th, 1927." The day of my birth. I recognized the handwriting as my mother's. The book was a ledger. There were columns labeled "Date," "Amount," and "Place." Entries under the latter were mostly from the little bank in Burr where my folks kept their money, although there were others: "Gift from Aunt Irene in Nashville," or "Piggly Wiggly in Alva." Around the date of my mother's death, the handwriting changed from her clear hand to Dad's near illegible scrawl. As the years passed, the entries became fewer and harder to read. The last one had been made only the day before. Under "Amount" Dad had written "5.00." Nothing was written under "Place." I rummaged through the stacks on the floor, looking for a loose bill. I didn't find one.

I stuffed the bundles back in the bag and threw out the moth balls. The boys from Pate's took Dad away and left me alone. I started to fold the blanket that had been on his lap. A five-dollar silver certificate like the others fell on the floor. I put it in my wallet.

At the wake, I showed it to Dad's best friend Jerry, and told him about the bag I'd found.

Jerry smiled. "My Lord, I haven't thought about that in years. Your dad started socking away those silver certificates the day you were born. He and your mama used to search high and low for those damn things. Had to be five dollars, too. Don't ask me why. I can't imagine the government printed all that many of them. I reckon your folks cornered the market. Your dad always thought they'd be valuable one day. You should look into cashing those in. I'll bet they're worth something."

I said they were worth at least 10 grand.

He said: "I wouldn't be surprised if they're worth more than that."

I took the bag to the bank the next day, curious to see what they were worth. The cashier directed me to the bank president, Deke Bixby. Deke's the younger brother of Edgar Bixby, who I put in jail for murder about eight years ago. We aren't bosom pals.

Deke met me at his office door. He wasn't in the mood to reminisce about old times. I told him why I was there. "Have you counted it?" he asked.

I said I had.

"How much?" he asked.

"$10,000," I said.

"Then they're worth $10,000," he said, and shut the door in my face.

Simmie Blevins was witness to our exchange. Simmie's been a teller at the bank longer than I'd been alive. She pulled me aside and told me my father had just been in a couple of days earlier. "He always insisted I call him whenever I came across one of those five-dollar silver certificates," she said. "I hadn't seen one in years, but I got one earlier this week and called him first thing. He came by and wrote me a check for five dollars in exchange. He saved those for you. Did you know that?"

I said I did.

"He was a fine man, your father."

I thanked her, then went to the Burr Public Library to do some research. Come to find out, those silver certificates never appreciated in value much. They were still worth five dollars apiece.

Dad probably didn't know. Or maybe he knew and just didn't care. Either way, something about those five-dollar silver certificates compelled him to get up out of his fancy recliner and drive to the bank on the next-to-last day of his life.

I cried some more after I left the library.

CHAPTER 13

My pickup was in the driveway when I got home. Red, however, was nowhere to be found. Her car was gone, though, leading me to the conclusion I'd have to fend for myself, dinner-wise. I changed out of my uniform and got in my pickup. I listened to Champion Jack Dupree sing the tragic tale of Frankie and Johnny while I drove around trying to decide where to eat.

It was the early evening of a typical August day, meaning it still felt like God was training sunlight on me through a magnifying glass. With gas prices so high, I try to drive without the air-conditioner when I can get away with it. But after a couple of minutes of insects blowing into my mouth, I broke down and turned it on.

I decided a Quarter Pounder sounded good, so I headed for McDonalds. My addiction to fast food rivals my weakness for bourbon. The problem with McDonalds—besides making me fat—is that it's not a drive-in, so even if I want to take it out, I have to go inside, which means I'm forced to talk to people I'd rather not talk to. Ultimately, my craving for a burger and fries outweighed my urge to be left alone.

It was dinnertime, so there was a considerable line at the counter. I fell in behind a couple of boys about junior high school age having an animated conversation about something. After a few seconds, I realized they were talking about Frankie Gately.

"Yeh, man," one of them said loud enough for me to hear, "I saw Frankie riding around with Braley last night."

"Gettin' high, probably," the other one said at a lower volume.

"Braley's an asshole," the first kid said, then looked around to make sure Mr. Braley wasn't within hearing distance. He saw me instead, which in his view that might've been just as bad. He elbowed the other kid, who then turned around. Both clammed up. They got their food and found a booth by the front window. I got mine and joined them.

"You two boys mind if I sit with you?" I asked.

They stared wide-eyed at one another, burgers frozen in midair, probably wondering if a night behind bars lay in their immediate future. Having kids be afraid of me is on the always growing list of things I don't like about being a cop.

"Ok," one of them said. He was skinny and short, with big teeth and shaggy dark blonde hair sticking out of a blue and white Pabst Blue Ribbon baseball cap. The other was taller and stouter, with a round face, small brown eyes and dark hair tamed into a helmet by what must've been half a jar of Dippity-do.

I sat down next to the skinny one, opened the foam clamshell and dumped my fries into the open half. "They sure make good french fries here, don't they?" They said "Uh-huh" in unison. I Introduced myself and asked their names. The short one was Kevin, the big one, Jeff.

"Y'all about ready for school to start?"

They both said "Yeh," uncertainly, hoping it was the right answer. I reckoned I'd just as well get to the point.

"I heard you talkin' about Frankie Gately. I guess you know what happened to him last night."

They nodded.

"Did either of you know him?"

"We both did," Jeff said.

"He a friend of yours?"

Jeff looked at Kevin for help. Kevin said hesitantly, "I wouldn't say we were friends. He's a lot older than us."

"But you've seen him around, I expect."

Jeff swallowed a bite of burger and said: "He hangs around at Chrisler's. I see him there sometimes. Play him at foosball."

"What do you think of him?

"I don't know," said Jeff. "He stinks at foosball. He's ok, I guess."

"For a retard," Kevin added. They both laughed.

I gave them a stern look. "That's not very nice."

They stopped laughing

"Yeh, I know," said Kevin. "I'm sorry. He's actually a nice guy. I guess in some ways he's the nicest grown-up I know. Was the nicest, I mean."

"What's nice about him?"

"Oh, he's just nice, you know," said Kevin. "Friendly. He's always happy."

"Yeh," said Jeff. "I don't know if I'd be so nice if I was as poor as he is and didn't have a mom and dad."

I nodded and waited.

"Yeh, it's kind of scary, what happened to him," said Kevin.

"Well, we're going to find whoever did this," I said, meaning to put their minds at ease, although I knew events could end up making a liar out of me.

None of us spoke for a few seconds.

"I heard you talking about Randy Braley. Is he someone Frankie rides around with?"

Kevin glared at Jeff, who had little choice but to answer. "Yeh, he hangs around with Braley."

"One of you said you saw Frankie and Braley together last night."

Jeff looked at Kevin like he was asking permission to talk. Kevin threw up his hands and said, "Go ahead. Tell him. Get us beaten up, I don't care."

"Yeh," said Jeff. "I saw him last night on my way home from the movie."

"You went to the movies last night?" Kevin said.

"Yeh, my brother took me."

"What'd you see?"

"The Exorcist."

"Ah, man! You saw The Exorcist? Why didn't you ask me to go?"

"I knew your mom wouldn't let you."

"Ah, man," Jeff said, frowning. "Yeh, you're probably right."

"What time was it that you saw Frankie and Randy?" I asked.

"On the way home. I guess a little after ten o'clock."

"Where'd you see them?"

"They were pulling out of the Sonic as we were driving in."

"Ah, man!" said Kevin. "You went to Sonic, too?"

"Ok boys, let's stick to the subject," I said. Kevin gave Jeff a sideways look. "I get the feeling you don't care much for Randy Braley."

Kevin said in a low voice, "He's a big jerk. Don't tell anyone I said that, though." He paused. "Especially him."

"Don't worry. This is purely confidential. What is it you don't like about him?"

"The way he messes with everyone," said Jeff. "Not just Frankie."

"He picks on younger kids," added Kevin. "I mean a lot younger. Not just like us, but elementary school kids, too."

"And he sells them drugs, too," said Kevin.

"That's a serious charge."

"Everyone knows it," said Jeff. "He doesn't hide it."

"How'd he treat Frankie?"

They both shrugged. "Ok, I guess," said Jeff.

"He bossed him around a bunch," said Kevin. He lowered his voice again. "I think they did drugs together."

"Any idea what kind?"

"Pot, probably," said Kevin.

"You ever see Braley hit Frankie?"

They shook their heads in unison. "Nah," said Jeff. "Frankie was too big to beat up. But Braley yelled at him a lot. Frankie didn't seem to mind. Usually, he just laughed. At least the times I saw." He looked at Kevin for confirmation. He nodded in agreement.

I finished my burger, wadded up the refuse, and stuffed it into the paper bag.

"I'll let you boys finish your food in peace." I wrote down their full names and phone numbers for possible future reference. "Don't worry. You're not in trouble. I just don't know many kids your age, is all. I reckon you might be able to help me out at some point."

They obviously didn't like the sound of that, probably because they'd been seen talking to me. We'd been keeping our voices down, but the joint was packed with kids their age and every eye was fixed on the two of them.

"Just don't tell anyone," Kevin said through stiff lips, his face as red as the hair on the life-sized Ronald McDonald statue by the door.

"Yeh," added Jeff. "No one likes a narc, ok?"

"Would it help if I made it sound like you two were in trouble?" I whispered.

They looked at each other and came to an unspoken agreement..

"Yes," said Jeff.

I slammed my hands on the table. All noise in the room ceased. "Don't let me see you two doing that again," I said loudly.

Jeff was confused. "What'd we do?"

Kevin kicked him under the table and said, "Okay, Chief Hardy. We're sorry. We'll be careful next time."

"You'd better," I said, feeling sad we live in a world where a twelve-year-old boy would rather be thought of as a petty criminal than as an ally of law enforcement.

I left them to their own devices. I hoped I hadn't ruined their reputations, but if I did, it was for a good cause.

I went to the counter and bought another Tab on my way out. I got in my pickup, thinking I was going to drive home. After putting on the Champion Jack tape and hearing him sing about all the evil things he'd done, however, I started feeling like doing something a little evil myself.

I drove to the site of our new police station. I reckoned no one would think it strange seeing the police chief's pickup parked outside the new police station under construction. I got out and looked around. The construction workers had quit for the day. Considering how much rain we'd gotten earlier, they might not have been there at all.

I grabbed my Tab and secreted my bottle of Smirnoff in a paper bag. The building had no roof, although the outside was starting to look like something. There still weren't any doors in the doorways or glass in the windows. The inside walls were made of the same cinderblock as the outer walls. The rooms were recognizable as such, except there weren't any ceilings or tile on the floors. I took a brief tour before settling down on an old couch someone had dragged into the space that would one day be my office. I tried to detect the smell of marijuana but could not. Everything was wet from the rain, but I managed to find a piece of plastic to cover the couch. I sat down and topped off my Tab with vodka.

I'd gotten drunk in worse places.

I relaxed for a bit, drank my drink, and considered the next step of my official-unofficial murder investigation. At some point, I must've fallen asleep. My mind is foggy on the matter.

The next thing I remember, Kenny was shaking me by the shoulder and shining a flashlight in my face. My first thought was to hide the bottle of vodka. I felt around in the dark but couldn't find it. Kenny held it up and said, "Looking for this?" When I'd started, it was half-full. Now it was empty.

I remembered an old *I Love Lucy* episode and said, in English more fractured than Desi Arnaz's but in a different way: "I guess I have some explaining to do."

"Don't you think you ought to go home?" asked Kenny. "Mrs. Hardy is climbing the walls worrying about you."

Mrs. Hardy was my mother, I thought, and she's been dead over twenty years. Then I realized he was talking about Karen.

"Oh, hell, what time is it?"

"Nine o'clock."

Dammit to hell anyway. I'd been laying on that couch for more than three hours. In my panic, I stood up too fast. The floor seemed to open under my feet, and I fell backwards. The couch was where I'd left it and broke my fall. I dimly understood I would, at the very least, need to down a pot of black coffee before I dared show my face to Karen.

Kenny got hold of Karen and told her he'd found me, sparing any but the essential details. He then proceeded to lay into me a bit.

"Chief, whether or not you drink isn't any business of mine, although I've been around long enough to remember how it caused you a lot of problems."

I growled something mean about him being right. It was none of his business. He said, "Ok, I just care about you, is all." I felt bad when he said that. I should've apologized but didn't.

He then took me back to McDonald's and pumped me full of coffee. When I'd gotten at least some of my wits about me, he drove me back to the construction site to pick up my truck. I drove home carefully, prepared to meet my doom.

Red started in on me before I could say a word.

"You mean to tell me you've been sleeping in your new office on some dirty old couch? How does that work, exactly?"

I reckon the fact that I wasn't dead in a ditch somewhere gave her permission to be mad. My best way out of this jam was to be as truthful as I could without dropping the fact I'd been drinking, which I expected would set off an explosion that makes an atom bomb look like a lady finger.

CHAPTER 14

I've spent a good chunk of time over the years sitting on my back porch and watching the sun go down. I haven't spent near as much time watching the sun come up, since I like to sleep as late as I can. After the reaming out Karen had given me the night before, however, I thought it best that I put some space between us. I couldn't remember exactly what either of us said, but I knew it wasn't a polite exchange of opposing views. When I woke up and saw she was still asleep, I made myself some coffee and dragged a kitchen chair onto the front porch.

The view of the eastern horizon is obscured by the houses across the street. It's not as quiet as the backyard, either. Our across-the-street neighbor raises goats, so I got an earful of bleating. The fella next to him has a chicken coop beside his house, so there was also a crowing rooster and clucking chickens. There's a pump jack in the vicinity making a rhythmic thumping and creaking noise as it sucks oil out of the ground. Between all that and the flock of noisy birds that had taken up temporary residence in the cottonwood tree in our yard, I got quite the sunrise serenade.

I sipped my coffee and brooded over who might've killed Frankie Gately. Jim Chrisler had incriminated himself up to a point when he admitted he'd had an altercation with the boy just hours before his body was found. There was something about Sam Carter that made me think he could've done it. Maybe it was that ugly scar across his face and the fact that he dressed like a member of a motorcycle gang. Of course, Randy Braley had to be in the frame since he picked up Frankie that night.

But maybe it wasn't any of them. Maybe it was whoever had killed that family in Kingfisher and that hitchhiker in Idabel. I was dead certain Dwight and Amanda hadn't killed anything but the occasional cockroach in that dump of an apartment they shared. Still, it might be true that Frankie was killed with the same gun as those other folks. In that case, a mass murderer might live in Burr. At the very least, he'd been here a little more than 24 hours earlier. He could still be around.

The thought gave me a headache. But that might have been from the previous evening's over-consumption.

I considered Frankie's killing separate from the others. Why would someone shoot in the back of the head a mentally retarded young adult male who never hurt anyone and leave his body in the back row of a drive-in movie theater?

It could just be the act of a random crazy person, I thought.

I answered myself: Well, of course whoever did it was crazy. The only killers I ever met who weren't were the young men I fought with in the Marines. They killed to survive.

That's not to say there weren't a few flat-out nuts who seemed to enjoy it. Maybe whoever shot Frankie was like that. A psychopath.

Was Frankie a physical threat to someone? That story Chrisler told about him attacking that girl was ridiculous, according to both her and Kenny. The girl had no reason to lie, and I'll take Kenny's word over Jim Chrisler's any time. I reckoned we could cross self-defense off the list.

How about revenge?

Who would've felt the need to revenge themselves upon Frankie Gately—a twenty-something man with the mind of a child? Frankie scared Glenda, and she didn't like it, but she'd practically forgotten about it almost as soon as it happened. She said she laughed when she told Chrisler about it. Did she have a boyfriend who decided to teach Frankie a lesson? Over such a little thing? I tended to think not, although it might be something we should check out.

Could Frankie have stolen something and been killed by the person who wanted it back? I didn't think so. Frankie wasn't the type, and anyway, it's unlikely that a person with his issues would be clever enough to pull off a theft that would inspire such violence.

So what was left? Craziness, I guess, or sheer meanness, which might be opposite sides of the same coin. I might not be any kind of Sherlock Holmes, but I'm smart enough to know that if you eliminate the impossible, whatever you're left with—no matter how improbable—must be the truth. I hadn't eliminated the impossible, but at this stage, some things seemed more likely than others.

It got to be 7:30. The sun still had not made an appearance above the roofs across the street. A band of coyotes started howling, sending a chill down my spine. Sunrise is for roosters, not coyotes. I took it as a sign and went inside to face the music.

My fears were unfounded. Karen was in a pretty good mood, or at least she pretended to be. She didn't even bring up what had happened. Neither did I. We didn't talk much, but she was more pleasant than I had any right to expect. We typically take turns going in to work at eight o'clock. Today was my turn, so we didn't spend too much time together.

Cindy held the phone out to me as I walked through the door.

"Agent Cruickshank of the OSBI," she said. "For you."

I told her I'd take it in my office.

I sank back into my chair, picked up the phone, and asked Isabel if there was any news.

"It's looking like that tip about the Cottrells was fraudulent," she said. "A family feud. An agent in the city tracked down Billy Wayne. He didn't get him to confess, but apparently Billy Wayne's a terrible liar. Anyway, as luck would have it, the Cottrells got caught by a local cop in Perry having sex in the back of a van on the north-bound side of I-35 at the time of Frankie's death. I think we can safely rule them out."

"Even for the Idabel and Kingfisher deaths?"

"Yeh, well, that's the thing. We got the final ballistics on the bullet that killed Frankie Gately. It came from the same gun as those from the other homicides. If the Cottrells didn't kill Frankie, they didn't kill the others."

"I guess that means you're back at square one."

"Yeh, to a certain extent, although we have two independent witnesses who recall seeing an old beat-up blue pickup near the scene of both the Idabel and Kingfisher killings."

"That's something."

"Better than nothing."

"What do you suggest I do, assuming you still want my help?"

She sighed. "Well, I'd like us to work alongside one another, but I'm under some pressure to include this guy I'm training."

"By the way, what's that fella's name again?"

"Probationary Agent Merle Raksin."

I wrote it down on the desk blotter.

"Anyway," she said, "I've got to hold his hand, so I believe we could get more done if you and I run separate tracks. I'll keep you informed and vice versa."

"What's your main line of inquiry?"

"I'll run down the lead on the pickup, ask around to see whether one like it was seen in the vicinity of the drive-in the other night."

"What would you have me do, if you had your druthers?"

"You know this town. Keep your head down and do what you can. If you see any troopers or OSBI agents on your travels, though, head in the opposite direction."

"Got it. Whatever I do, I do it quietly and on my own."

"Any ideas?" she asked.

"I've got the guy who might've been the last person to see Frankie," I said, "this fella named Jim Chrisler. He runs an arcade here in town, where we know Frankie was at some point between nine and ten o'clock. Chrisler ran him off for scaring some girl who works for him. He says all he did was basically tell the kid to get off his property, but I have my doubts. I also have a witness who saw Randy Braley drop off Frankie at Chrisler's."

"From what I can tell, Braley hasn't been seen since that night."

"Yeh, Karen talked to his mama. She says she hasn't seen him. The old gal's a real piece of work but Karen thinks she's genuinely worried. We'll keep looking."

"As will I," she said. "All that sounds promising. Just investigate it on the sly. In fact, the fewer members of your team involved the better. Karen's fine, but make it an exclusive club."

"What about Kenny?"

She sighed. "Well, I guess he's already into it pretty deep. But just those two."

"No problem. We'll keep Lester on regular duty. Maybe we'll call in our part-timer, too. We've got to have someone left to deal with the usual sacks of sh—" I caught myself. "You get the idea," I continued.

"I do," she said.

"I'll get after it and try to stay out of your way."

"Sounds good, Chief. I'll be in touch."

"Backatcha."

CHAPTER 15

I only had one murder I was helping to solve, and nobody even knew I was working on it. Isabel had five—she was the chief investigator on the Gately homicide and assisting on the Kingfisher and Idabel cases—and everybody knew. The spotlight was on her. I was working in the shadows. If I helped find the killer, great. If I didn't? No harm, no foul. Basically, all I needed to do was avoid engineering a Bay-of-Pigs level screw-up.

That didn't mean I wasn't putting pressure on myself.

Isabel had agreed to let me rope-in Karen and Kenny, which I intended to do. Since this would be my focus for the next few days at least, I'd need Red to run things around the station. She's help in other ways, though. As for Kenny, I didn't want to put too much on his plate, given that he was still upset about losing his friend. I intended to use him as needed, however, if he felt up to it.

Red had walked in while I was on the phone to Isabel. We went back to my office and shut the door. I reckoned the best way to avoid rehashing my ill-advised nap from the day before would be to get straight to the point.

"I just got off the phone with Isabel," I said. "They've cleared the Cottrells."

"No surprise there."

"Nope. Also, the ballistics report came in on the Gately case. The same gun that killed him also killed that family in Kingfisher and the fella in Idabel."

She didn't flinch. "So we're looking for a spree killer, then."

"You might call it that. I don't know. This fella seems to target specific people."

"How do you figure?"

"Why would someone go to all the trouble of breaking into someone's house to shoot a man and wife and their little daughter, if he's doing it just for kicks?"

"Hmmm. That doesn't compute, does it?"

"No it doesn't. Frankie and that hitchhiker seem random enough targets, but the family? I can't help but believe there was a reason behind that one."

"And if there's a reason behind one, there's a reason behind them all."

"That's what I'm thinking. Which makes me believe there's got to be a connection. We just need to find out what it is."

"Does Isabel think the same thing?"

"What, that there's a connection? I don't know. It only occurred to me after I got off the phone with her."

"Well, it makes sense to me. Do you want me working with you on this?" She cut me off before I could reply. "Just remember I got a pile of paperwork three-feet-high waiting for me. Plus, someone's going to have to run the show if you're helping Agent Cruickshank."

"She doesn't want me bringing in any of our folks, anyway, since officially we're not supposed to be working on it."

"Good," she said, looking somewhat relieved.

"She did say I could use you and Kenny."

She rolled her eyes and shook her head. "Great."

"Don't worry, I won't ask you to do much. Maybe a phone call or two. Run down license plate numbers. Stuff like that."

"Whatever," she said wearily. "Just keep it to a minimum, if you don't mind."

"I'll have Kenny help me, too, if he's able."

"You're the boss."

"Right now I'm going to head out to Delia Wishon's place to see if her son's shown up since you talked to her."

"Oh joy. Have fun."

***

I slipped a tape into my truck's tape deck. Not Champion Jack this time. That stuff was too dour for the mood I was in. I put in another tape Kenny gave me by a fella named Buddy Guy. Buddy's blues are the kind that make the blues go away, if you know what I mean.

The music didn't help much, though. I was feeling down, noticing everything that was wrong—with my life, with my job, with my town.

Driving through town on my way to Delia Wishon's, I started noticing how dirty everything was. When did that happen? It wasn't that way when I was a kid. At least I don't think so. The trucks and cars were dirty. The windows in the stores were dirty. Caked red dirt covered everything in sight. You'd think with all the rain we'd gotten, it would've washed away a lot. But Oklahoma red isn't like that. It's tenacious. You can be washing your car and get right up on it with the spray. That dirt'll just give you the middle finger.

Maybe that's part of getting old, noticing dirt all over everything.

All the trailers in the trailer park where Delia Wishon lived were dirty. Hers was the dirtiest.

The doorbell was broken, so I had to knock. She came to the door in a clingy turquoise-green lace dress. It might've looked good on a burlesque dancer half her age, but on Delia Wishon it looked like she'd started to get dressed, then decided it wasn't worth the trouble. The tops of her light blue felt bedroom slippers were embroidered with the outline of a swan. Her hair was bleached yellow blond and lacquered into a Jayne Mansfield-type style. I suspect it had not been brushed since Mrs. Wishon had last visited a beauty salon, which, I conjectured, might well have been when Miss Mansfield was in her heyday. That was a while back.

"Yeh?" she asked, looking at me through puffy eyes. Her breath stank of many things, most noticeably beer and cigarettes. "If you're looking for that little bastard son of mine, he could be anywhere, but he's not here, so I'd appreciate it if you'd get out of here and leave me the hell alone."

All this before I could even introduce myself.

"Mrs. Wishon, my name is Emmett Hardy. I'm the local Chief of Police. My Assistant Chief was here yesterday asking about Randy. We were just wondering if you'd heard from him since."

"No, I haven't," she slurred. "If you see him, tell him to bring back my ice chest."

I made no promises on that count. "When was the last time you saw your son, Mrs. Wishon?"

"I don't know," she said, then muttered a series of angry sounds that did not resemble any language I'd ever heard. Her leathery face had caved in on its geographic center, her mouth. Apparently, Mrs. Wishon only puts in her false teeth on special occasions.

"Has it been in the last 48 hours?"

She shook her head.

"Any idea where he might be?"

"Gettin' inna trouble," she said.

"Does he have any friend who might have an idea where he is? Any family?"

"He's always hangin' around with that little retard who got killed." She wiped away a string of drool trickling down her chin. "Is that why you're lookin' for him? You think he killed that retarded kid?"

"We're concerned for his safety, ma'am, although we are hoping he might help us in our inquiries."

"Oh, hell," she said, without seeming to hear a word I'd said. "I wouldn't exac'ly be surprised if he did kill that kid. His step-daddy shot an Indian for looking at him crossways."

Already I was thinking she wouldn't be much help, but I kept asking questions, anyway.

"I understand he drives a blue pickup. You wouldn't remember the make and model, would you?"

She rested the side of her face on the doorframe. "It's blue."

I reckoned I'd have to settle for that.

"Would he have any reason to travel to Idabel? Family? Friends?"

She pushed herself away from the doorframe. It left an indentation on her cheek.

"Oh hell, no, he don't know nobody in Idabel. He might've gotten a wild hair across his ass and gone to visit his step daddy in prison." The state penitentiary in McAlester is a couple of hours north of Idabel. "That is, if his piece of shit truck'd make it, which it prolly wouldn't."

"How about Kingfisher?"

She shook her head. "I'n't know why he'd go there."

"My colleague says he used to work for a Mr. Chrisler."

"Yeh, at that whorehouse downtown. He might still. He don't never tell me anything." She started to cry.

I told her that to the best of my knowledge, there wasn't a whorehouse downtown.

"Oh hell, you know what I mean," she sputtered through the tears. "That puss ball place."

"You mean foosball?"

"Puss ball, foosball," she sputtered. Little droplets of spit hit me in the face. "What the hell's the difference? He worked there, that's all." He expression turned hopeful. "Maybe he still does. Y'all think you could go there and check?"

I said I could. I didn't say I already had, and he wasn't there.

"If you find him, tell him to bring back my ice chest. And put some ice in it. My refrigerator's busted. My beer's all warm." She turned her head and spat on her carpet. "Jeez Louise, I hate warm beer."

***

If Randy Braley killed Frankie, he'd have had to kill that accountant's family in Kingfisher and the hitchhiker in Idabel, too. He either killed all of them or none of them.

I leaned toward believing the latter. No matter how much of a punk Braley is (and according to sources as varied as Kenny Harjo and the boy's mother, he won't be winning any good citizen awards), I can't imagine he'd travel the width of the state for no discernible reason just to kill someone he'd never met. Not knowing him at all, I guess I could see him killing a local kid, especially one who trusted him and wouldn't put up a fight. But a stranger? Depending on how depraved he is, he might kill for kicks, but I can't see him going to the trouble of driving 300 miles to do it.

Even if he wasn't the one who killed him, Randy Braley was one of the last people to see Frankie alive. That was reason enough to talk to him.

Trouble was, no one could find him.

There was also the matter of the blue pickup spotted near the other two crime scenes. That could've been Braley's. Or it could've been someone else's.

Jim Chrisler claimed not to have seen Braley that night, but if Braley was working for him, he might well have a reason to cover for the kid. I figured it couldn't hurt to talk to him again and press him on the matter.

The same orange Trans-Am I'd seen the last time I was at Chrisler's was leaving just as I got there. I made a mental note to ask Chrisler about it.

The sign said they were closed, but I tried the door and it was unlocked. I let myself in. The place was empty of people, but I could hear clinking and clanking coming from the office.

I found Chrisler doing the same thing he'd been doing there when I was there last—leaning over his desk, screwing little plastic soccer men onto long chrome rods. A plume of fresh blue smoke merged near the ceiling with Ghosts of Cigarettes Past. Chrisler's gray work pants covered even less of his rear end than before.

"Still working on that?" I said.

He gave me a dirty look. "Trying to. I keep getting interrupted." He put down the screwdriver. "Where's Officer Geronimo? Out collecting scalps?"

"You're a regular Bob Hope, Mr. Chrisler."

He grinned wide enough for me to see more of his tobacco-stained teeth than I cared to. "Oh hell, I'm way funnier than Bob Hope," he said.

"I keep hearing Randy Braley worked regular for you."

His grin vanished. "You heard wrong, pardner."

"Randy Braley never worked here?"

"Like I said, he just hauled away some junk for me a couple of times."

"His mama says he did more than that."

"His mama's wrong."

"You sure about that?"

He picked up the screwdriver again. "Why're you asking me about that punk? I hardly knew him."

"Why do you say knew? Don't you know him?"

"Oh, c'mon now. Knew. Know. What's the difference? All he did was a little hauling for me. It ain't like I was his daddy or nothin'." He pretended to get back to work.

"The difference is, Randy's been missing since the night of Frankie's murder. We're trying to find him. His mama's worried."

He chuckled and said under his breath, "I'll bet she is."

"Does that mean you know Randy's mom?"

"What do you mean?"

"When I said she was worried about him, you laughed and said, 'I'll bet she is.' Sounds like you know her."

He slammed the screwdriver down. It bounced off his desk and clattered onto the floor. "I don't know what you're tryin' to say, but no matter how many times you ask me if I knew or know Randy Braley, or if I know where he is, or if I know his mama, the answer's always going to be 'No.' Now, would you please leave me alone so I can get some work done?"

"When was the last time you saw him?"

He cursed. "I done told you. I don't remember."

"Ok then, Jim. Do you mind if I call you Jim?"

"Call me whatever you want."

I planned to do just that. "Jim, I've been seeing an orange Trans-Am going in and out of your parking lot the last couple of days. Would that be your silent partner?"

"If I told you, he wouldn't be silent anymore."

"All I have to do to find out is run the license plates."

"Run 'em then, because I ain't going to tell you."

I hadn't expected he would, but it was worth a shot. "If you see Randy in the coming days, I want you to deliver a message. Can you do that for me?"

"I won't see him, but if I do, fine, I'll deliver a message."

"Tell him we need his help in finding who killed his friend, and that it would be a whole lot better for him if he came in on his own."

"Oh, hold it, let me write this down." He pretended to pick up a pen and scribble. "Ok, what I got so far is: 'Bullshit-bullshit-bullshit-bullshit.' Is that all?"

"You're a real funny guy, Jim. A real funny guy."

"You're a barrel of laughs yourself."

I'd have liked to have arrested the SOB right then and there, but as yet I had no valid reason.

I remembered one more thing as I was leaving. "Hey Chrisler," I yelled. "Tell Braley his mama wants her ice chest back."

CHAPTER 16

I stopped at a pay phone after leaving Chrisler. I felt like I'd been splattered with raw sewage after talking to that sleazy SOB. Sadly, Southwestern Bell Telephone has yet to add shower heads to their phone booths, so I had to settle for a simple call to the station. Red picked up.

"What's going on?" I asked.

"We're working and we're busy. What's going on with you?"

I told her about my conversation with Chrisler.

"I was talking to Wes Harmon earlier when I was putting gas in the car," she said. "I asked if he knew Randy Braley. Turns out he did. He said Braley was quite a football player in junior high but started getting into mischief and quit when he got to high school."

"Interesting," I said, "but not much help."

"No, but get this: According to Wes, Jeff Starns took Randy under his arm—"

"Under his wing."

"Under his arm or wing. Whatever, that's not the point," she said. "The point is, Jeff tried to get him straightened out. I imagine that's why Randy's mom said he's going out for football this year."

"So Jeff might be close enough to the boy to know where he might be."

"That's what I was thinking."

"Didn't this come up when you went looking for him at football practice?"

"You'd think so, wouldn't you?"

Same old Jeff, I thought.

"Maybe I'll go over there now," I said. "Last I heard, they were having two-a-day practices. Jeff should be easy to find."

"Go find him, then."

"I'm already halfway there."

***

I stopped by the library on my way, hoping to find a picture of a Russian Nagant revolver to get an idea what they looked like. Kate Hennessey, the librarian, found one in a book about guns used in the World Wars. I made a few Xerox copies and thanked her for her help.

From there I drove to the high school to talk with Jeff Starns. At one time, Jeff moonlighted as a part-time officer for me. He was the Dick Nixon of cops, but once he went full time at the high school, he proved to be a top-notch football coach. Before Jeff took over, Burr High hadn't won a state title since the '40s, which coincided with my tenure as team captain. Not long after that, the program fell on hard times and was downgraded to eight-man. Things started to turn around when a stud transfer from Enid moved to town eight or nine years ago, but the team really caught fire when Jeff took over. Not that I care, because I dislike football, but they've won two of the last three state eight-man championships. There's even been talk of them going back to 11-man now that the town's getting bigger and school enrollment is up. With Jeff at the controls, I reckon they'd manage to be plenty competitive if they took that route.

The sky was looking like an upturned bowl of dark gray mashed potatoes, which likely portended rough weather. The heavens opened up almost before I got back to my truck. It rained buckets all the way to the high school. The red clay path leading to the football field was a mess. My tires slipped and slid, trying to gain traction. There wasn't any action on the football field, but knowing Jeff, they'd have moved practice inside. I parked close to the gym. Even so, by the time I got to the door, I was soaked to the skin.

Sure enough, that's where everybody was. Jeff had the bigger boys—linemen, mainly—running up and down the bleachers. The more athletic kids—quarterbacks, halfbacks, and receivers—were going through plays step-by-step on the basketball court. One of the latter tried a jump shot with a football when Jeff's back was turned. The ball got hung up in the net. When Jeff saw that, he chewed the kid out and made the entire crew join the linemen running steps. He smiled when he saw me.

"How you doin', boss?"

"Doin' fine, son. Runnin' 'em ragged, I see."

"No pain, no gain," he said. "What brings you here? Itchin' to suit up?"

"Thanks very much, but my football days ended long before any of these fellas were born. Actually, I wanted to talk to you about Randy Braley."

"Randy Braley, huh? Sure." He motioned for us to sit on the bottom row of the bleachers, out of range from the boys clomping up and down.

"So you want to know about Randy. That kid," he said, shaking his head. "What a waste."

"Why do you say that?"

"He could've been a player, is why. When I coached him in junior high, I thought he might turn out to be the best linebacker Burr's ever had. Then puberty hit—" He sighed. "Something happened. Whatever it was, he changed. For the worse."

"What was it that made him change?"

"Drugs. I'm almost positive. He used to be a terrific player and a decent student. Don't get me wrong. He was always a little mean. You've got to be mean to play middle linebacker. But he always dialed it down when he was off the field. I'd been waiting for him to get his growth. I figured once that happened, he'd be all-state material. When he did, though ..." He shook his head. "He stopped being able to turn off the mean. That was the year they made me principal, so I felt an added responsibility to set him straight. I'd pull him aside and try to talk to him. Before, he'd always been quiet and humble. Now there just wasn't any way of talking sense into him. I eventually had to kick him off the team."

"Why? Did he hurt somebody?"

He paused. "You'd have thought that mean streak of his might be useful when it came to football, but it wasn't. It's like he just lost interest. To make matters worse, he didn't stop being mean off the field. He was getting his fill of violence somewhere else. Bullying little kids is what I saw, but there might've been other things I wasn't aware of. I benched him, thinking that might get him to focus. He didn't care. He'd act strange, and I suspected he was high on something, but there was no way of being sure. It wasn't so much that I cut him from the team, but that he just stopped showing up. I tried to set him straight, but he just clammed up. That was it."

A few feet away, a mountain of a kid with a belly the size of a hot-air balloon bent over, grabbed his knees, and teetered from side to side like an old-growth redwood sawn at the base. Jeff told him to take a break.

He turned back to me. "I assume the reason you're asking about Randy is that he's in trouble."

I shrugged. "He may be, but I need to find him to know. Nobody's seen him since you saw him drop Frankie off at Chrisler's the other night."

"Huh," he said. "The first thing that occurred to me when I heard Frankie Gately had been killed was how it would affect Randy. Frankie was one of the few friends he had. I would've thought since he dropped Frankie off a few hours before the body was found, he'd be in the clear."

"He probably is, but I still need to talk to him."

"Yeh, I guess you would."

"Could he have done it?" I asked.

He looked uncertain. "Maybe, but I don't think so. For one thing, Frankie was his friend, and Randy didn't have many friends. Frankie was a pretty big kid, too, and Randy didn't exactly like a fair fight."

Bullies seldom do, I thought.

"On the other hand," he said, "give a kid like that a gun, and who knows?"

Who knows, indeed? I've seen how guns can artificially inflate a man's courage.

I asked Jeff how well he knew Frankie.

"Frankie went out for football when he was in high school," he said. "Poor kid couldn't run, couldn't block, couldn't throw or catch. Had lots of enthusiasm, though, I'll give him that. I was coaching JV, which was just a bunch of eighth and ninth graders and Frankie. He almost never got in a game. Coach Graham let him be varsity manager. He did ok with that."

"Randy's mama tells us he was supposed to play football this year."

Jeff smiled a sad smile. "He showed up here the same day I saw him with Frankie."

"In the morning?"

He chuckled. "If he'd shown up in the morning, I'd have put him right to work. No, it was at the end of the afternoon practice. He asked for a second chance, said he'd messed up, and he wanted to straighten himself out. I got the feeling he felt like he was running out of time. Maybe because he's going to be a senior this year. Anyway, I told him I'd give him a chance, but with a zero-tolerance policy. I said the first sign of him dogging it and I'd throw him out on his rear end. More than anything, I said, he had to cut out the drugs. He said he already had." He chuckled. "I'll tell you what, he seemed thrilled I was willing to let him back on the team. Then I saw him that night dropping Frankie off at Chrisler's. I thought that was a bad sign; if he'd been serious about playing, he'd have been home in bed at that hour. When he didn't show up the next morning, I reckoned he must've decided he liked sleeping in better than practicing twice a day in 100-degree weather. Of course, that was before I heard about what happened to Frankie."

For a moment, we listened to the rhythm of stockinged feet. The tempo was getting slower.

"I don't think he did it," I said. "In fact, according to what little evidence we have, it's about as likely as me flying to the moon on roller skates. That said, we need to talk to him. He's missing. I'm worrying something might've happened to him, too."

"You've checked with his mama, I assume."

I nodded. "She hasn't seen him in a couple of days."

"She's a piece of work, ain't she?"

"She is that."

He stood and stretched. I stood as well. "Well, I'd better back to work," he said with a yawn. "Sorry I couldn't be of more help, but I have no idea where he'd be." We watched the boys trudge up and down the steps for a few moments. "Hey, you know what?" he said. "I saw him one more time that day. Have you talked to that new fella of yours? The guy who replaced Bernard?"

"Lester Filer. He was the one who found Frankie's body. Why?"

"I drove by Randy on Main Street about an hour after he came to see me. He'd been pulled over by that Filer guy."

I'd meant to talk to Lester yesterday, to see how he was holding up, but my vodka-fueled nap had thrown me off schedule. "I haven't talked to Lester since that night," I said. "I'll ask him about it."

"You don't think the same thing happened to Randy that happened to Frankie?"

"I don't even want to think about that. I'm concentrating on finding him. Safe and sound."

Bleacher-climbing had petered out. "I got to get back to work," Jeff said again. "Good to talk to you, Chief. Like old times."

With me and Jeff, 'old times' usually comprised me finding him asleep in my holding cell, or in his squad car behind the billboard outside town. Or him playing an unfunny practical joke on somebody who couldn't defend himself. Talking to him now, however, I had to admit, he seemed more thoughtful. More mature.

"If you think of anything else," I said, "you know where to find me."

"Uh-huh," he said, suddenly preoccupied. He grabbed a wet towel that'd been lying next to him and snapped it against the thigh of the kid who'd been about to keel over. "Break's over!" he shouted with sadistic glee. The kid said "Ow!" and rubbed his leg.

I could be wrong about him being more mature.

CHAPTER 17

I radioed Cindy from my truck and asked her if she had a record of Randy Braley being stopped the day of Frankie's murder. She did not.

By now, the rain had slowed to a sprinkle, but the dirt road was slicker than snot and the ruts were filled with water six-inches deep. If I'd been driving one of our cruisers, I'd have probably gotten stuck. Since I was driving my pickup, however, I didn't have much trouble.

I wanted to check on Lester before he went on duty, to see how he was coping with his recent shock, and to ask him about having pulled over Randy Braley. I'd driven by the little white farmhouse Les rents on one of the county roads off US 14, but I'd never been inside. He's shy and keeps to himself, which I can respect.

It was too early in the afternoon to expect him to be up. He's been working those double shifts, getting home around eight AM or so and going back to work at five PM. Honestly, we could probably do without someone working overnight now that Bernard's around, but Les says he needs the work and doesn't mind the long hours. If our budget can afford it, I'm happy to have the extra coverage.

I returned to the station and pulled Red away from a pile of paperwork. She resisted, but I told her a person's got to eat and she couldn't think of a good argument to the contrary. We walked across the street and down the block to The Piazza, Burr's oldest sit-down eating establishment. Red had a club sandwich. I had chicken-fried steak. "Say hello to that new notch on your belt," she said. She's right, of course. I should eat better. Maybe someday.

We dawdled and for a change had a friendly conversation about things other than work. Afterwards, we went back to the station. She got back to what she'd been doing. I remembered the picture of the Nagant and went out to my truck to get a copy. I showed it to Karen. She said something about how old it looked and tacked it up on the wall beside the dispatcher's desk.

I went back to my office, returned a few calls, and filled some forms required by the state. Kenny came in and we talked over the latest developments. It was after 3:30 before I finished with everything. Lester would be rolling out of bed and getting ready for work. I said my goodbyes to Cindy and Karen and headed out.

The drive out to Lester's would only take a few minutes, so I killed time by listening to some of the music Kenny gave me and driving around town looking for Randy Braley's junky old blue pickup. I saw lots of people driving junky old blue pickups, but none of them were Randy Braley. I saw a few parked in driveways, so I'd knock on the door to see who they belonged to. None of them belonged to Randy Braley.

I pulled up to Lester's place around 4:00. His landlord keeps a horse and a couple of cows in a fenced-off pasture behind the house. Three big cottonwood trees stood in a straight line in the front yard, a few feet from the road. Beside the house was a carport with a rounded metal roof. Fifty feet from that was a corrugated metal barn.

The Fury was parked in the carport. I've been letting Lester drive it home. Kenny and Karen both prefer the Javelins, so the Fury's kind of become Lester's personal vehicle. I expect he has his own car or truck, but he likes to drive the Fury so he doesn't have to switch cars when he drives back and forth to work. It's no skin off my backside, so long as he puts gas in it. I tiptoed through the mud and knocked on the door.

Lester yelled, "Who is it?"

"Emmett Hardy, Les."

"Be right there."

He answered the door in his uniform, although the shirt was untucked and partially unbuttoned, so I could see the white T-shirt underneath. Still wearing long sleeves, I noticed.

"Hey, Chief, c'mon in," he said, holding the door open and standing aside to give me room. "You got to excuse me. I just woke up."

I wiped my boots on the welcome mat and followed him inside.

The living room was small and neat, with a comfortable looking brown suede couch, a matching recliner, a coffee table, and a pair of end tables. A small air-conditioner ran full blast. August rains tend not to cool things down much.

He motioned for me to have a seat on the couch. He sat leaning forward in an armchair. "What can I do for you, Chief?"

"Well, a couple of things, really. The first is, I haven't talked to you in a couple of days. I wanted to see how you were doing."

He shrugged. "Ok, I guess. Still thinking about it."

"It's not something you'll forget," I said. "I know from experience."

"Yeh, I guess," he said, trailing off. His toes started tapping.

"I just want you to know if you ever want to talk about it, I'm here."

He nodded. "I appreciate that, Chief."

I asked him if he'd talked further to Agent Cruickshank or anyone else from the OSBI.

"Yeh, I've had to tell that story a few times."

"You'll have to testify in court, of course. Assuming they catch whoever did it."

"Right. Hopefully that'll be the end of it."

I nodded.

"There's another thing," I said. "Someone told me he saw Randy Braley being pulled over the day Frankie was killed. He thought it was you who made the stop."

He looked surprised. "Yeh, that was me."

"I called Cindy at the station and asked if she had a record of it. She didn't."

"I figured I didn't need to since I didn't give him a ticket."

"You're supposed to record all interactions with the public."

"Yeh, I get that," he said. "But that kid's been up to his ears in trouble since I've been here. I thought I'd give him a break."

"You gave him a break by not giving him a ticket. Why'd you stop him, anyway?"

"He was going a little over the speed limit. It wasn't a big deal. I just wanted to remind him to be careful, that's all."

I asked if he'd seen him since.

"Nah, I haven't. Should I be looking for him?"

"Yeh, you should. Not only is he one of the last people to see Frankie alive, he seems to have disappeared into thin air. No one's seen him since Jeff Starns saw him dropping Freddie off at Chrisler's that night."

He frowned. "I'll keep on the lookout. I hadn't been told he was missing."

"I realize that, and it's my fault. I should've told you." I paused. "Did you notice anything strange about him? Was he in a hurry, do you think? Was that why he was speeding?"

He thought on it. "Now that you mention it, he seemed to be trying to chase down this fancy orange Trans-Am that was driving through town. I asked him if that's what he was trying to do. He said he wasn't, but I'm not sure he was being straight with me."

Mention of the Trans-Am got my attention. "You ever see that car before?"

"A couple of times. He always drives slow through town, then floors it when he reaches the city limits."

"I don't reckon you know who the driver is?"

He shook his head. "No, I don't." He took a swig from a can of Pepsi sitting on the table next to him. "I'm sorry, Chief, I should've offered you something to drink."

"I'll take one of those Pepsis, if you got any left."

"Coming right up." He went to the kitchen and brought back a Coke. "This is all I got," he said.

"That's fine." I stood up. "Alright then, you have a safe night, and remember, I'm always here if you need to talk. Karen, too. She's even a better listener than I am."

"Thanks again, Chief."

He walked me out to my car. As I got behind the wheel I said, "Hey Les, you're not looking too great. You sure you're getting enough sleep?"

He smiled a sad smile. "I haven't been sleeping too well, but not because of that. It's just that I've just been having a lot of bad dreams."

"I guess I can understand that," I said. "Would it help if I took you off overnight?"

He shook his head. "Nah. Work keeps my mind off things."

I reckoned I knew what he meant. "You let me know if you want to cut down on those hours."

He said he would. We shook hands, and he went back in the house. When he was out of sight, I fished my bottle of Smirnoff out from under the seat. I chugged half the Coke and replaced it with vodka. It was only four-thirty.

Oh well. Somewhere it's five o'clock.

CHAPTER 18

I made one last return to the station after making my usual post-vodka stop at the 7-11 for a pack of gum. It was 5:00 and, to my great surprise, George, my relief dispatcher, had already crammed his Sumo wrestler bulk into the narrow space behind Cindy's desk. She was nowhere in sight, meaning he must've gotten to work on time. Early, even.

"Cindy told me to give you this," he said, and pushed something across his desk. I picked it up. It was a photograph of Randy Braley. He was dressed in a suit and tie, so I reckoned it must've been his senior picture. I thanked George and went back to my office.

Karen was sitting at my desk behind a pile of paperwork.

"How was your day?" I asked.

She shrugged. "The usual," she said. "Our favorite pregnant detective called a few minutes ago, wanting to talk to you. I asked if she wanted to leave a message. She said no, just to have you call her back."

"Any idea what it's about?"

"I assume Frankie Gately, but she was in a hurry, so I didn't ask. She won't be in her office." She shuffled through some papers. "Here we go," she said and handed me a scrap torn off the corner of a newspaper with a phone number written on it. "It's a motel. Don't ask me where."

I dialed the number. "Highway Three Motor Inn," chirped a cheery female voice. I asked for Isabel Cruickshank's room. They put me on hold. Isabel picked up after about a minute.

"It's Emmett Hardy," I said. "Where in heck are you?"

"Idabel," she said, sounding none too happy. "Of course. They couldn't send me to Kingfisher, which would've been an hour's drive. It had to be Idabel. Took me all day to get here."

"Karen said you called."

"Yes, it's about that hitchhiker who got killed. Travis Ballard. The local cops had forgotten to turn over some items found on his person. My boss sent me here to pick them up. Turns out the guy had some things that connect him to Burr."

"Like what?"

"A receipt for $202.56 from The Big Chief Motor Court. That's in Burr, right?"

"It is," I said.

"Also a business card for someplace called Guardsmen Drilling. Ring a bell?."

"No, but that doesn't mean anything." She gave me the address. "Anything else?" I asked.

"No, just those two things, but I think that's suspicious enough, given the circumstances."

"For sure. I'll go to The Big Chief and track down this Guardsmen Drilling to see if there's any connection. What's that fella's name again?"

"Travis Ballard."

"Think you could get me a picture of him?"

"I'll find a way to get you one tomorrow. You might want to get an early start on this. I told my boss about it a half hour ago, so I expect he'll send someone to Burr first thing."

"Gotcha," I said. "We don't want to be bumping heads with your team." Red was trying to tell me something. I asked Isabel to hold on. "What? I asked.

"Ask her how she's feeling!"

I asked Isabel how she was feeling.

"Like there's a Russian gymnast in my belly."

I laughed. "Got yourself a little Olga Korbut, huh?"

"It sure feels like it."

We promised to keep each other posted and said our goodbyes.

"What's going on?" asked Red.

I described Isabel's side of the conversation.

"I don't like the sound of that," Karen replied, referring to both the victim's Burr connection and Isabel's pregnancy issues, although she obviously sympathized with the latter.

"Could be a coincidence," I said.

"I suppose. Pretty big one, though."

I nodded. "I might as well check them out on my way home. They're probably closed, but you never know."

"Want me to come?"

"I'd rather you go out and ask Shannon Gately if she can pin down the time Braley picked up Frankie. If you're not too tired."

"I'm tired, but I can do that. Anything else you want me to ask?"

"It wouldn't hurt if we could get a better idea of the relationship between Frankie and Braley. And her, for that matter. I'm wondering if maybe she and Randy had something going."

"I've thought the same thing."

"I don't need to tell you to be gentle. She's been through a lot."

"You're right. She has. And you don't have to tell me."

***

The Big Chief Motor Court was built in the '30s, a piss poor time to build anything in this part of the world, especially something that catered to travelers. John Steinbeck's Okies camped out on the side of the road. They didn't stay in motels. The Big Chief went out of business in the early '40s, about the same time unattached men in town started going off to war.

It never got torn down, I suspect, because it was so unique. The Big Chief's cabins weren't the usual little four-sided cracker boxes; they were built to resemble teepees. The local Indians think it's disrespectful of their culture. Kenny hates it, I know that.

Those teepees stood empty and abandoned for going on three decades, until a few years ago when some rich rancher from Alva bought the place, fixed it up and reopened it. If you can ignore the insult to our Native American friends, it looks great. Here lately, with the oil boom and cattle boom and all the other booms, it's done pretty good business.

When I got there, I found an ambulance from Pate's Funeral Home backed-up to the door of one of the teepees. A pair of medics were pushing a gurney with a slender middle-aged gentleman as a passenger. One medic was holding a cloth against the side of the man's head, which was bleeding profusely. He looked to be unconscious. A woman rushed to his side tried to grab his hand, but one of the attendants pushed it away. She wailed while they loaded him into the ambulance.

I asked a male bystander what had happened.

"Some guy was jumping around in his room trying to put on his underwear and he fell and bashed his head on the edge of a table."

We looked at each other and shook our heads, each probably thinking something along the lines of: There but for the grace of God go I.

Being clumsy isn't a crime or they would've locked me up a long time ago, but I reckoned I should check on things and make sure the wife hadn't clocked her husband in the head and tried to pass it off as something else. I hailed George and told him to send help. Lester showed up a minute later. I had him get a statement from the wife and survey the scene to make sure there was no foul play involved.

I spied a round-faced, round-bodied young woman hovering near the scene. Her name tag read: "Becky—Motel Manager." I introduced myself and said I'd like to ask her a few questions.

We walked into the office. She went behind the check-in counter. I stayed on the lobby side.

"I'm sorry about what happened to that poor man, but there's not much I can tell you. His wife burst in here, yelling and pulling out her hair, and told me had happened. I called the ambulance." She shrugged. "That's all I know."

"It's a shame what happened to those people, but they're not what I wanted to talk to you about. I'm here to ask if you remembered someone who stayed here about a month back."

She started shaking ahead before the words were out of my mouth. "Chief Hardy, we get so many people through here, I can't remember who was here yesterday, never mind a month ago."

"If it helps, this fella ran up a bill for over $200. I reckon he was here for a while."

She shook her head again. "I'm sorry, but that doesn't narrow it down much. With all the new oil field work going on around here, we get a lot of long-term guests."

"Well, let me tell you his name just in case it jogs something loose. Travis Ballard."

"Hmmm," she said. "Doesn't ring a bell. It might help if you had a picture."

"I don't have one yet, but I should tomorrow. You keep a guest register, don't you?"

She gave a reluctant nod. "We do, but ..."

I leaned on the counter and gave her what in my fantasies I imagine being an irresistible smile. "I sure would be obliged if you could check it for me."

She smiled back. "I guess we could go through it, if it's important. You say he was here about a month ago?"

"Yes."

She pulled out a thick ledger from under the front counter and began thumbing through its pages. "Here he is," she said. "Travis Ballard. June 1st through July 4th." She turned it around and showed it to me. "Now I remember," she added. "Normally we ask for the type of car and license plate number, but this gentleman didn't drive. That almost never happens, where we get a guest who doesn't have a car. When it does, we ask for an employer."

She turned the ledger back around ran a finger across the page. "He wrote it in, but I can't make it out." She let me see it. The writing was sloppy, but I could read it, because it said what I expected it to say.

Guardsman Drilling.

CHAPTER 19

I drove to the address I had for Guardsman Drilling. It was locked up tight with no one there, so I went home for the day. Red had picked up some fried chicken from the Dairy Mart, which, before we got a Sonic and McDonalds, was the only place in town you could get takeout food. She still prefers it to those newcomers. I reckon I do, too, when it comes right down to it.

We sat down with plastic utensils and paper plates. I asked what she'd gotten out of Shannon.

"I have no idea what that poor girl was like before she lost her brother," she said, "but she's a mess now."

"I'm pretty sure she was a mess before."

"Well," she said, "she's worse now. She's confident it was Randy Braley who picked up her brother."

"I'm a little confused about that. First she didn't know who picked him up, then she thought it was Braley. Now she's sure it was Braley."

"She said she'd been drunk the night before and y'all had gotten her out of bed and she was all mixed up. But now she's certain it was Randy Braley."

I thought back on our encounter. "She didn't show any signs of being hungover that I remember."

"Yeh, well, she doesn't seem to be a fanatic truth-teller," said Karen. "I imagine she was just grabbing any old excuse that floated by."

"I reckon so," I said. "Did she have any idea what time Braley picked Frankie up?"

"She says she was watching Nixon's speech when she heard a horn honk and saw Frankie get into Braley's pickup."

"That would put it around 8:00 or 8:15."

"Yup."

"What's her opinion of Braley?"

"She says she doesn't much like him, but I'm not sure I'm buying it. He was pretty much Frankie's only friend—besides Kenny, of course, but Braley was closer to Frankie's age. Frankie followed Braley around like a puppy, she says. He had trouble speaking clearly. Braley was one of the few people who could understand him."

"How well does she know him?"

"According to her, hardly at all." She paused. "She made it a point to say he was never inside her trailer, only that little one of Frankie's. I thought that was kind of strange, the way she brought it up out of nowhere. It made me think it wasn't true. Most of the time she seemed sincere, but she was a little squirrelly about that. I wouldn't be surprised if they had something romantic going on and she didn't want to own up to it." She paused. "Something's going on there."

"Has she seen Braley since that night?"

"She says no."

"You believe her?"

She thought for a moment then said, "I'm not sure."

We were quiet for a few minutes.

"Hey," I said when I'd finished, "have you seen an orange Trans-Am driving around town lately?"

"I have, as a matter of fact. I wonder who owns that?"

"No idea."

"Why do you ask?"

"Oh, just curious. You don't see one of those every day."

While we cleared away the mess, she asked about my inquiries into Guardsman Drilling and The Big Chief Motor Court. I told her about the hairy brouhaha at the Big Chief, then gave her the gist of what I'd discovered about Travis Ballard's stay, and his employment by Guardsmen Drilling.

"Never heard of Travis Ballard or Guardsman Drilling, but I guess that's where you'll be headed first thing in the morning." Karen said.

"That means you'll have to run things tomorrow."

"What else is new?"

Guardsman Drilling's office was located on the end of a four-store strip mall off the main drag, next door to Aunt Fifi's House of Kitty Worship, a defunct pet-grooming store. From the day it opened, Aunt Fifi's was picketed day and night by members of a local church, who considered the name an affront to the Lord. Aunt Fifi's coughed up its last hairball after only a month in business. Burr's always been more of a dog town, anyway.

Guardsmen Drilling looked as unoccupied as it had the day before. The only sign of occupancy was a small card above the door buzzer with "Guardsman Drilling" typed on it. The glass door was covered in aluminum foil on the inside, and a lime-green curtain hung in the large front window, making it impossible to see who or what was in there.

There were no cars in the lot when I pulled in. I pressed the buzzer a few times to no effect. I'd almost decided to try again later, when a big late-model gun-metal blue Cadillac lurched into the parking space next to mine. A portly gentleman got out. He had a full head of slicked-back gray hair and smoked a cigar as long and wide as a Little League baseball bat. The fella himself was so big, it almost made the cigar look regular-sized. He wore a shiny shirt covered in a floral pattern that clashed with his brown, orange, and yellow plaid suit. His pants were bell-bottoms, and his white patent leather belt matched his shoes.

I'd never seen an oilman dress so much like an unusually prosperous circus clown.

"You waitin' for me?" he asked in a friendly manner.

"I am if you're the man in charge of Guardsmen Drilling."

"You're lookin' at the one and only." He unlocked the door and invited me in.

The room was only medium-sized, but since it was so sparsely furnished, it seemed bigger than it needed to be. The floor was generic off-white tile, like you see in schools or other public buildings. The only furnishings were a small desk with a pair of metal folding chairs, one in front of the desk and the other behind it. On the desk was a big metal and plastic contraption that looked something like a reel-to-reel tape recorder with a telephone attached. The walls were covered in cheap, dark brown plywood paneling. The only decorations were a Phillips 66 calendar, a surveyor's map of Tilghman

County, and a poster of a kitten holding on to a tree branch for dear life. The caption read "Hang in there, baby!" There was a closed door in the back of the room.

The man jammed the cigar into the side of his mouth and stuck out his hand. "Rodney Whizzer, President and chief bottle-washer, Guardsmen Drilling. And who might you be?" I introduced myself. We shook and sat on opposite sides of his desk.

"You wouldn't be related to the famous Wisner family, would you?" The Wisner family founded Whizzer Gas, a chain of gas stations found in pretty much every itty-bitty town in Oklahoma except Burr. I've always thought of Whizzer Gas as a place you go only when the needle on your gas gauge dips below "Empty." One time I drank a complimentary cup of coffee at a Whizzer station. It tasted like used crankcase oil. (Yes, I have tasted used crankcase oil. By accident, and that's all I'm going to say.)

"I'm a distant nephew of the founder's step brothers's aunt's boyfriend," he said with a wink. "They always treated me like I was a blood relative, though. I changed my last name to Whizzer when I left the company." He gave me a knowing nod. "That name means something in this state."

Yeh, I thought. It means watered gas and filthy restrooms.

"Nice place you got here," I said to be polite. He noticed my eyes had wandered to the kitty poster. "Ain't that somethin', a cat hangin' from a branch like that?" he said. "Got that from Aunt Fifi when she shut down. Didn't cost me nothin'." He smiled and stuck out his chest.

"I wanted to ask you about a former employee of yours, a man named Travis Ballard."

He laughed. "Travis Ballard? Where'd you hear he worked for me?"

"He listed you as his employer when he rented a motel room here about a month back."

"Aw hell, I guess he did kind of work for me earlier this summer." He tapped cigar ash on the floor. "I hired him on a Monday. On Tuesday he called in sick. On Wednesday he quit."

"One of those deals, huh?" I said. "What was the job?"

"Oh hell, nothing a monkey couldn't do. I put an ad in the local paper looking for people with experience in the oil business. He said he'd worked as a nuclear engineer for Kerr McGee. Sounded like he knew what he was talking about, so I hired him."

"Did you check his references?"

"Nah, he didn't have none. I didn't care. All I really needed was someone to answer phones and scrub the toilet." He crooked a thumb over his shoulder at the door in the back.

I couldn't let that pass. "You didn't think it was strange that a man trained as a nuclear engineer would take a job answering phones?"

"Shee-yit. He wasn't no more a nuclear engineer than I am president of the General Motors. I knew it, and he knew I knew it. I just needed someone in a hurry. I figured if all he was doin' was answerin' the phone and not counting my money, he'd be alright."

He smiled wide enough to reveal a big black hole where one of his upper front teeth should've been. He wedged the cigar into the gap. "Know any good dentists?" he asked and laughed so hard one of the buttons on his flowery polyester shirt popped off. "Whoops!" he said and laughed even harder. "Looks like I'm going to need a new shirt!"

Something about his appearance and irrationally good nature gave me an almost panicky urge to get the hell out of there.

"Did this Ballard fella tell you why he left?"

"I'll hand it to him," he said. "He didn't just disappear. He came in on that Wednesday and told me to my face. Said he'd gotten a better opportunity with another business here in town."

"Did he say what it was?"

He laughed. "I didn't give a good goddam. Didn't ask." He puffed on his cigar. "But guess what?"

"What?"

He slapped his desk and guffawed. "Sumbitch told me anyway! Said he'd be working for a delivery service."

"Delivery service?"

"That's what he said."

"What? Like United Parcel Service, something like that?"

He leaned back in his chair and propped his snakeskin Tony Lamas up on his desk. "Sorry there, Mr. Police Man. He didn't say, and I didn't ask."

I asked him if he saw or heard from Ballard after that. He said he hadn't, then asked why I was asking about him.

"He was shot to death near Idabel a while back. We're looking for his killer."

Whizzer's perpetual ear-to-ear grin faded just a little. "That's a damn shame," he said. "Seemed like a nice enough fella."

"Nice fellas get murdered just that same as mean fellas," I said.

"I reckon that's true," he said, nodding sagely.

I got up to leave. "Hold on a minute, Chief," Whizzer said, grinning once again. "I didn't introduce his replacement."

By now I was afraid Rodney Whizzer's nuttiness might rub off. I half-expected members of the Dallas Cowboys' offensive line to burst out of the bathroom, adorned with pasties and pink tutus. Instead, he pushed a button on the metal and plastic contraption on his desk.

A voice recognizable as his said: "Hello, you've reached the offices of Guardsmen Drilling. We're not here, so ya'll had best leave a message after the beep." Something beeped.

"It's called a Code-a-Phone." he said and patted it like a proud papa. "Answers the phone and takes messages. Holds 20 at a time. Works with tape, like the kind that records music. Set me back $375.00, but I reckon it'll save me millions down the road."

I tried to imagine how many hours Travis Ballard would've had to work to make $375.00, and how many phone calls that machine would have to answer to make it worth the expense. My brain started to cramp, and I abandoned the attempt.

Clearly, I'm nowhere near smart enough to be a successful businessman like Rodney Whizzer.

CHAPTER 20

Karen, Kenny, and Cindy were at the station when I returned after my conversation with Rodney Whizzer. Karen filled me in on a few mundane details that had transpired overnight. No more murders, thankfully.

I asked if there was any word about the man who busted his head while putting on his underwear. Kenny and Cindy hadn't heard about it, so I filled them in.

"He's hanging in there," said Karen. "The doctors put him in what they call a medically induced coma to help with the swelling on his brain. But he's in critical condition."

"Are you saying he could die?" said Kenny. "From getting his feet tangled up while putting on his jockey shorts?" said Cindy.

"They were boxers," said Karen, "but yes, that's what I'm telling you."

I took a moment to ponder the randomness of the universe.

"If you're thinking you're lucky to be alive after all the times I've seen you do the same thing," Red added, "it's crossed my mind, too."

I changed the subject back to the business at hand. Isabel hadn't wanted me to bring in anybody but Karen and Kenny, but I figured Cindy wasn't going to blab. I told them what had been discovered about Travis Ballard and his connections to Burr, including his short-lived association with Guardsmen Drilling. In the middle of the story, Isabel's partner, Probationary Agent Raksin, walked in.

He handed me a manila envelope and told me his boss asked him to give it to me. "It's that hitchhiker who got killed in Idabel," he said.

Inside was a small Polaroid photograph of an average-looking man in thick, black-rimmed glasses—the kind of person you'd chat with while in line at Safeway, then five minutes later forget what he looked like and what you talked about. Raksin shuffled his feet like he didn't know what to do with himself. I thanked him and told him to say hi to Isabel for us. He took the hint and left.

"Rodney Whizzer said he quit to take some kind of delivery man job," I said. "Who here in town uses a delivery man?"

"Dairy Mart," said Kenny.

"Anyplace else?" I asked.

There weren't any more restaurants that delivered. We made a list of other businesses that did. The post office, of course. A couple of local dairies, and two or three trucking firms that work with small oil-related companies like Guardsman Drilling. We came up with a list of a dozen. I split the list and gave half to Kenny and half to Karen.

"I'll go across the street to the library and make Xerox copies of this picture. You should both take one with you. It might help jog some memories."

"Emmett, I've been meaning to ask, where's Sheriff Belcher been through all this?" Keith Belcher is the Tilghman County sheriff and a close friend of mine. We've bailed each other out of a few scrapes over the years. I hadn't seen him since the night of Frankie's murder. There was so much going on, I didn't get to talk to him.

"If you're asking if he's working on this, I don't know. I'm sure Isabel's got him doing something, although I couldn't tell you what. I should give him a call."

"You should," said Karen. "I'll leave a note on your desk."

I asked if I'd forgotten anything. No one could think of anything. "Let's get after it, then."

Karen grabbed the phone book and thumbed through the Yellow Pages, looking for relevant numbers and addresses. I followed Kenny out the door to one of the Javelins. I told him to stay put until I gave him a copy of Ballard's photograph. I crossed the street to the library, apologized again to

Kate Hennessey for not having time to talk, and made several copies. I trotted back and handed one to Kenny.

"Hey boss, I just thought of something," he said. "Didn't Chrisler say Randy Braley had been doing delivery work for him?"

"I believe he said he hired Braley to haul some stuff to the dump."

"That could be construed as delivery work, don't you think?"

Considering how suspicious I was of Chrisler anyway, I was easy to convince. "I guess it could," I said.

"Don't you think we ought to talk to him?"

"Well, if you're going to twist my arm."

***

I told Kenny I'd do it myself and sent him on his way. I gave Karen the rest of the copies, told her of Kenny's revelation, and said I was going to Family Fun Center to talk to Chrisler. She tried to get me to take someone, but I wanted her and Kenny to ask around about Ballard. Now that I'd gotten the measure of Chrisler, I wasn't too concerned about going at him one-on-one. He was mean, but I'm bigger than he is, and—when I get mad—probably meaner, too.

The Family Fun Center was locked up, but there was a fancy car parked out front, a metallic gold Chrysler New Yorker—brand new, by the looks of it. I reckoned it must belong to Chrisler. Chrisler drives a Chrysler. Of course he does.

I looked through the glass door but didn't see anybody. I pounded on it and saw Chrisler stick his head out of his office.

"Just a second," he yelled. His head disappeared, then reappeared. He came and let me in. I'd never seen him standing up. He was a head shorter than me. Unless he was packing a machine gun, I should be able to handle him pretty easy. I let my hand wander to the grip of my .45, just to be safe.

"That your car out front?" I asked.

"Yeh," he said, in the same suspicious way he'd answered every question I'd put to him.

"Nice. Business must be good."

"It's ok," he said. "If this is about that Braley kid, I still haven't seen him."

We both folded our arms and leaned back on foosball tables a few feet part. As I looked at him I was reminded of someone, but I couldn't put my finger on exactly who.

"This isn't about Randy Braley," I said. "Not directly, anyway. I wanted to ask you about this fella." I handed him the picture of Travis Ballard. "Did he, by any chance, do some work for you about a month back? Maybe some delivery work?"

He glanced at it. "Never seen him."

"You sure? Look real close. His name's Travis Ballard."

Chrisler held the photo an inch from his face so I'd know he was taking a closer look. He handed it back. "Never seen him, never heard the name. Is that all? I got work to do."

"You're sure?"

"Yeh, I'm sure." He pushed himself away from the foosball table. "I ain't seen him or heard of him. What's this about, anyway?"

"This is a fella who was killed in Idabel not long ago. It looks like he night have ties to Burr. I'm asking around, hoping someone might recognize him."

He shrugged. "Alright," he said in an exasperated tone. "Let me look at it again." Again, he pretended to take a longer look. "Is this that guy who got shot and left on the side of the road? Don't the cops think it's some mass murderer or something?"

"That's right. He was hitchhiking down by Idabel when someone picked him up and put a bullet in his head."

"You ain't accusing me of doin' it, are you?"

"I'm not accusing you of anything. Like I said, he might've had Burr connections. We have reason to believe he worked as a delivery driver for someone here in town. I remembered you said you'd hired Randy Braley to do some deliveries."

"I said I had him haul some stuff to the dump."

"Right," I said. "I figured you might've used this fella to do the same sort of thing. But you're saying you didn't."

"I'm saying I didn't."

He handed the photo back to me.

"One more thing," I said. "You wouldn't know the name of the fella driving that orange Trans-Am around town, would you?"

He shook his head. "I told you before. No."

"Really? Because I just saw him again and it got me thinking whether he's that silent partner you were talking about."

"Listen, I don't know anyone who drives a Trans-Am. Now, could you leave me alone? I've got work to do."

"I'm sorry to have taken up your time. I appreciate your help." I smiled. It was not a friendly smile. He glared.

"Alright," I said, "you take care now."

"Yeh, right."

It hit me who he reminded me of on my way out. Calvera, the bandit chief in *The Magnificent Seven*. I love that movie, although I hear the Japanese movie it's based on is even better.

CHAPTER 21

Agent Cruickshank and I passed each other on the highway, going in opposite directions. She pulled a U-turn and fell in behind me.

She parked beside me in front of the station. It took a good amount of effort to disengage herself from behind the wheel. I would've offered to help but had the feeling she'd rather do it herself.

She said she was ok before I could even ask. I had my doubts. She was as pale as a blind cave fish. "Are you sure?" I said.

"Yeh," she said. "It's just that the air-conditioner in this piece of junk puts out nothing but hot air." She took a step and her knees buckled. I took her elbow and helped her into the station. She didn't resist.

Fortunately, the town replaced our old air-conditioner with one I expect would cool the Burr High School gymnasium. I escorted Isabel back to my office and left the door open so as not to block the flow of cold air. Cindy brought her a cup of water. Isabel downed it in a single gulp.

"Shouldn't you be taking it easy?" I asked.

"Thanks, but I'm fine. Just a little headache." I asked if she wanted some aspirin. She said yes. We were out, so I walked down the street to Miller's Drug and brought back a bottle. When I got back, Isabel was resting on the cot in our holding cell, with Kenny and Red hovering over her. I got her another cup of water. She sat up and knocked back a couple of aspirin.

"Better?" Karen asked.

Isabel half smiled. "I'm fine," she said. "How did it go with the motel manager and Guardsman Drilling?"

I gave her a straightforward account of my talk with the manager and Rodney Whizzer. In the interest of time, I left out descriptions of Whizzer's colorful attire and the incident with the man who critically injured himself putting on his underwear.

"I assumed you and your people had already talked to them," I added.

"I'm usually the last to know," she said.

"Aren't you the boss?" Kenny said.

She gave him a withering glance. "Yeh. So what?"

Kenny made an "Ok, I get it" gesture.

I related my conversation with Chrisler. "I'm about as sure as I can be that he was lying when he said he'd never met Ballard."

Isabel started to comment, then hesitated, like she was weighing whether to chime in. Finally, she said, "Chrisler has been on the Bureau's radar for a while. Not about this, but for other things."

"Like what?" I asked.

"This can't get out, understand?" she said and waited for us to acknowledge. We did.

"I'm not telling you anything new when I say there's been an influx of illegal drugs coming into Tilghman County. We've been investigating. I'm mostly outside the loop, but from what I've been told, Chrisler is a person of interest.

Karen said, "That's no surprise."

"I've suspected the same thing," said Kenny.

"The investigation is in its early stages," Isabel said. "All I can say for sure is Chrisler's name has been mentioned. Prominently."

Karen said to me, "Why do you think he was lying about not knowing Ballard?"

"His expressions. His attitude. I don't know. He's not the type you trust about anything, so that could be what it was. I guess it's just a feeling."

"If you're right, though, and he knew Ballard," said Isabel, "that connects him with two of the five victims."

"It might be good to find out if he has any connections to that family in Kingfisher," Kenny said.

"What was that family's name, again?" I asked Isabel.

"Fechner," she said.

"What did the husband do for a living?"

"Managed an auto parts store."

"Did the wife work?"

"Outside of the home, you mean?" added Karen.

I smiled and nodded. "Right."

"She didn't work outside the home that we know of," said Isabel.

Cindy stuck her head in the door and asked if anybody wanted coffee. No one did. I asked her to run across the street to the drug store and get me a Tab.

"Chrisler had a run-in with the victim the night of the murder," continued Isabel. "He admits as much. It's suspicious, but there's nothing tying him to the shooting."

"Did the medical examiner ever fix an approximate time of death for Frankie?" I asked.

"He estimates between midnight and 1:00."

"That rules out Chrisler, don't you think?" said Kenny. "That girl working for him was sure he'd been in the store when it closed at midnight."

"She could be lying to protect her boss," I said.

"It would help if we had physical evidence connecting Frankie and Chrisler," said Isabel. "But let's not get lost in the weeds. I probably shouldn't have brought up this drug thing. Right now, Chrisler's not even an official suspect."

Cindy came back with my Tab. I asked how much it cost. She said a quarter. I shook my head and told her to take it out of petty cash.

"Ballard and Frankie were killed with the same gun, right?" asked Kenny.

"No question," said Isabel.

"So whoever has the gun must be the killer, right?" he said. "Maybe Chrisler has it. Maybe we could search—"

Isabel cut him off. "It's too early to ask for a search warrant. We need to get something that ties him to a crime, first."

"What if we could get him on something connecting him to drugs?" I asked.

"Then we'd have something. But right now we don't."

"I'll see what I can do about that," I said.

Isabel gave me a skeptical look. "I don't mind if you investigate the drug connections on your own. It's your town. But do it by the book. Coming back with something that won't stand up in court won't do us any good."

"Emmett's just great at following rules," said Karen with a truck's worth of sarcasm.

That got a chuckle out of Isabel. "Oh, I trust him. To a point."

"I trust him to not get caught," said Kenny with a wry smile.

Isabel stood. "I don't know about you people, but it's time I got back to work."

"You sure you're ok?" I asked.

"I'm fine," she said for the umpteenth time. "You'd better believe I'm going to trade-in that piece of junk I'm driving for one with a functioning air conditioner, though."

Karen and I walked her to her car. "I suppose I don't need to remind you to keep a low profile," she said. "You see one of my guys, head in the opposite direction."

"I believe you've mentioned that a time or two," I said. "That's fine. We're used to being officially unofficial."

"In other words," said Karen, "we're used to being ignored."

***

I saw the note Karen had written, reminding me to call Sheriff Belcher. I dialed and got his secretary. He wasn't there, but she said she'd have him return my call. I asked her what he'd been working on. She said he'd been working with Agent Cruickshank on a few things, which is what I'd figured.

While I was doing that, Karen called Randy Braley's mom. He still hadn't shown up. Karen volunteered to drive to the high school and ask Jeff Starns if the boy had shown up for football practice. The odds were against it, but it wouldn't hurt to check. The longer he was missing, the more I was worried his disappearance had something to do with Frankie's murder.

Karen left. I grabbed the keys to one of the cruisers and shanghaied Kenny. I do some of my best thinking when I'm driving, and it helps to have someone to bounce my ideas off.

At first, instead of talking, we listened to the Champion Jack Dupree tape. When it got to what I'd thought was the last song, I started to turn it over.

"Aren't you going to listen to the last song?" asked Kenny.

"I thought that was the last song."

"No, there's one more."

"I didn't realize. Let's give a listen." I pushed it back in.

"It's called 'Junker Blues'," said Kenny.

We listened. Over a rickety, old-timey beat, Champion Jack sang about drugs — specifically, I expect, heroin. Let's just say it delivered a mixed message. During the verses, he sang about how he loved to get high. Later, underneath the sax solo, he muttered how the junk is killing him and he should've listened to his mama and stayed away from it. The performance gave me chills.

"I think I've about had my fill of Champion Jack Dupree," I said.

"Why? Because of the songs about drugs?"

"Yeh, but not just that. I don't usually have the world's rosiest outlook on things, but that fella makes me look like Little Lord Fauntleroy."

Kenny shrugged. "Yeh, I guess it can be depressing."

We rode in silence for a while.

"You get any blowback about the other day?" he asked.

"About what?"

"You know ... about me finding you ... asleep ... in your new office."

"Why would I?"

"Well, I just figured ... Mrs. Chief, you know ..."

"What Mrs. Chief doesn't know can't hurt her."

He didn't say anything for a few seconds.

"So she don't know?"

"Nope."

I turned on the air conditioner. We listened to it blow for a while.

"Am I the only one who knows?" He wouldn't leave it alone.

A dog ran in front of the car. I stopped short. While the dog's owner corralled his pup, I said to Kenny, "If you're asking if you're the only one who knows I've decided I can have a drink now and then, then yes. I'd appreciate it if you'd keep it that way."

The dog's owner waved an apology and led it away. I drove on.

"Don't get mad at me, Chief," said Kenny. "It's just that I was here when you almost lost pretty near everything because of drinking. I don't want it to get to that point. No one does." He paused. "You got people who care about you, you know?"

When I felt I could trust my voice, I said, "I know, son. I appreciate that. But that was a long time ago. I've learned a few things. One of them is how to handle it. Don't worry, I'll be fine."

He said, "Ok, I won't," but I could hear doubt in his voice.

We came upon a county deputy pulled over on the side of the road being whacked over the head with an umbrella by an elderly woman. I did not recognize the deputy, but I recognized the woman: 70-something Gena Mae Jeffries. Gena's so mean even her boss, Deke Bixby—Burr's own Mr. Potter from *A Wonderful Life*—is afraid of her. It looked like the deputy had pulled over Gena's coral blue Studebaker coupe and she was not too happy about it.

I crept up next to them and had Kenny roll down his window. Gena Mae saw it was me. She tromped over, fire in her eyes. I asked if I could be of service.

"Emmett Hardy, first this arrogant young man turns on his flashing lights and almost runs me off the road, then he tries to tell me I'm going 40 miles per hour in a 30 miles per hour zone. I told him he's mistaken, that in all the 60 years I've driven an automobile, I've never driven faster than 30 within the town limits. I've never gotten a ticket, and if he thinks he's going to be the first to give me one, he's got another thing coming."

She kept yapping, sounding like a chihuahua that'd learned to speak like a human. Her red lipstick was smudged, although every other aspect of her appearance remained impeccable. Gena Mae's as well-known for her stylishness as her foul temper. I got out and pulled her aside, while Kenny did the same with the deputy. We got it squared away without bloodshed.

The humor of the encounter had melted the tension between Kenny and me.

"I love that old car of Gena Mae's," said Kenny as we drove away. That reminded me of something.

"Speaking of cars, have you seen that fancy Chrysler of Chrisler's?"

"Are you telling me Chrisler drives a Chrysler?" He chuckled and shook his head. "I never noticed. What about it?"

"Don't you wonder what happened that toy badge you told me about? The one Frankie used to wear?"

"Yeh, I do, as a matter of fact." I could hear the misery in his voice.

"What if Chrisler loaded Frankie into his car and drove somewhere?"

He nodded thoughtfully. "The girl who worked that night says Chrisler was back no later than 12. Agent Cruickshank says Frankie wasn't killed until after midnight."

"Maybe one of them's wrong. Chrisler could've driven Frankie to the drive-in, shot him, then gone back to his store and closed up."

"I guess it's possible," admitted Kenny.

"Frankie might even have left something for us to find in that car."

"Like that badge?"

"That's what I'm thinking."

"You're not saying we should search his car?" he said. "We can't do that without a warrant."

"Not officially," I said. "But what we're doing isn't exactly an official investigation, is it?"

He smiled faintly. "I remember someone saying something about it being 'officially unofficial.' I also remember Agent Cruickshank say something about following the rules."

I chuckled. "The way I figure it," I said, "if whatever we do is unofficial, we might as well go all the way."

"That depends on what you mean by 'going all the way.'"

"In this case, it means: You and I are going to Chrisler's. You're going to distract him while I search his car."

CHAPTER 22

The traffic on Main Street was a steady parade of trucks carrying pipes and other pieces of drilling gear; mud-stained pickups driven by tired-looking, unshaven men with cigarettes hanging out of their mouths and suntanned left arms dangling out the drivers' side window; women in cars searching for parking in front of the stores lining Route 14.

The sky was leaden. The air stunk like oil and gasoline. We'd had rain off and on, but it was still as hot as the devil. Steam rose off the asphalt like fog in a Sherlock Holmes movie. We'd driven several miles out of town toward Butcherville in the opposite direction of Chrisler's, so it took us a few minutes to get there.

I used the time to outline my plan.

"Ok, this is going to be easy."

Kenny stopped me. "You realize if we do this without a warrant, nothing we find will be admissible in court."

"I wasn't born yesterday, son. If I come across evidence, I'll leave it where it is and not tell anybody. I'll be the only one who knows it's there."

"I'll know."

"Not if I don't tell you."

He thought for a moment. "Nah, I want to know."

"I'm not making any promises," I said. "I'm only doing this to save time. If I find something, I'll know Chrisler was involved, and we can focus on him. If I tell you and then get caught, you could get in trouble, too."

"What if the evidence you find is all the evidence there is?"

"We'll cross that bridge when we come to it."

He heaved a sigh. "Fine. You're the boss."

"Ok, here we go. First, we'll pass by the place and get the lay of the land. I'm driving, so I need you to be my eyes and ears. Check things out. If there's a bunch of kids hanging around, or if there're too many people going in and out, we'll do it another time. I don't think there will be, though. That place doesn't usually get busy before nightfall."

I slowed down as we approached so Kenny could get a good look.

I asked him if he saw that blue Chrysler.

"No, not yet. Wait." He paused. "There it is."

The car was parked at the rear of the building, partly obscured by a gray dumpster. That meant I wouldn't be able to see anyone go in and out the front door. Someone could be right up on me before I knew they were there. I'd have to be quick.

We drove past, made a loop, and drove back. I parked in front of the Chrysler, so it couldn't be seen from the highway.

"Go in and keep him busy for a few minutes," I said.

"You want me to ask him anything specific?"

"Anything that makes him nervous. I don't care what. Just don't mention his car or say anything that'll make him want to come out here. I won't need much time. Five minutes. Ten at most."

"What if the car's locked?"

I reached into a pocket in the door. "I've got this," I said, and pulled out my Slim Jim—a thin strip of metal I use to jimmy open locked cars for folks when they lose their car keys.

Kenny shook his head. "You're just trying to get us in trouble, aren't you?"

"We aren't going to arrest ourselves."

"Alright," he said with an exaggerated shrug and got out of the car.

I waited for him to disappear around the corner. I gave him a few seconds, then got out and looked around to see if I was being watched. Except for the glass front door, Family Fun Center doesn't have windows, so no one could see me from inside. There was an emergency exit in the back, a few feet away from where we had parked. If someone came out that door suddenly, I was cooked. There was no reason to think that'd happen, though, unless we were incredibly unlucky and the place went up in flames. The only living thing in view was an old swaybacked horse on the other side of the fence separating Chrisler's from the pasture behind it. Not even he was paying any attention.

I sidled over to the Chrysler. The crunch of gravel under my feet seemed louder than it probably was. I looked in the driver's side window. Chrisler might not be an especially neat person, but he kept his car clean.

The windows were tinted, making it hard to see much. No matter. I intended to open the door anyway.

For just a second, I started to doubt myself. Kenny was right, I thought. This is a bad idea. I tried to put it out of my mind.

I held out some hope I wouldn't have to break into the car, but the doors were all locked. I looked around again, saw no one, and used my Slim Jim.

The car's inside was as hot as a blast furnace. There wasn't anything in the front seat or on the floorboards. I ran my hand in between the seat back and seat cushion. Didn't find a thing. The glove compartment was locked. I figured trying to break into it was a bridge too far, so I left it alone. All I found were Pall Mall butts in the ashtray.

I opened the driver's side back door. There wasn't anything laying out in the open. I got down on my knees so I could search under the front seat.

The parking lot was paved with those big chunks of gypsum, like on the country roads around here. The stuff's everywhere these days. It's what we found Frankie lying face-down on. The edges can be as sharp as razor blades. They about ripped my already-gimpy knees to shreds.

I reached under the front seat and felt around. Nothing. I lifted the floor mat. Nothing. I moved to the passenger side and got the same results.

No badge.

My heart sank down into my shoes. I got up and was about to shut the car door when something caught my eye. A small piece of metal had fallen between the seat and the door molding. I used the Slim Jim to nudge it within reach. I nudged too hard. It fell onto the ground beside the car. I picked it up.

It was an old, tarnished dog tag, minus the chain. It looked a lot like the one I wore as a Marine when I served in Korea, the main difference being the initials before the ID number read "RA," for Regular Army. There was the date this fella got his last tetanus shot: 1951. Also his religious preference:

"P" for protestant. Most interesting, however, was the name stamped into the metal.

Gately, Francis V.

Chrisler, you bastard. I've got you.

CHAPTER 23

But I didn't have him. Not yet. All I had was the confirmation of a hint of a suspicion that had only popped into my mind an hour ago. A flash of inspiration. Evidence, perhaps, of my Phillip Marlowe-esque powers of deduction, but not something we could take to court.

Not yet, anyway.

As I gloated over my find, I heard loud voices on the other side of the emergency exit. Someone rattled the knob like they were having a hard time opening the door.

I put the dog tag back where I'd found it, only this time I shoved it a little deeper so Chrisler wouldn't see it. I got up off my knees and eased the car door shut as quietly as I could. I limped back to the Javelin, folded my arms, and leaned casually against the car. The sounds from behind the door stopped. Seconds later, Chrisler appeared from around the corner, with Kenny on his heels.

"C'mon, Geronimo, I'll show you," he said, stomping toward me Godzilla-like. "It must've got thrown away by mistake."

He lifted the dumpster lid. "Well, shit, I guess they picked up the garbage already. But I'll bet you 20 bucks that's what happened. Those numb-nuts kids working for me last night threw it in the trash by accident."

I winked at Kenny. "You ready to go?"

He winked back, then barked at Chrisler: "All I know is that it'd best be posted in full public view next time I come in."

"Mr. Chrisler," I added, "I hear you call him 'Geronimo' one more time, I'm taking you in."

He smirked. "On what charge?"

"I'll find one."

He spat on the ground and walked away.

Kenny and I got in the Javelin.

"What in hell was that all about?" I asked Kenny.

"Oh heck, don't make me tell you the whole story," he said, then told me the whole story. "I noticed he didn't have one of those state certificates he needs to sell food, and it set him off. I was just looking for something to rag on him about. He insisted it had been there yesterday and that it must've accidentally gotten taken out with the garbage. Before I knew it, he was stomping out the back door. I tried to tell him to let it go, but he wouldn't. He was going to show me." He grinned. "How 'bout you? Find anything?"

I didn't answer.

"Yes? No?" he insisted.

"I'm going to take the fifth on that one."

He slapped his thighs. "Oh, c'mon Chief!"

"Let's just say: What you don't know won't hurt you."

"Seriously?"

"Leave it!" I snapped.

"So that's how it's going to be," he said under his breath,

We sat for a moment, neither of us saying anything.

"What do you know about Frankie's father?" I asked.

"Not much," he grumbled. "He deserted the family not long after Frankie was born."

That would've been '50 or '51, I thought.

"What'd he do for a living?" I asked.

"What difference does it make?" Kenny asked. "He might've ruined Frankie's life, but he didn't kill him."

"Do you know what he did for a living or not?" I asked.

"He was in the Army, ok? A career non-com, is what Shannon told me."

"Was Frankie named after him?"

"Yeh, the name on his birth certificate is Francis Vernon Gately, Jr."

I tried to keep my face expressionless but did not entirely succeed.

"You found something, didn't you?" he said.

I kept my mouth shut.

"What was it?" he said in an exasperated tone. "Was it the badge?"

"The less you know the better," I said. "Let me ask you this, though: Did Frankie own anything of his dad's? A memento? Something he might've carried with him?"

He thought about it. "Not that I know of," he said. "Can you give me a hint?"

"I'm not roping you into this, son. All I'm going to say is I know for a fact Frankie was in that car. Chrisler might not have killed the boy himself, but he had something to do with it. He could've handed him off to someone else who did the actual shooting. Maybe his silent partner, the guy in the orange Trans-Am."

Kenny shook his head and looked out the window. "You can trust me not to tell. You know that, right?" He sounded hurt.

"It's not a matter of trust, Kenny. It's a matter of keeping you clean. The less you know about any shenanigans I pull, the less trouble you're liable to get into."

That didn't satisfy him. We rode the rest of the way in uncomfortable silence. Rain was coming down hard by the time we got to the station. "Do me a favor and send Karen out, will you?" I asked him.

He nodded and went in. Seconds later, Karen came out, holding a magazine over her head. "Lost my umbrella," she said as she got in the car. "What's up?"

"You and I are going out to talk to Shannon Gately."

She made a face. "Can't we leave that poor girl alone? She's not the one who killed her brother."

"Maybe not, but she can help us find who did."

"How's she going to do that?"

"You'll see."

I decided to save the news about finding the dog tag for later. Instead, I put on a Willie Nelson tape. Red's a fan. Maybe she feels a kinship based on the color of their hair. I kind of like him, too, if I'm to be honest. Anyway, *Blues from the Gutter* was starting to hit too close to home.

It didn't take long to get to the road leading to the Gately Estate. It did, however, take a good amount of time to reach our destination. Driving on a wet country road can be as treacherous as driving on asphalt in an ice storm. Sometimes county workmen drive heavy rollers over the roads to smooth them out and tamp them down, but only after the rain's stopped. Right now I inched along, the car floating on top of the mud like a surfboard. I kicked myself for bringing the Javelin instead of my pickup.

I steered around the pair of deep, water-filled ruts that comprised Shannon's driveway. The rain had slowed to a drizzle. Shannon and Frankie's trailers looked even sadder in the rain.

Shannon came to the door dressed in a T-shirt with a Budweiser logo on the front. Her cut-offs looked to be the same as last time. Streaks of eyeliner snaked down her cheeks.

"What do you want?" she asked in a pouty voice.

"We'd like to ask you a few questions about Frankie," I said. "Mind if we come in?"

She shrugged and stood aside. Karen offered consoling words. Shannon wiped her nose with her forearm and shrugged.

Inside, the trailer looked like the Burr landfill. Apparently, you don't need a permit to dump in Shannon Gately's living room. I looked for a clean place to sit. I couldn't find one, so I cleared the remains of a Swanson's Hungry Man Salisbury steak TV dinner from the couch and made room for Karen and myself. Shannon sat in a battered easy chair across from an old black-and-white television turned up full blast. I asked her if I could turn it down. She shrugged again. The TV's knobs had all broken off, so I had to guess which screw to turn. I got lucky and picked the one that turned it off.

"So Shannon," I began, "I want you to know we're doing everything we can to find who did that to your brother."

"Them other people keep coming by every fifteen minutes saying the same thing, but they always have questions for me, like I'm the one who done it. Whyn't y'all just leave me alone? Go out and find whoever really done it."

"We're sorry to bother you, hon," said Karen. "I know it must be hard."

"Darn right, it's hard," Shannon mumbled.

"No one's seen Randy Braley since he dropped off Frankie at Chrisler's that night. He hasn't been home. No one's seen his truck. He was one of the last people to see Frankie alive. We need to talk to him. We're hoping you can help us with that."

"How could I help?"

Karen said, "We just figured since Randy was friends with your brother, you might know something about him. You know, like where he hangs out, or if he has friends he might be staying with."

"I don't know where he is," said Shannon defensively. "I barely knew him. He just hung out with Frankie. He never came in this trailer or nothin' like that." That last remark was strange, I thought.

"Shannon, would it be ok if I used your rest room?" I asked. She waved toward the back of the trailer. "Over there. Down the hall on the left."

I stepped over the junk on the floor and walked down the hall. I looked back. Shannon couldn't see me, but Red could. I motioned to her to keep Shannon talking. She caught my drift. I opened a door. Shannon's bedroom was the housekeeping equivalent of a Jackson Pollock painting. Stuff was strewn all over.

On the floor next to her bed was a stack of high school textbooks, which I thought was strange, since both Shannon and her brother were long past high-school age. I picked the books up one by one, and looked inside. They'd all been issued to the same person, and it wasn't Shannon or Frankie Gately. I carried one back to the living room.

"Shannon, you said you barely knew Randy Braley, right?"

She nodded.

I showed her the book. "What's this, then?"

She turned red.

"What is that?" asked Karen, nodding at the book.

I opened it and showed her the inside front cover. It said, "This book is the Property of Burr Public Schools." Underneath were lines of dates and names, each scribbled by a different hand. The most recent, for the 1973-74 school year, read "Randy Braley."

"Shannon's got a whole pile of Randy's books back there," I said. "Either she knows him better than she says, or we're going to have to run her in for possession of stolen property."

CHAPTER 24

Shannon's face twitched like it had been hooked-up to a car battery. "You can't do that, can you?" she said.

"What? Arrest you for stealing textbooks?" I asked. "I probably could, but I'd rather you just tell me the truth about your relationship with Randy."

She pretended to sniffle, probably hoping it might inspire me to go easier on her. "I was afraid if I told you I knew him, you'd think I had something to do with killin' my brother."

I must admit: As pathetic excuses go, I've heard worse.

"So, does that mean you think Randy had something to do with it?" Karen said.

"I ain't sayin' that exactly." She reached for a pack of Marlboros and a lighter on the end table beside her. She lit up with shaking hands. "Randy couldn't have hurt Frankie. Frankie was his friend."

"What was your relationship with Randy?" I repeated.

"He stayed here sometimes to get away from his mom, who is just a horrible person. I used to help him with his homework. That's why his books are here."

The idea Shannon was helping Braley with his schoolwork was either ridiculous or scary, take your pick. Something else was going on there, but I let it pass for the moment.

"Ok then, let's start over," I said. "You know Randy better than you were saying, is that right?" She nodded.

"Ok, then. Can you think of another reason why he would have disappeared after Frankie's murder?"

"I don't know. Maybe he was afraid people would blame him." She shook her head. "I'm worried the person who killed Frankie might've done the same thing to Randy."

The thought had occurred to me, as well. I didn't tell her that.

Karen asked, "Do you have a romantic relationship with Randy Braley?"

Shannon nodded again and started to cry. "Never mind the books," I said. "I could take you to jail right now for lying to me. In fact, I might do that very thing unless you come clean and tell me where Randy Braley is."

"I don't know where he is!" she wailed. "I promise!"

Judging by the quality of her hysterics, I was inclined to believe her.

"I swear I don't know where Randy is," she sobbed again. The smeared eyeliner had now formed spiderweb-like patterns on her cheeks. "But I can tell you something else."

Red gave me one of her "be nice" looks.

"It better be good," I said.

"It ain't good," she said in a tortured voice, "but it's true."

**

I probably should've been surprised at how easy Shannon was to break, but I wasn't. Karen suggested we give Shannon a minute to compose herself. I went to the tiny kitchen and rinsed out the least-dirty plastic cup in the sink. I filled it with water from the tap. When I got back, Shannon was smiling faintly through the tears. Red must've said something funny. I handed Shannon the cup. She thanked me and took a drink.

I asked if she was ready to talk. She nodded.

"Ok, well, first thing is, Randy's a nice person. He's just had a hard life, is all. I don't know if you've met his mama, but she's just horrible, and his step daddy's in prison. Anyway, I know Randy's done bad things, but it ain't all his fault." She sniffled. "At least I don't think so."

I nodded, even though I'd heard similar excuses used to justify an infinite number of misdeeds over the course of my career.

"Was killing Frankie one of those bad things?" I asked.

She shook her head emphatically. "No, no. He'd never do that. I told you. Frankie was his friend." She took a sip of water. "I was talking about the drugs."

Here we go, I thought.

"Does Randy use drugs, Shannon?" asked Red.

She slapped the chair cushion. "No, that's not what I ..." She paused. "I mean, yeh, he smokes pot and does a little angel dust once in a while. But what I meant was, he sells drugs."

"To you?" I asked.

"No, not to me." She shrugged. "Well, he shares his own stash with me sometimes, but he doesn't make me pay."

It must be love, I thought.

"You're right, Shannon," said Karen. "Selling drugs is bad, but right now we're looking for who killed Frankie. Are you saying Randy's drug dealing has something to do with it?"

She moved her head like she couldn't decide to shake it or nod. "No. At least I don't think so."

"What drugs does Randy sell?" asked Red.

"PCP and pot, I know. Some pills."

I could think of a million reasons a drug dealer might kill someone. Most of them had to do with the drug dealer trying to stay out of jail.

"Is it possible Randy thought Frankie was going to tell someone and get him in trouble?"

She pounded the arms of her chair with both fists. "No!" she yelled. "There ain't no way Randy hurt Frankie! Y'all just shut up about that. There's nothing Frankie could've done that would've caused Randy to hurt him."

"Hon, calm down," said Karen. "We believe you." She looked at me for confirmation.

"Sure, we do. We're just trying to find whoever killed Frankie, is all. Randy saw him last, and now Randy's disappeared. You understand why we need to find him, don't you?"

"I guess, but you're wasting your time if you think Randy did it."

I was thinking we needed to either to wind this up or move it outside.

The stink of the place was giving me a headache—mostly the same rotten banana smell from when Kenny and I had visited.

"Where did Randy get the drugs to sell?" I asked. She tensed. "Please don't make me tell you that."

"So you know?"

She started crying again. "Randy told me, but he said if I ever told anyone, the person would kill me."

I moved close and took her hand. "Shannon, if that person would kill you, don't you think he'd have been willing to kill Frankie?"

"Frankie couldn't have told no one because Frankie doesn't know Randy sells drugs."

"Are you sure about that? They were friends. Couldn't he have found out?"

"Yeh, I guess," she said reluctantly.

"Don't you think it's possible this person might've killed Frankie?"

She frowned and nodded. "Mm-hmm."

"So don't you think it might be a good idea to tell us who it is?"

She nodded again.

"Alright, then. Who supplied Randy with the drugs?" I asked, knowing what the answer would be.

She gnawed on her bottom lip.

"Jim Chrisler."

Boy, was I ever not shocked.

CHAPTER 25

For a while when I lived in New York City, I had a cat named Steve. One time I heard him scratching around in the bathroom. I went in to see what was going on. Steve had trapped a mouse in the tub. I watched him for a minute. The poor little mouse would windmill and thrash his legs and almost reach the top, then Steve would swat it down and make it start over. I tried to snatch the mouse away. Steve didn't like that. He picked it up in his mouth and carried it under the bed. By the time I could finally affect a rescue, all that was left of the mouse was its ropy little tail.

I wondered if, in some fashion, that's what had happened to Frankie at the hands of Randy Braley.

***

"Did Randy tell you he got the drugs from Jim Chrisler?" I asked.

She gave us a tentative nod. "Uh-huh."

After what we'd been hearing and speculating about Chrisler, the revelation didn't come as a shock.

"What kind of drugs were they?"

"I already told you, all I know about is the pot and angel dust. And some pills, I think. Randy didn't like to talk about it."

"Ok, Shannon, from here on out, it's very important that you tell the truth. Ok?"

She gave a little bobble-headed nod.

"Have you seen Randy since the night Frankie died?"

"No, last time I seen him is when he picked up Frankie that night."

"You sure?"

"I'm sure."

"When was the last time you saw him before that?"

"That afternoon."

"Did he say anything about having plans for that night?"

"He said he was going to come by and pick up Frankie and take him cruising, that's all."

"When you say 'cruising,' you mean they were just going to drive around? Not going any particular place?"

"Yeh, you know this town. There ain't much to do in the summertime."

"What kind of stuff did Randy and Frankie do together?"

"Oh, I don't know. Guy stuff, I guess."

"Did Frankie help Randy sell drugs?"

"No. At least, I don't think so."

My head was starting to throb. I motioned for Karen to take over.

"Do you have any idea where Chrisler gets the drugs?" she asked.

Shannon looked more scared and pitiful than ever.

"If I tell you, they'll come after me," she said in a small voice.

"Shannon, darlin', whoever it is doesn't even know you exist," said Karen. "They'll have no way of knowing it was you who told us, and even if they did, I'm sure that OSBI lady you've been talking too, Agent Cruickshank, she'll fix it so you'll be protected."

Shannon produced an old rag and wiped her nose. "You're sure?"

"We're sure," said Karen. I nodded in agreement. I was sure. Kind of.

"Ok, well, Randy says that Chrisler gets his merchandise from the man who delivers potato chips. Wednesdays at 4:00. He hides the drugs under the bags of chips."

Today's Wednesday, I thought. Red and I looked at our watches, then at each other. It was ten 'til four.

We told Shannon to expect someone from the OSBI to come by soon, and that she should tell them what she told us. Red grabbed a crumpled brown paper bag on our way out the door. I felt a new appreciation for fresh air after being stuck in that trailer. When we got in the Javelin, however, the overripe stench from Shannon's trailer followed us.

"What the hell is that smell?" I said.

Karen held the bag open where I could see. Inside was a twisted tube of model airplane glue.

"Geez, I thought it was a rotten banana," I said.

"There might've been one of those in there, too, but this is what caused that smell."

"So she's a glue sniffer," I said.

"That's what it looks like."

We headed towards town. The sun peeked through the clouds, but the road was a muddy mess until we got to the highway.

"Let's figure out how we're going to handle this," I said.

"Without a warrant, there's not much we can do but watch."

"I guess we could pull up beside the potato chip truck and hope they drop some drugs in front of us by accident."

She chuckled. "Yeh, right."

"I expect the best thing to do is watch from a safe distance. Try to get an idea of what their routine is, but stay out of sight."

"Should we call Isabel?"

"There's not enough time. If Shannon's right, they'll be doing it again next week. I'm sure Isabel can get a search warrant before then."

"I'd hate to have to wait a full week."

"We might not have a choice."

For the third time that day, I drove past Chrisler's. His Chrysler was still the only car in the lot, parked in the same place as before. It was four o'clock on the dot. There was an oil lease road about 50 yards south of Chrisler's on the opposite side of the highway. I turned onto it and parked the car so it was hidden by a couple of oak trees. I could see Chrisler's car tolerably well. I cut the engine and waited.

We didn't have to wait long.

I'd expected one of those big delivery trucks with the name of the potato chip company painted across the side. What we got instead was a plain emerald green Ford Econoline van. It parked near the back door by the dumpster. A tall fella with long black hair, wearing jeans and a t-shirt got out. Even from a distance, I could tell he was using one of those big wallets that attach to a belt loop with a chain. The kind bikers wear.

"That's the guy who runs the drive-in," I said. "His name's Sam Carter."

"Are you sure?"

"I just talked to him the other day."

Chrisler appeared from behind the building. They talked. Chrisler looked angry. Carter seemed to be explaining himself.

"I'm sorry," I said and started the car. "I can't just sit here and watch this."

Red grabbed my arm. "I thought we were going to watch from a safe distance and observe."

"Yeh, well, I'm making an executive decision."

She let go of my arm. "I want to go on record that I think you should wait until you get a warrant."

"Noted," I said. I hit my emergency lights and crossed the highway over to Chrisler's. I told Red to stay where she was, put on my hat and got out of the car.

"What's the problem, officer?" said Chrisler said with the usual note of contempt in his voice.

"I was in the mood for some potato chips when I noticed your potato chip salesman pull up," I said. "I thought I'd get him to sell me a box."

"What makes you think this fella sells potato chips?"

"Doesn't he?"

"Yeh, but how'd you know? The truck's not marked."

"Lucky guess."

Carter's head swiveled back and forth between Chrisler and me like he was watching a tennis match. Chrisler looked like a card-player measuring the odds. He turned to Carter. "Get the man a bag of chips."

Carter shrugged and smiled. "Fine," he said. He opened the van's back door, reached into an open cardboard box, and pulled out a bag of potato chips. "Heads up," he said and tossed it to me.

I caught it. "Thank you, Mr. Carter," I said, "but I reckon I didn't make myself clear. I wanted a whole box." I tossed the bag to Chrisler. "See, I really like potato chips."

Carter looked at Chrisler. "What do you say? Can you spare a box?"

Chrisler smiled. "Hell, Sam, he doesn't want a box of chips. He wants whatever else he thinks is in them boxes. Ain't that right, Chief?"

Chrisler walked to the back of the truck and elbowed Carter aside. He pulled out a box and dumped the contents onto the ground.

"What're you after, Chief? We got Lay's, we got Ruffles, we got Cheetos. Take your pick. Or have them all. I don't care. But it ain't chips you're looking for, is it?"

I walked closer and peered inside the truck. There were at least a dozen more boxes, the same size and shape as the one Chrisler had dumped out.

"I expect I'd need a warrant to go through all those boxes, wouldn't I?"

Chrisler cocked his head and stuck out his chest. "Don't know why you'd want to, but yeh, I reckon you would."

"OK, then," I said. "You wouldn't mind if my colleague and I sit here while you unload, would you? I mean, I wouldn't need a warrant for that, would I?"

Chrisler spit on the ground. "Well, Chief, that's the thing," he said. "Old Sam here brought me the wrong shipment. We was just having a talk about it when you drove up. Weren't we, Sam?"

Carter gave me smug grin. "Yeh, sure," he said. "Sorry about that, Mr. Chrisler." He stabbed a hand into his pants pocket and pulled out his car keys. "I got your order mixed up with someone else's."

"You're burning the candle at both ends, aren't you, Sam?" I remarked. "Running that movie theater at night and delivering chips by day."

"With the economy the way it is," he said, "a man just about has to work two jobs to get by." He picked up the bags of chips on the ground and put them back in the box. "I'd better get going. I've got lots more stops to make. Be seeing you, Mr. Chrisler."

"Seeya, Sam."

Carter got in the van and drove away. Chrisler disappeared through the back door without a word.

I got back in the Javelin and drove after Carter. I caught up with him in less than a minute. I got close so he'd know I was following him. He'd seemed cool and collected around Chrisler, but the way he kept looking back at me in his rearview mirror, I expect he was plenty hot and bothered. He drove through town, past Butcherville toward Alva.

"I expect he'll keep going until he sees we're not following him anymore," I said to Karen.

"Probably," she said.

We got halfway to Alva before I finally turned around.

"That was a thrill," said Karen.

"Not exactly *The French Connection*, huh?"

"No," she said. We were quiet for a moment, then she added, "I guess The Burr Connection doesn't have the same ring, does it?"

I said I reckoned it didn't.

CHAPTER 26

Cindy handed me a piece of paper with a phone number scribbled on it. "Agent Cruickshank says to call," she said.

On our way back to my office, Red and I talked about what to do about Shannon. I thought it'd be a good idea to have whoever was on patrol duty roll by her house a few times every shift, and maybe knock on her door to see if she was ok. As for the bag of airplane glue: possessing it wasn't a crime, but people have died from inhaling that stuff. At best, it rots your brain faster than daytime television. We agreed she needed help and vowed to get her some when this was all over.

I picked up my phone to call Isabel, but I couldn't get a dial tone, so I went back out front and used Cindy's.

Isabel said the reason she'd called was to tell me they'd let the Cottrells go. I'd almost forgotten about them. She also said they'd investigated any connection between the Fechners in Kingfisher and Travis Ballard. So far, they hadn't been able to find one.

"I'm also looking for anything that connects those killings to Jim Chrisler," she added. "So far, I haven't come across anything there, either. What about you?"

"Nothing concrete connecting him to the killings," I said. I couldn't share my discovery of Frankie, Sr.'s dog tags. "Karen and I dug up something else, though." I told her about our talk with Shannon and her relationship with Braley. "According to her, Braley's been selling drugs for Chrisler. She told us they're delivered by a potato chip salesman, Wednesday afternoons at 4:00."

She paused. "That was twenty minutes ago."

"It was," I said. "Karen and I dropped by. Turns out, Chrisler's potato chip guy is Sam Carter."

"The owner of the drive-in?"

"The same."

"Wow." The word sounded funny coming from her.

I related the talk I'd had with Chrisler and Carter.

"That's interesting, but why didn't you call me?"

"We didn't find out until just before 4:00. We just barely had time to rush over there. I'd intended to watch the transaction from a distance, but I couldn't resist going over there and poking them a little."

"That wasn't a good idea," she scolded. "Chances are you scared them off. They'll find a new way to deliver the goods."

"Yeh," I said. "I was just so mad I couldn't help myself." I turned to Red. "Why didn't you stop me?"

"Uh, excuse me, Chief Hardy, but I tried."

"Oh, right." I felt like an idiot. "Well, I'm sorry. That wasn't very smart of me."

She asked if I'd gotten the van's license plate number. I gave it to her, along with a description of the van.

"Well, at least it's another piece of the puzzle," she said. "Lord only knows how it fits."

"It should be enough for a search warrant, right?"

"I hope so."

"I'd like to be there when it's executed, if that's alright."

"I'll make sure," she said. "Meanwhile, I'll have to think this over."

"Need any help?"

"I think I'll call it a day. My little friend is about to kick my insides out."

"Are you staying here in town?"

"Yeh, at that Big Chief place you recommended."

"I *told* you about it. I don't recall recommending it."

"Whatever. It's fine."

"One more thing," I said. "You know anything about an orange Trans-Am that's been driving around town the last couple of days?"

"Actually, I have noticed. A car like that sticks out."

"Any idea who's behind the wheel?"

"No idea. Why do you ask?"

"Because I've seen it driving in and out of Chrisler's. I'm wondering if it might be the silent partner Chrisler told me and Kenny about."

"Hmmm, let me make a note," she said. I could hear her pencil scratching. "Ok, next time I see it, I'll jot the license number down and run it through the system. Anything else?"

"Speaking of Chrisler's silent partner, I wonder if it could be Sam Carter?"

"That's a good question. I'll have Raksin look into his background."

"How's ol' Probationary Agent Raksin working out?"

She snorted. "Don't ask."

We agreed to meet the next morning.

Isabel's mention of The Big Chief Motor Inn again reminded me of the guy who busted his head open while putting on his undershorts. I asked Red if she knew how he was doing.

She shook her head. "Still in critical condition, last time I heard."

"What's the story on that couple?"

"You mean, what were they doing in Burr?"

"Right."

"On their way to Boiling Springs State Park," she said. "Vacation."

"Do you think I ought to go visit him in the hospital? Maybe comfort the wife?"

"You can if you want," she said, "although they don't know you from Adam."

"Maybe I'll just send a card."

"I'm sure they'd appreciate the gesture."

***

Bernard rolled in a little before five o'clock. Cindy, Karen, and I talked with him for a few minutes before Karen took off to run some errands. George was late as usual, and Cindy was anxious to leave. I told her to go ahead.

Bernard and I talked a bit about the case. I told him some—but not all— of what I'd learned since we'd last spoken. I mentioned my suspicions about

Chrisler's drug activity. I didn't tell him that Shannon had more or less confirmed them. I also asked him about the orange Trans-Am and if he knew the driver. He'd seen it but didn't know whose it was. "Why don't you just have Lester find an excuse to pull him over tonight?" he said.

"Maybe I'll do that."

"Speaking of Les, how's he doing?"

"You'd know better than me," I said. "Haven't you run into him on patrol?"

"Not much. Just to wave, mainly."

"I was over there earlier. He seemed a little down, but not too bad. I reckon missing his girlfriend is his biggest problem."

"Maybe. I reckon it wouldn't hurt to talk to him, though. Just to make sure."

"Couldn't hurt, but if he's going to let the first dead body he sees get to him like that, maybe he should consider a new line of work."

Bernard chuckled. "Don't give up on him yet. I know I made some major screw-ups when I was starting out."

"I don't recall firing you for any of them."

"That's my point."

"I'll talk to him."

Lester walked through the door.

"Now's your chance," said Bernard.

"Now's your chance for what?" asked Lester.

"Oh, we were just talking." Bernard nodded goodbye and took off.

I asked Les how he was feeling.

He shrugged. "I'm fine."

"I need to get home to Mrs. Hardy, but you and I should talk. You're working a double tonight, right?"

"Yes sir."

"Don't go home tomorrow morning until you've talked to me."

He smiled wanly. "10-4 on that, Chief."

I told him to have a safe night and went home to the wife.

***

I tossed and turned half the night, until I finally got up, tip-toed out to my truck and chugged some Smirnoff. That put me down quick, but the sleep wasn't restful.

Red got up when I did and cooked me some scrambled eggs, hash browns with little pieces of fried onion, and thick slabs of bacon. She's no Julia Child, but it might have been the best meal she'd ever cooked for me.

I stuck my head in the office, said hello to Cindy, and told her I was going to sit outside on the bench and wait for Lester. He drove up in the Fury shortly thereafter.

"Hey, Chief," he said with a tired smile. "I reckon I know what this is gonna be about."

"You're a mind reader, huh?" I said. "Come on and take a load off." I scooted over and made room.

He sat. "I expect folks've been telling you how out of sorts I've been."

"One or two have mentioned it, yes."

"I'm sorry. It's just …" He scratched his arm absent-mindedly. I noticed he still hadn't picked up his short-sleeved uniform shirts. Neither had I, for that matter.

"Since that thing the other night, I don't think I've gotten an hour's sleep," he said with a sigh. "Maybe I made a mistake, being a cop."

I was thinking along those same lines, but like Bernard said, it was too soon to give up on him.

"It's not easy," I said, "but dealing with death is part of the job. The good news is, it gets easier. This was your first one and, who knows, it might be your last. Let's hope it is. If not, well, each one will bother you a little less than the one before."

He hung his head. "I can't wait for that to happen."

I remembered the sick feeling in the pit of my stomach when I saw Frankie lying face down in the dirt and suddenly wished I could take those words back. "Don't want it too much," I added. "You need to have feelings in this job, or you don't have any business doing it. I've promised myself the time I stop caring about people dying on my patch is the time I get a job pumping gas. I haven't gotten there yet."

"Yeh," he said, his voice flat.

"It might be good if you talked to someone," I said, thinking of my time at the VA hospital. The headshrinkers there did me some good, even if I hadn't realized it at the time.

He shrugged. "Maybe," he said.

"We'll look into it," I said. "For now, though, how about you take some time off?"

He shook his head. "No, we don't have enough people as it is."

"You let me worry about that. We can always call in Eugene if we have to." Eugene Hughes is a part-timer we only use in emergencies. He's a little too much like a real-life Barney Fife to be trusted on a regular basis, but he's fine as an occasional fill-in.

Lester half-nodded, half-shook his head. His handsome features had become nearly zombie-like. "No, I don't want to take time off," he said. "I need to work."

"You're in no fit shape to work. You need time to think and rest." The thought of how Red helps me when I'm down gave me a flash of inspiration. "How 'bout you go visit your fiancé for a few days?"

He laughed mirthlessly and shook his head.

"You two having trouble?"

"Nah, not really."

"Alright then. Take three or four days. Go see your girl. If, when you get back, you're still not one-hundred percent, we'll look into finding a doctor who can set you straight. How's that sound?"

He gave me a despairing look. "Sounds like I ain't got a choice."

I gave him a hearty slap on the back. "I reckon you don't, bud. Don't think of it like that, though. Consider it a vacation. Everyone needs a breather now and then." We got to our feet. "You going to need a bus ticket to Kansas?" I asked. "We're going to need the Fury while you're away."

"That's ok, I got my own truck."

"Well, gas it up, call that gal of yours and tell her you're on your way."

He nodded. "Ok, Chief."

In asked if he needed a ride home. He did. I commandeered a Javelin and we hit the road. We listened to one Kenny's blues tapes without saying much. I didn't see a vehicle when we got there. I asked where he parked his truck. "It's in the barn," he said.

"If you decide you want to talk, or if there's anything else I can do to help," I said, "just let me know. I'm not the best in the world at making people feel better, but I'm willing to try."

"That's ok, Chief," said Lester. "I feel a little better, talkin' to you."

I was fairly certain he was just being polite. The boy's got good manners.

CHAPTER 27

The rest of the day was uneventful. Things didn't start going to hell until the sun went down.

***

Isabel and her people had their hands full trying to find the driver of that van and getting the warrant to search Chrisler's place. She called us twice. The first time it was to tell me they'd gotten an ID on the owner of the green Econoline; it was part of a fleet that belonging to an actual snack food distributor based in Weatherford. They were still awaiting confirmation that Sam Carter was an employee. Her second call was to confirm that he was.

I ran into Bernard late in the day and told him I'd had a talk with Lester, and that I was giving him time off to visit his fiancé. Bernard thought it was a good idea. He asked if I was letting him drive the Fury to Kansas. I said of course I was not, which relieved Bernard a great deal. Even though it wasn't his to drive anymore, Bernard still feels as protective as a mother hen when it comes to that car.

By this time, I reckoned Randy Braley could officially be considered missing. His mama had yet to file a report, but I figured enough time had gone by that someone should, so I did it myself. Red tracked down his vital statistics, including the plate numbers of that old junker truck of his that I'd heard about but couldn't remember having seen. I relayed copies to the sheriff's office and the highway patrol. We'd been looking for him and had come up dry. It was time to bring in the big boys and girls.

Speaking of girls, it was Karen's night out with her friends. I lose track of who "the girls" are; they tend to vary from week to week. Red's always on hand, however, so I guess it's fair to say she's the leader of the pack. Red doesn't drink and is generally well-behaved in social situations. I can trust her not to raise too much hell, no matter what foolishness they're up to.

I, on the other hand, drink. Lately I'd been using girls' night out as an opportunity to indulge.

Crime-wise, Thursdays are usually the calm before the storm—the storm being Friday and Saturday nights, when it's not unusual for a week's worth of mischief to occur. On Thursdays, I have Lester or Kenny holding down the fort. In an emergency, Bernard's no more than radio call away. If I'm going to drink to excess, Thursday's the night to do it.

Girls' night typically lasts until about ten, but this time they decided to go to a movie in Temple City, so Red said they'd be late. That would give me extra time to cover my tracks—return my bottle of Smirnoff to its place under the seat of my truck, brush my teeth, and crawl under the covers before she gets home.

Karen had put a TV dinner in the oven before she left. I ate the chicken and the mashed potatoes but stayed away from the peas and carrots. Nor did I partake of the so-called apple cobbler included for dessert. I washed what few dishes there were and watched a little of *The Waltons* on the little portable black & white set we keep in the kitchen. It was eight o'clock before I was ready to kick back and relax.

I poured myself an economy-sized vodka and Tab on the rocks and retired to the couch in the living room We had recently purchased a brand-new Magnavox Spirit of '76 color TV, which is about as close to going to the movies as you can get in the comfort of your living room. By the time Karl Mauldin and Michael Douglas were chasing drug dealers up and down the streets of San Francisco, I was on my second drink. Like most real-life cops, I scoff at TV's portrayal of law enforcement. Liquor increases that propensity, although, to be fair, I do remember thinking: What in hell do I know about policing in a big city?

Anyway, by the time the ten o'clock news came on, I was well on my way to being three sheets to the wind. Sadly, God, or fate, or whoever oversees such things, chose that moment to infringe upon my alcohol-fueled bliss.

The phone rang. It was George at the station.

"Chief, Laverne Colley just called in, says she let her dog out to do its business, and it came back carrying a hand in its mouth."

I guess I'm drunker than I thought, I said to myself.

"Come again, George?"

"Laverne Colley called in and said her dog came home with a hand in its mouth."

I almost asked if the hand was human, then I caught myself. With the slow-motion and exaggerated sense of logic you tend to exercise when you're inebriated, I realized that, except for monkeys, humans are the only animals *with* hands. Most others make do with paws or claws or fins or whatever.

"I assume it was unattached," I said.

"Uh, well, yeh, I think that's why she was so upset," said George. He added, "I thought you'd like to know."

Like to know? I could've lived a happy and fulfilled life had I never heard of the dog that carried home a severed hand.

Need to know?

Yeh, well, I guess I did.

CHAPTER 28

My dog Dizzy was a Labrador retriever. True to her breed, she used to retrieve all manner of dead animals and discarded objects, and deposit them on my front porch. Squirrels. Old work boots. And birds, of course.

She never brought home a hand, though. I've never been so drunk that I wouldn't remember that.

It'd been years since I was so soused that I couldn't drive, but this night I was.

"George," I said, careful to enunciate every word, lest he deduce my impairment, "Karen's got my truck tonight. Could you have whoever's on duty come by and pick me up?"

"That'd be Hughes."

Right. Eugene's covering for Lester.

"Fine. Have him pick me up."

"He's already at Laverne's, but I'll have him circle back and get you."

"You do that."

I could've walked if I'd wanted. The town's grown, but it still isn't so big you can't walk about anywhere in five minutes. That includes Laverne Colley's, who lives on the corner of 6th Street and Bud Wilkinson Way, a couple of blocks off Main Street, right behind Jesus is Lord Hair Salon. I wanted to keep the number of people who saw me staggering around to a bare minimum.

It was a little after nine. I remember thinking it was too early for me to be as intoxicated as I was. I recall seeing about an inch of vodka left in the bottle and realizing while I was knocking it back that I was making a terrible mistake. Oh well, I thought. No use cryin' over spilt vodka. I laughed to myself. I heard a voice say, "What's so funny, Chief?" and I realized George was still on the line.

"Nothing," I said. "I'll be waiting for Hughes to pick me up."

George might've said goodbye, but I can't be sure. All I know is I hung up. I was already thinking about how I was going to make myself presentable. I was still wearing most of my uniform, although it looked like I'd been sleeping in it. I tucked in my shirt, brushed the fried chicken crumbs off my chest, and pulled on the Dingos I wear since I can't wear pointy-toed boots anymore. Ingrown toenails.

I went into the bathroom and gargled with the Lavoris I keep for emergencies. I put on my fedora and gave myself a good look in the mirror. I squinted hard and thought myself presentable. I put my hand over my mouth and smelled my breath. Cinnamon. Good ol' Lavoris.

I carefully extricated my keys from the hook by the door, opened the door and locked it behind me in time to see headlights light up the porch.

It was the Fury, with Eugene Hughes behind the wheel.

I got in the car and Eugene pulled out. "What do we got, Eugene?"

"It's the dangdest thing, Chief," he said. "You know that little ol' dachshund of Laverne Colley's? Burt Reynolds? Laverne leaves him tied up outside Jesus is Lord while she's workin'."

Laverne's a beautician at Jesus is Lord Hair Salon. She named her dog Burt Reynolds after the fella who posed naked in that women's magazine a couple of years back.

"Yeh, I know Burt Reynolds. He's a good little dog."

"Well, he don't like me much, but I suppose he is," replied Eugene. "Anyway, Laverne let Burt Reynolds out to do his business before she went to bed. He was gone a long time, and she was getting worried about him, so she went out to find him just in time to see him trotting up onto her porch with something in his mouth. Guess what it was?"

"A hand?"

"Oh, I guess George already told you," he said, sounding disappointed. "That's what it was. A human hand. Don't that beat all?"

"I reckon it does," I mumbled.

I rolled down the window and kept my face turned away from Eugene for the duration of the drive. I thought I'd caught him looking at me funny. I might've been wrong.

Laverne Colley is far and away the most stylish employee at the Jesus Is Lord Hair Salon. As far as I know, she was the first and so far only woman in town to wear hot pants, which she augments with the most up-to-date (by Burr standards, anyway) colorful blouses, jewelry, and fancy boots. She's inching toward middle-age and no great beauty, but she's good at doing her own hair and making herself up, which in part explains why she's one of the more popular beauticians in town. She's even cut my hair a few times. That's how I met Burt Reynolds. Laverne's also a horrible gossip, which is important to mention in this context.

When we arrived, she was sitting in a metal rocking chair on her front porch. She wore short red nylon pajamas and was smoking a cigarette out of a long black holder. Last time I'd seen her, she had long, straight brown hair. This time, it was cut into a shag and dyed ash blond. Burt Reynolds lay on the porch beside her. He didn't even bother to bark when he saw us. He'd had a long day.

"Hey there, Laverne," I said, speaking carefully. Last thing I needed was for Laverne to tell the gals down at the beauty shop I'd shown up drunk. "Eugene tells me little Burt brought you an early Christmas present."

She gave me a haughty look. "Chief, his name is *Burt Reynolds*, not Burt."

"That's right," I said and addressed the pooch directly: "Sorry about that, Burt Reynolds."

Laverne gave me an annoyed look, but I'm pretty sure Burt Reynolds accepted my apology.

"Also," she said, "you might think it's funny to joke about, but I about had a heart attack when Burt Reynolds brung up what he did."

"A hand."

She exhaled a plume of smoke. "That's correct, Chief Hardy," she said. "A hand."

"What'd you do with it?"

She gestured with her cigarette holder at a brown paper bag sitting at the end of the porch.

"It's in that bag," she said. "Careful when you open it. It smells bad."

I peeked inside. Sure enough, it contained a dismembered hand. It did indeed give off an unpleasant odor—I'd describe as a dead possum stuffed with rancid hamburger meat. I shut it as quick as I'd opened it.

"Any idea where Burt Reynolds found it?"

"No idea, except he came running from that direction." She nodded toward the north.

I held my breath and looked inside the bag again. The hand wasn't especially dirty. It didn't look like it had been buried, necessarily.

"Does Burt Reynolds do a lot of digging, Laverne?"

"Well of course he does." She took a pull on her cigarette and exhaled elaborately. Laverne does everything elaborately. "That's what dachshunds do," she drawled, pronouncing it *dash hounds*. "They dig. It's genetic or something."

"I see. Does Burt Reynolds have any special places he likes to dig?"

"Not in my yard," she said. "He knows better than that. He goes somewhere else, I suspect. I don't know where."

I looked at Burt Reynolds' stubby little legs and concluded he hadn't gone very far.

"Did you notice how long was he gone?" I asked.

"Oh, a half hour, I guess. That's why I was worried. He hardly ever takes that long, especially at night. He's scared of the dark."

I tried to calculate how much time it would've taken Burt Reynolds to dig up that hand, then how long it would've taken for him to get there and back, but that last inch of Smirnoff had turned my mind to sludge. Laverne and Eugene and Burt Reynolds were swaying up and down and side to side. I pulled out my little black notebook, concentrated as hard as I was able and wrote down Laverne's story, knowing I'd have trouble remembering it in the morning.

My writing was squigglier than usual, but I reckoned I'd be able to read it. "Alright, Laverne, thanks for callin' this in. That'll be all for now. We'll be talkin' to you soon."

"That's it?" she said, surprise written on her face. "Don't I have to make a statement? On TV shows, the witnesses always have to make a statement."

By now, my lips were numb, and I was seeing at least two of everything. "That's what you jus' did and what I jus' did, Laverne. You stated somethin' and I wrote it down. I reckon Bernard's some'eres within shouting distance. I'll go back to the car and give him a shout."

I remember Eugene calling after me as I walked to the Fury: "Shouldn't we call out a sheriff's deputy, Chief?" I ignored him. Somehow—don't ask me how—I made it to the car. I must've gotten through to George or Bernard, but I don't remember doing it. I either fell asleep or passed out, because the next thing I knew, Bernard was half-walking—but mostly carrying—me to my front door. Karen's car was in the driveway.

Even through the fog of drink, I knew my goose was cooked.

CHAPTER 29

I opened my eyes the next morning, only to shut them again as fast as I could. The blinds were open. Sunlight bored into my head like an icepick. No more than I deserved, but uncomfortable—no, not uncomfortable—*painful*, nevertheless.

I called out to Karen, but all that came out was a phlegmy cough. I cleared my throat and tried again. My voice was there, but she wasn't.

I opened my eyes again, using my hands to shield the sun. It helped a little. I started shivering. All I had on were my BVDs and a t-shirt. The air-conditioning was on full blast. Whoever had put me to bed—Karen, presumably—had not bothered to cover me up. Or put a pillow under my head. I was laying on a made bed. I moved my arms and legs. They ached but functioned as they should.

A minor victory.

I tried calling out to Karen again. I sounded like a sick little boy yelling for his mama. Still no answer.

I managed to sit up and swing my legs over the side of the bed. I smelled bacon, which I love. Today it made me want to throw up. I went to the bathroom and did just that. The thought, 'I'll never do that again,' echoed in my mind, even if I did not immediately remember what I'd done.

Oh yeah. Drank half a bottle of vodka.

I put on some pants and went outside. Going from the air-conditioned house to the heat and humidity of a late-August day felt like walking into a sauna fully clothed. The sun seemed higher in the sky than I thought it should be. I stepped back inside and checked the time. The clock on the stove said ten o'clock.

I was two hours late for work.

I checked myself out in the bathroom mirror. I saw someone I hadn't seen in a long time. Someone I didn't much like.

I washed down a few aspirins with a glass of water and promptly heaved up my guts.

I decided to wait before trying it again.

Ignoring the pounding in my head as best I could, I finished getting dressed. Somehow, I managed to primp myself into something presentable.

The thought of eating made me feel even worse, so all I ingested was an envelope of BC Powder dissolved in a glass of orange juice. This time I kept it down. I looked around for my keys, couldn't find them, and went out to check my truck.

It wasn't there. Karen must have driven it to work. She never does that, but she did this time. Her Falcon sat in the driveway, but I don't have a key to it.

I went back inside and found a note on the refrigerator: "Bernard told Isabel about the hand. I'm at work."

Short and to the point.

I could call the station and have someone pick me up, or I could walk. It wasn't a tough call. I was too embarrassed to ask for a ride. I put on a pair of sunglasses, pulled down my fedora as low as it would go, and headed out on foot, taking side streets to avoid running into anyone I knew.

Memories of the night before began peeking through the fog. My primary concern—besides finding out who that hand belonged to—was that Laverne Colley would blab all over town about me being drunk. There was a time when I could've charmed my way out of such a mess. Not anymore. The town government has changed. I used to know everything there was to know about the mayor and members of the city council. Hell, they'd known me since I was a kid. Unfortunately, those fellas have all died or retired. Half the time I forget the names of this new group. They're a more ambitious bunch, I know that. They'd be just as happy to cut me loose and replace me with someone who's as slick as they are.

The walk took five minutes. It felt a lot longer.

Both Javelins were gone when I got there, as was my pickup. A young woman and her little boy wearing a toy badge walked past me on the sidewalk. I thought of Frankie.

"It's about time," said Cindy as I came through the door.

"Yeh, sorry I'm late."

"That's fine. Mrs. Hardy said you might not be in since you were feeling sick after finding that hand. I guess that must've been pretty gross, huh?"

At least Red wasn't so mad that she wouldn't cover for me.

"Yeh, I'm still smelling it. Where is everyone?"

"202 Maple Street, corner of West Santa Fe. They found the body that hand belongs to."

"Who?"

"Laverne Colley's little dog Burt Reynolds found it." She paused and lit a cigarette. "Last I heard they hadn't ID'd the body, although I can guess."

I could, too

***

202 Maple Street, at the corner of West Santa Fe, is just past the outermost edge of what passes for civilization in our town. Laverne Colley lives one block over, at 201 Elm Street, which is also on the corner of West Santa Fe. The houses on Elm are old, but generally in pretty good shape. The houses on Maple are mostly unfit for human habitation. Those that aren't abandoned should be.

An alley runs between backyards of Laverne's Colley's house and 202 Maple. The latter's only occupants are rats and possums and snakes and drug addicts looking for privacy. Recently, Maple Street had evolved into a place the hardcore users go—those who use needles—to scratch their itch. If you'd told me a few years ago that Burr would one day have its own Skid Row, I'd have said you were crazy. I'd have been wrong.

A fleet of law enforcement vehicles were parked in front of the house: Isabel's unmarked car; a green Tilghman County Sheriff's Department cruiser, and a black and white Dodge Diplomat used by the Highway Patrol; our own Fury and the other Javelin.

Also, a red and white Ford F-150 pickup belonging to me.

I parked on the corner and picked my way through the jungle of weeds in what used to be the front yard. A cinder block held the front door open. Inside, Isabel huddled with a couple of men in ugly suits who I took to be her OSBI colleagues. A few state troopers scattered themselves about. Kenny and Karen stood together next to a pair of rusty metal poles that had once supported a gate.

"What's going on?" I asked.

"How you feelin'?" asked Kenny. "Karen tells me you were throwin' up all night."

She didn't look at me.

"Oh, I'll survive," I said. "What have we got here?"

"A body," he said, nodding toward the house. "Chopped up, put into plastic garbage bags, and stuffed under the floorboards."

"So that's where Burt Reynolds got the hand."

He chuckled and shook his head. "Who names their dog Burt Reynolds? Yeh, Laverne Colley followed him when she let him out to do his business this morning. He went straight to this place. There's a hole in the back door big enough for him to get through. It was unlocked, so Laverne followed him inside. Whoever cut the body up didn't do a very good job hiding it. Burt Reynolds went right to it. Tore through the plastic bag and pulled out the other hand, with Laverne standing there watching."

"She called it in?"

"Yeh, she did, although we'd already decided to check the houses on the street." He looked at me, concerned. "You ok, Chief? Because you don't look ok."

I didn't feel ok, either, especially with Red standing there ignoring me

"I'll survive," I said. "Any idea who it is?"

"Randy Braley."

"I figured. So this is where he's been."

He nodded. "I didn't like the kid, but I wouldn't have wished this on him."

"Cause of death?"

"Too soon to tell, I expect, although if they have any idea, they're not sharing it with us. Agent Cruickshank and the rest of the state boys shooed us out as soon as they got here." He shook his head. "I don't know. They haven't told us anything. I didn't look too close when I got here because I didn't want to disturb the remains."

I asked Kenny if he'd give Karen and me a minute. He walked over to a state trooper and tried to wheedle some information out of him.

"You mad at me?" I asked her.

"Hmmph." she said, still not looking me in the eye. "Mad doesn't begin to cover it."

"Well, if it means anything, I'm mad at myself," I said. "Why'd you take my truck?"

"Because I didn't want you to kill yourself or someone else driving drunk," she said through clenched teeth. "That's why."

There didn't seem any point in telling her I only had a hangover and was fine to drive.

"That makes sense," I said instead. "I can't tell you how sorry I am."

She made a gesture like she was trying to push me away. "Ok, we'll talk about it later. Now's not the time."

"Home? Tonight?"

Her laugh didn't express a speck of amusement. "You're not sleeping in my bed, buster. Go sleep at your daddy's house."

"Tomorrow, then?"

She frowned. "I don't know. We'll see. Right now, you need to get away from me. I'm so mad, I'm afraid of what I might say."

I couldn't think of anything to say that wouldn't make things worse. I tried to touch her cheek, instead. She slapped my hand away.

"Don't," she said. "Just go."

***

I waited on the fringes of a conversation Isabel was having with a couple of other plainclothes folks. She turned to me when they'd finished.

"You healthy enough to work?" she asked. I thought I detected a hint of sarcasm. Maybe I imagined it.

"Yeh, I'm fine," I said. It was partly true. The headache had faded, although my stomach still felt like it was trying to digest kerosene.

"Have you seen the body?" she asked.

"Just that hand the dog dragged in last night."

"Come on."

She led me to a room at the back of the house. A few used syringes lay scattered about. Weeds and tall grass grew between rotten wooden flooring. In the middle of the room, someone had pulled away several planks to reveal a couple of torn plastic bags containing a human body that had been butchered like a chicken.

"Randy Braley," she said.

"How do you know?"

"Officer Harjo recognized him."

I looked closer. "Where's the head?"

"The crime scene investigators removed it," she said. "Officer Harjo saw it before they took it away. Whoever killed him made sure Braley's wallet was stuffed in there with him."

"That's strange, don't you think?"

She shrugged. "If it was a robbery, you'd expect the wallet to be missing, but this obviously isn't that. The killer might've figured it didn't matter. He might even have wanted the body to be identified."

"Why would he want that?"

"He could be sending a message."

To his silent partner? I wondered. To Sam Carter? Hell, could Sam Carter be his silent partner?

I asked why she thought the murderer had cut the body into pieces.

"Easier to transport, for one thing," she said. "The victim obviously wasn't killed here."

"Why wouldn't he have just buried it?"

"You ever try to dig a hole big and deep enough to bury a human body? I'm suspect he decided it was just easier to cut it up, stuff it in a couple of garbage bags, and stow it somewhere it wouldn't be found. Like this place."

I guess he wasn't counting on Burt Reynolds, I thought. "Do you think this is connected to Frankie Gately?"

She nodded. "It would be a heck of a coincidence if it wasn't."

"Jim Chrisler's got to be involved. How's it going with that search warrant?"

"It's going," she said. "We should get it today."

"I don't mean to tell you how to do your job, but make sure it's for his car, too."

She gave me a suspicious look. "Don't worry. We'll include the car."

The way she said it was a little snippy. Maybe Red told her why I was in the condition I was in.

"Ok, you've got your hands full," I said, backing away. "I'll let you do your job and let you know if we find anything."

She gave me one of her Sgt. Joe Friday nods. "We'll keep you apprised of any developments."

I could be wrong, but judging by the way she said it, I reckoned she was just trying to be polite. We Okies are always polite.

CHAPTER 30

Somehow, I managed to convince Red I was fine to drive. The way she threw the keys at me, it might've been she just wanted me out of her sight. It seemed apparent I wouldn't be working with her for a while. Kenny was on patrol, and Isabel didn't seem interested in my company. I reckoned I was on my own.

That's ok, I tried to rationalize. Gives me freedom to roam.

Yeh, you keep telling yourself that, Emmett.

I dropped by station and asked Cindy to remind me of the name of that Kingfisher family who'd been killed. "Fechner," she said. "Bill and Patsy. Their little girl was named Rita." I thanked her and told her I'd be out of radio range for the rest of the day.

***

From Burr to Kingfisher takes a little over two hours. The route goes past some of my favorite places to visit. For some reason, passing them by made me feel homesick.

At one time, Kingfisher was a big city compared to Burr. We've inched up on them the last few years. Kingfisher's still twice as big, but we've closed the gap. They've got a sign on the road leading into town: "Welcome to Kingfisher: The Buckle of the Wheat Belt." More like the Buckle of the Bible Belt, but I'm sure they have reason to be proud of their wheat, as well.

My first stop was the police station. Kingfisher is the seat of Kingfisher County, meaning I had the local police and the sheriff's department to choose from. I chose the town police. Downtrodden small-town departments tend to want to help one another.

I introduced myself to a uniformed woman at the front desk. I asked if I could talk to whoever investigated the Fechner killings. "No one here really investigated it," she said. "Soon as something like that happens, the OSBI and Highway Patrol zoom in and take it off our plate."

"What about the county?"

"They didn't have much to do with it, either, if I remember correctly."

"Do you remember who answered the initial call?"

"That'd be Karl Mezzatesta," she said.

"Would there be a way for me to talk to him?"

"Hmmm," she said. "Let me look." She looked at a Xeroxed piece of paper taped to the wall. "Today's his day off, looks like. You might could stop by his house, though."

She gave me an address and directions. I eventually found it—a small, neat red brick house located a couple of blocks from the town's primary tourist attraction, a mansion once lived in by an early governor of Oklahoma territory. I forget his name.

A blue and white Chevy pickup and a trailer with a Chris Craft motorboat were parked side by side in the driveway. Kingfisher must pay their cops better than Burr does.

Officer Mezzatesta was a big man—a foot taller, at least fifty pounds heavier and ten years younger than me. He wore a yellow sports shirt and blue plaid Bermuda shorts. A thick head of dark brown hair added a few more inches to his height. Judging by his biceps, I expect he could juggle cannonballs if he had a mind to learn. He seemed to look at a spot just over my head when he spoke, which threw me at first. He was friendly, though. I told him who I was. He was quick to invite me in.

He offered me a can of the Lone Star beer he was drinking. I rubbed my still aching head and said thanks but no thanks.

"So what brings you to our neck of the woods?" he asked. "You're from one of the Tilghman Counties, right?"

"Yup. The northern one."

"The one up against the Texas panhandle."

"That's it. Spelled 'T-i-l-g-h-m-a-n,' not 'T-i-l-l-m-a-n.'"

That our state has two counties pronounced the same but spelled differently is frequently a matter of confusion.

"Chief Hardy, how can I help you?"

I told him a little about the killing of Frankie Gately and how we thought it possible that it was connected to the murder of the Fechner family. "The lady at the station told me you were the first one on the scene."

"Yeh, I was," he said. "I wish I wasn't, but I was."

"I expect the OSBI and state troopers took over pretty quick."

"They did, and that was fine with me, although I think it ruffled the sheriff's feathers a bit."

I chuckled. "Yeh, they like to get their hands on those big cases, don't they?"

"Politicians," he said with disgust. "Anyway, I can't tell you much. I found the bodies, is all."

"How'd that happen,? Did you get a radio call?"

"No, I wasn't even on duty. I was asleep. The shots woke me up."

That gave me pause. "They were killed nearby?"

"Oh, yeh. Their house was just down the street a ways. I could show it to you if you want."

That, I hadn't expected.

"I would appreciate that immensely."

He excused himself. After a few minutes, he came back dressed in his uniform. "Just in case someone sees us going in," he explained. "So if they see us, they'll know it's official and won't call it in. Folks have been very paranoid since it happened." He took a last draw on his beer. "That includes me. C'mon."

I followed him out the door. "We can walk," he said. He pointed across the street at a diagonal. "The one with the blue trim." We crossed and walked around the side of the house, through a gate leading to a backyard surrounded by a seven-foot-high stockade fence. "This is the where the killer gained entrance," he said.

The latch and lock on the back door were broken. A strip of yellow crime-scene tape held it shut. Officer Mezzatesta peeled it away and let us in. "No one's going to care," he said. "Whoever's doing the investigation hasn't been here in weeks. Just watch where you step."

The door opened into the kitchen. Besides smelling stale as you'd expect of a house that had been shut up for a long period, there was a tinge of something else, something metallic. The blinds were drawn in the room's single window. The room was dark. Mezzatesta didn't bother to try the lights. I assumed the electricity had been cut off. "Nothing to see here," he said. He waved me forward. "This way."

The living room was a little lighter than the kitchen, though it was still hard to see. I noticed the layout was similar to Officer Mezzatesta's house and made a comment to that effect.

"Not similar," he said. "The same. The builder tried to make the houses look different on the outside, but inside, every house in this development is identical."

We reached the hallway. He stepped to one side. "Have at it. I've already seen it a few times too many." He sat down on the couch. "Take your time," he added. "I'll be out here when you're done."

The hall was about 15 feet in length. There were four doors, two on each side. The only light came from a half-open door on the end. The others were shut tight.

I opened the first door on the right. The curtains were open, so the room was well lit. It was decked out as a home office. A plain wooden desk was positioned against the right wall, catty-corner to the window. A chest-high file cabinet occupied the wall opposite. Next to the window was a floor-to-ceiling bookshelf containing a few dying houseplants and about a dozen books. A framed college diploma hung on the wall, along with photographs of folks young and old, smiling and carrying on without a care in the world. There was no sign the room had been disrupted.

I shut the door behind me and opened the one across the hall. It was a bathroom. The only window had pebbled glass and open blinds, so it too was brightly lit. The sink, tub, and floor were spotless.

I exited into the darkened hallway. As I did, I reached for a light switch. To my surprise, the light came on. I could see everything nice and bright.

Well, bright at least. There wasn't anything nice about it.

CHAPTER 31

I went the first 18 years of my life without seeing a dead body. Then I joined the Marines and got shipped to Korea. For more the next two years, it seemed like that's all I saw.

There weren't any bodies in the Fechner's bedrooms. But there obviously had been. It didn't take much imagination to see them in your mind's eye.

Two sets of muddy footprints the color of red Oklahoma clay led down the hall—one set coming, one going. The carpet was light blue, but there was a large purple bloodstain on the carpet in front of the half-open door on the right. On the white doorframe was a small red handprint.

I stepped in and turned on the light. It was the little girl's room. Rita Fechner's room. It looked how you'd expect an eight-year girl's bedroom to look: pink and girly, with dolls on the shelves, a framed print of Winnie the Pooh and his pal Piglet, a small bookshelf holding what seemed like every book Dr. Seuss ever wrote. Toys on the floor and in a toy box. There was no sign of violence inside the room. Only in the doorway.

I crossed the hall, opened the door, and turned on the light in the parents' room.

The queen-sized bed had a dark walnut headboard shaped like the bow of an old-time sailing ship. The bedding had been removed, revealing the mattress and box springs, covered in bloodstains. The pattern they made looked like a map of some alien world—islands of white surrounded by oceans of red, darkening to crimson where the victims' heads had lain.

Except for a few drops on the bedstands, the blood was confined to the bed. On the carpet, there were muddy footprints like the ones in the hall. One set coming, one going. The shape of the prints was vague, as if whoever had left them had wrapped his feet in plastic. I have my people do that when they enter a crime scene.

The parents were shot first, in their bed. The little girl got up to see what was going on. The killer shot her in the door of her bedroom.

I returned to the living room. The footprints crossed the floor into the kitchen.

I asked Mezzatesta who had left them.

"The killer, I suspect. They were fresh when I got here that night. They were on the back steps, too, but of course it's rained a lot since then, so they're long gone." He stood. "C'mon," he said. "I'll show you where they came from." I turned on the lights as we entered the kitchen. There were footprints, but they'd mostly worn away.

I followed Mezzatesta out the back door. He pointed at the concrete steps. "He tracked mud on the steps, too," he said, and continued to the backyard gate. "Right there," he said, gesturing toward a patch of dirt beneath the gate. "That was nothing but mud that night. That's where he picked it up."

We went back inside. I asked if it would be ok if I looked around some more.

He sat back down. "Take all the time you need," he said, still looking above my head, like he expected me to be as tall as he was.

Something bugged me about that office. I couldn't put my finger on what it was. The killer had apparently not gone in there. I expect he had no reason to.

I went in again. At second glance, I thought maybe it was slightly cluttered, as if someone had given it a light going over, perhaps looking for clues. Nothing serious caught my eye, however.

I looked at the books. A couple were paperback novels, but most had titles like *20th-Century Bookkeeping and Accounting*, or *Co-operative Bookkeeping*.

There were also three leather-bound volumes. Accounting ledgers. I started thumbing through them. Each had a name at the top, evidently referring to a specific person or business. Underneath were columns and lines with dates and monetary amounts. The dates were all at least five years old. None of the names were familiar.

I called out to Mezzatesta. "What did Mr. Fechner do for a living?"

"Oh, he managed a shoe store here in town."

"He wasn't an accountant, then?"

"Not that I know of."

"How about ..." Just then, my eyes rested on the diploma I'd noticed before. It was from Phillips University, a small college in Enid, about 45 minutes north of Kingfisher. It conferred upon one Patricia Fechner a Bachelor of Science in Accounting.

I called to Mezzatesta. "Did Mrs. Fechner work outside the home?"

"Not that I know of. I believe she used to be a secretary or something like that, but after she got married, she quit working. She was a housewife, is all."

I pulled out the last ledger. I got chills when I saw the name on the first page. *Family Fun/JC.* As in Family Fun Center. As in Jim Chrisler.

I turned the pages. The most recent entry had been made a week before the Fechners had been murdered.

I called out, "Officer Mezzatesta, is there a business here in town with the words 'Family Fun' in the name?"

"Family Fun?"

"Yeh, you know, like Family Fun Center, or something like that?"

He was quiet for several moments.

"I can't think of one. Why?"

"Oh, my mind just works in strange ways, that's all."

I put the ledger back where I'd found it and returned to the living room. Mezzatesta was still on the couch.

"I'm sorry for putting you to work on your day off," I said.

He stood and hitched up his pants. The buckle about came up to my nose. "That's no problem at all, Chief," he said, still looking at that spot over my head. "Glad to help. Learn anything?"

"Maybe. Maybe not. Gave me a lot to think about, though, I'll say that."

We walked out the way we'd come in and crossed the street back to his house.

Mezzatesta smiled as I got into my truck. "Why do I get the feeling you found something you don't want to tell me?"

"Probably because I did," I said. We both laughed. "Trouble is, I'm not too sure what it means. I've got to add it to some things I discovered earlier and see what it all amounts to. Maybe nothing. But I've got to think it through before I go shootin' off my mouth." I paused. "If I told you, it'd take the rest of the day, and I've taken up enough of your time as it is."

"Fair enough," he said with a smile. We shook hands and said our goodbyes.

Driving out of town, I thought: He'd be hearing about what I'd found. No doubt about that.

But it probably wouldn't be from me.

CHAPTER 32

It was after five o'clock when I got back to Burr. I stopped by the station. George was the only one there, sitting at the dispatcher's desk with a copy of *Guns and Ammo*. He didn't ask where I'd been, and I didn't offer an explanation. I just announced my presence and asked who was on duty. He told me Eugene. I let him get back to his reading.

Going home—to *my* home—was not an option, so I drove up and down Main Street a couple of times. I ran into Eugene going in the opposite direction. We stopped alongside each other. I asked what was going on. He said, "not much," or words to that effect, and asked where I'd been. "Long story," I said. That was the extent of our conversation.

I saw Bernard filling up at Wes Harmon's Sinclair. I pulled up to the other pump and told Wes to fill 'er up.

"Guess where I've been?" I asked Bernard.

"The whole town's been wondering that," he said. "Kenny said you disappeared without telling anybody where you'd gone."

"Yeh, I reckon I should've told someone."

Wes was hanging around a few feet away from us, trying to listen in.

"So where were you?" Bernard asked.

I lowered my voice. "Let's not talk about it here. Meet me at the Dairy Mart in about five minutes and I'll give you the rundown."

"Sounds like a plan."

Bernard drove off. Wes tried to pull me into a conversation, but I wasn't in the mood to chat. I felt bad, but once he gets talking, he'll just go on and on.

Unlike the Sonic, which has separate stalls where you pull in and place your order, the Dairy Mart experience is more of an every-man-for-himself deal. There aren't any marked parking spaces, only a small gravel patch where anyone can park anywhere. It was dinnertime, so I ended up out by the highway. Bernard pulled up next to me. I got out and opened my tailgate. We sat down.

"Ok," he said. "So where were you?"

"Kingfisher."

"What were you doing in Kingfisher?"

"Oh, nothing much," I said. "Just solving a bunch of murders, is all."

I told him about visiting the Fechner crime scene and finding the ledgers. I did not confide my suspicion about Patsy being Jim Chrisler's bookkeeper, but said I believed she'd been working as a part-time bookkeeper, and that one of her clients had decided she'd been cooking the books and killed her.

I didn't tell him I suspected that client was Jim Chrisler, although I wouldn't have been surprised if he inferred it.

He acted agreeable. It might've sounded to him like I was grasping at straws in the middle of a tornado, but he respects me too much to say so. I'd tell him everything when the time came.

The conversation stalled.

"Karen told me about what happened last night," he blurted. I knew he wasn't talking about Burt Reynolds finding Randy Braley's hand.

"Which version?" I asked. "The one about me getting a stomach bug or the real one?"

"The real one."

I nodded.

"Has that version gotten around?"

"Kenny knows. This afternoon when you disappeared, Mrs. Hardy called Sheriff Belcher to see if he knew where you were. I reckon he knows, too." He shrugged. "Not sure who else."

All I could do was nod. He asked if I'd called home to tell Karen where I was. I told him I had not. He said I'd better.

I nodded again, afraid my voice would crack if I tried to say anything.

We sat in silence for a while and watched the cars go by.

He jumped down off the tailgate. "That's enough jabbering. I'd better get to work."

"Have a good one, buddy."

"You, too. If there's anything I can do to help ..."

"I don't think there is, but I appreciate the offer."

***

Before we got married, Red and I lived in separate houses. Hers had belonged to her parents. It was the one she grew up in. Mine was my grandparents' on my father's side. When we moved in together, we decided to sell one of them. She didn't have especially fond memories of hers, so we sold that one and lived in mine.

We held on to my dad's house, however. We talked about selling it when he died, but never got around to it. I keep the lawn mowed and the electric and phone bills paid. I'm not sure why.

Maybe because I expected that one day I'd need it. Like today.

I let myself in. It smelled like it hadn't been lived in for a while.

The phone still worked. I dialed my home number.

Karen answered. "Hello."

"It's me."

Silence on her end.

"You still there?"

"George called me about an hour ago," she said. "He told me you'd dropped by the station."

"Yeh, I've been to Kingfisher. Saw the house where those people were killed. I think I got an idea about how that case connects to Frankie Gately and Randy Braley."

She didn't respond.

"Aren't you going to say anything?"

"What do you want me to say? You found a connection. Great. Take it to Isabel."

Silence.

"Listen, I know you're mad and I know why. I'm sorry. It won't happen again. It was just a little relapse, is all. I can quit whenever I want."

She laughed bitterly. "You don't get it, do you?"

In fact, I did, but I couldn't bring myself to admit it.

"It's not just that you're back to trying to kill yourself, Emmett," she said in a trembling voice. "That's bad enough. But you're lying about it. If you've been lying about drinking, Lord knows what else you've been lying about."

"Nothing, I swear."

"Yeh, well ..."

More silence.

"When do you want to talk?"

"I don't know. Not tonight. Where are you, at your father's house?"

"Yeh."

"Are you drunk?"

"No, I haven't drunk anything, and I don't plan to."

She sighed. "Ok," she said. "I'll see you tomorrow at work."

"Can we talk then?"

She hesitated. "Tomorrow? We'll see."

I told her I loved her.

She said goodbye.

CHAPTER 33

My talk with Karen had me looking for a hole to crawl into.

I'd almost lost her once. It was only her patience that saved me. She'd warned me, though, that her patience had limits. She would not sit still for any backsliding—not because of any ill will, but because she had no intention of sitting back and watching me drink myself to death. That doesn't even take into consideration how I lied to her back then, which bothered her just as much, if not more. I started out drinking again, thinking that I could control it this time. Now? I don't know. I have to admit; I seem to be falling back into some bad habits. Anyway, I can't blame her for getting mad. I just hope I can straighten things out.

My stomach growled, temporarily bringing me out of my lament. I realized I hadn't eaten a damn thing all day. Except for feeling a little tired and achy, the effects of that morning's hangover had faded, and I was starving. There wasn't a single thing to eat in Dad's house. I wasn't feeling picky, so I drove to McDonald's and ordered a Big Mac and fries. I meant to eat it at home, but I started nibbling on the fries and before I knew it, the only thing left was the styrofoam box the hamburger came in.

There wasn't much to do at my dad's house except think and watch TV. I couldn't help but think, no matter how I tried not to.

I turned on the TV. An old Jean Harlow movie was on. Clark Gable was in it, so I suppose it was *Red Dust*, but the phone rang five minutes in, so I never found out for certain.

It was Keith Belcher.

"Hey there, sheriff," I said. "You don't believe in returning phone calls?"

He chuckled. "Yeh, sorry about that. Isabel Cruickshank's been running me ragged."

"That's funny," I said. "Seems like she likes to do most of work herself."

"She's darn good at it, ain't she?"

"I reckon she is," I said.

There was a moment of uncomfortable silence. "So how've you been?" he asked.

"I've been good. Wow 'bout you?"

"Oh, fair to middlin' I suppose. I hear you pulled a vanishing act this afternoon." He was trying to sound casual, but I knew better.

"Oh, you heard that, did you?"

"I did. Karen called me, told me y'all had a fight. She was worried you'd gone off on a bender."

"Nah, nothing like that." Then—because I'd rather chew on shards of glass than talk about my troubles—I asked if he knew Jim Chrisler. He said he did. "I think I've found something that ties him to those killings in Kingfisher."

"That's interesting. Have you told the OSBI?"

"I'd rather tell you first."

He chuckled. "Well, as it just so happens, I'm calling from a pay phone in front of the Seven-Eleven. I can be there in five minutes."

"You remember where my daddy lived?"

"Been there many times. See you soon."

***

Keith was wearing his uniform when he arrived. He carried a cold six-pack of Tab.

"I seem to remember this is what you've been drinking," he said.

"Keeps me skinny," I said, patting my not remotely skinny belly. He smiled and handed me one. "Take one for yourself," I said. "No thanks," he said. "I take my rat poison straight."

We sat down at the kitchen table. "So enlighten me," he said.

I told him about my trip to Kingfisher and finding the ledger.

"Hmmm," he said. "Family Fun slash JC." He rubbed his chin. "Did you check if there's a place by that name in Kingfisher?"

"I asked that cop who let me in. He said there wasn't."

"Huh," he said again. "I'll say this: I wouldn't put it past Jim Chrisler to do something like that. Of course, Family Fun could refer to something else."

"With the initials JC on the end?"

He frowned. "It would be a giant coincidence, that's for sure."

"Can you tell me anything about this investigation into drug dealing in Tilghman County?"

"That's more the OSBI's thing," he said. "Why, what do you know?"

"I know that Chrisler's name has come up."

"Has it now? Well, there you go."

I told him about our conversation with Shannon Gately, and how she'd told us Randy Braley sold drugs for Chrisler. I said, "I gave all this information to Isabel Cruickshank."

"Well, she didn't tell me this morning when they found Braley's body, but she was pretty snowed under. Maybe that's why."

"She was pretty closed-mouthed to me this morning, too," I said. "I got the impression she expected to get a warrant to search Chrisler's premises, though. Sooner than later. We need that search warrant. Especially for the car."

"Why the car?"

"I'd bet just about anything there's more to Chrisler's story about running Frankie off that night. I think he drove him somewhere."

"That would make him the killer, is what you're saying."

"Probably, yeh. I'm telling you, Keith, we need to search that car for evidence that Frankie was in it."

"What would you expect to find?"

"Who knows? Fingerprints? Strands of hair? Those forensic folks can work miracles these days."

"Hmmm." He leaned forward, resting his elbows on his knees. "Maybe on TV shows. This isn't *Mannix*, it's real-life Tilghman County, Oklahoma. I wouldn't get my hopes up."

I left it there. No need for him to know what I knew.

Not yet, anyway.

"So tell me what you think is going on?"

"I think Chrisler came to Burr and opened that foosball parlor to use as a front for selling drugs. With all the new workers in the oilfields and Cudahy's, he reckoned there was a market."

"Not to mention selling to kids."

"Right," I said. "Did Isabel mention that Travis Ballard had Chrisler's phone number on him when they found his body?"

"That fella who got killed down in Idabel? No, she didn't tell me."

"Yeh, he also had some business cards that tied him to Burr. Chrisler insists he never met Ballard, but I think he's lying."

"Ok, let me get this straight. The Fechner woman did the books for a business that was called 'Family Fun' something-or-other ..."

"And the initials JC on the end."

He nodded. "Jim Chrisler—JC—owns a business called Family Fun Center, right?"

"Indubitably."

He chuckled. "So tell me again, how is it this guy hasn't already been arrested?"

"That's for Isabel Cruickshank to know and us to find out, I guess."

"Waiting to get her ducks in a row, I imagine," he said. "So let's map this out. Frankie Gately was last seen being run out of Family Fun Center by Jim Chrisler. A few hours later, one of your officers found his body. A few days after that, the next-to-last person to see Frankie alive was found dead and dismembered under the floor of a vacant house."

"Randy Braley, who told his girlfriend Shannon that he sold drugs for Jim Chrisler."

"Right. And Shannon is Frankie's sister."

He was silent for a moment. "Does Chrisler know Shannon was Braley's girl? Could he know that she knows Chrisler was Braley's supplier?"

"Shannon told Red and me. I doubt she told anyone else. The only person I told was Isabel. And now you." I was starting to feel out of my depth, and not for the first time since this whole thing started. "I told Shannon that whoever was behind Chrisler's drug-dealing didn't even know she existed. Now I'm not so sure."

"You're sure you didn't tell anybody else?"

I thought about it. "I can't remember if I told Kenny or not. Maybe I did. But he's not going to tell anyone."

"Could someone have overheard you telling Isabel?"

"No one I don't trust." Inwardly I cursed myself for not being more careful. "It's possible Chrisler might put together the pieces himself."

Keith nodded. "I reckon he wouldn't have to be too paranoid to decide she might be a liability."

I felt sicker and sicker, and it wasn't the hangover coming back.

I got up from the table. "What say we drive out and check on Shannon? Just to put our minds at ease."

Keith got up with me. "Sounds like a plan."

CHAPTER 34

My late start to the day notwithstanding, I'm about as prompt a human being as you'll ever know. Unless, of course, I was drunk off my rear end the night before, there's always been something inside me that won't let me be tardy for anything. Give me a time and a place. I'll be there. Early.

My first impression upon entering Shannon's trailer was that we were late. Don't ask me why, but that's how I felt.

The place was still a disaster area but it looked a little neater compared to the day before. The rotten banana smell was still there, but fainter than it had been. Shannon must've gone on a cleaning binge, or at least the beginnings of one. The living room floor had been largely cleared of debris. Orange and brown shag carpet was visible where it hadn't been before. Someone had filled up a couple of large plastic garbage bags. One was closed with a twist tie. The other looked like it had been filled, then knocked over, with half the contents spilling onto the couch.

By civilized standards, the room remained a disaster area, but it was a heck of a lot better than before. Little old Shannon had put in some work.

Good for her, I thought.

"Anybody home?" I called.

No answer. I tried again. Nothing.

"My Lord, what a mess," Keith said.

"Believe it or not, it's 100% better than it was last time I was here."

"When was that?"

"Yesterday."

"That right?" He walked over to the overturned garbage bag. "Because if I didn't know better, I'd say this was the scene of a fight."

I meant to assure him otherwise, but then I looked closer. The garbage bag hadn't spilled but had been ripped open. The chair I'd sat in the day before lay on its side. Shattered pieces of glass lay all over the floor. A few had traces of blood. I felt the adrenaline flow.

"Look at this," said Keith. He pointed at a pink princess-type phone lying on the carpet next to an end table. The wire had been ripped from the wall. He pulled a pencil from his shirt pocket and poked at the handset. I bent down next to him. More blood, mixed with strands of blond hair. Shannon has blond hair.

"Looks like someone used this to defend herself," said Keith.

"That, or someone used it on her."

I thought of Frankie's little trailer. "C'mon," I said.

We rushed over. The front door was locked. I tried to look through the window in the door, but it was too dark to see.

Keith went back to his cruiser, got a couple of flashlights, and handed one to me. We shined them through a side window. No one was there, but nothing looked like it had been disturbed. It looked exactly as it had the morning after Frankie's death.

"That's a relief," I mumbled to myself. "I guess."

We searched the area around both trailers without finding anything of interest. We went back to Shannon's trailer and weighed our next move. My blood was pumping. I felt in a hurry to do something right then, even if I didn't know exactly what. At that moment, doing anything seemed preferable to doing nothing.

"What kind of car does she drive?" asked Keith.

"No kind," I said. "She doesn't drive, or at least she doesn't own a car."

"So if she went somewhere, someone would've had to take her."

"That's right."

The more I thought about it, the more I was sure I knew who that was.

"Let's go to Chrisler's," I said.

Keith nodded. "I was about to say."

Keith got hold of Bernard on the police band and told him to come out and keep watch over Shannon's trailer. "It might be nothing, so don't call in the state troopers just yet," Keith said. "While you're here, take a look around. We gave it a cursory search but might've missed something. Right now, we're going to Chrisler's and see what he has to say."

Keith hit his emergency lights but didn't use his siren. "No sense giving the SOB advance warning," he said.

Never warn an SOB. Words to live by.

The lot at Chrisler's was full. Cars were parked in front and along the side, all the way to the back door where he'd parked his Chrysler the day before.

"Let's go around back," I told Keith. "I want to see if Chrisler's car is still there."

Keith turned off his emergencies and drove along the side of the building.

"That's it," I said, spotting the blue Chrysler in the same spot as the last time.

Keith pulled up behind it, so it was blocked and turned off his engine.

"How do you want to handle this?" he asked.

"We can't talk to him in there. It'll be a madhouse. I say we ask him right off the bat if he's seen Shannon. If says no, which he probably will, we take him to the station and question him there."

"He's going to kick."

"Let him," I said. "Hold on a sec." I got out of the car with a flashlight and shined it through the Chrysler's windows. It looked as it had before: clean except for a full ashtray. I ran the light across the back seat over the space where I'd found the dog tag. Maybe it was still there, maybe it wasn't. There was no way to know.

We walked past a group of teenagers sitting in their cars, drinking from Dixie cups. "That'd better be Coca-Cola," I said. "Uh-oh," one of them said. "Mine's Sprite!" He put down the cup and held out his hands to be handcuffed. "Better lock me up!" They laughed, something I wasn't in the mood for.

"Those cups are getting the smell test when we come out," I said. They stopped laughing so hard.

"They'll be gone by the time we leave," said Keith under his breath.

"They'd better be."

Inside, loud music competed with excited shouts and screams, the rings and buzzes of pinball machines, and the thwack of plastic balls being whacked by little red and blue men. I couldn't understand the words of the song being played except for the chorus. Something about takin' care of business. I'm not a big fan of electric guitars unless they're played by someone like Roy Clark or Wes Montgomery, but I had to admit, it was a catchy tune.

The same girl who'd been scared by Frankie the night of his death was working behind the snack bar. I checked faces in the crowd, hoping to find Shannon, but didn't have any luck.

Keith and I dodged jutting elbows and made our way back to Chrisler's office. He was dressed in what by now I reckoned was his work uniform, the same dirty white T-shirt and gray work pants. He leaned over his desk, the last half-inch of a Pall Mall hanging out of his mouth, writing numbers into a ledger a lot like the one I'd seen at Patsy Fechner's house. The one with "Family Fun/JC" written on the first page. He must've seen us and slammed it shut.

He swiveled around in his chair, leaned back, and laced his fingers behind his head.

"Well, well. Another visit from Burr's finest," he said with a cocky smile. "I must be getting popular." He took a last puff and stubbed out the cigarette. "Brought the sheriff this time, did ya? Hey sheriff, you need to keep an eye on this fella. I don't think he knows how to do his job."

Keith drew himself up to his full height, which is considerable.

"Mr. Chrisler," he said in a voice so hard it could cut glass, "we're looking for a young woman by the name of Shannon Gately."

Chrisler smirked. "Never heard of her."

"Fine," I said. "We need you to come with us down to the station."

"What?" he sputtered. "Why?"

"We'll talk about it down at the station." I crooked a finger. "C'mon, let's go."

His eyes narrowed. "Are you arresting me?"

"Not yet, but we're headed there if you don't cooperate."

"Fine," he said in a tight and quiet voice. "Let's get this done." He locked the ledger in a small safe beside his desk, got up from his chair, and brushed past us. We followed him to the snack bar. He went behind the counter and said something to the girl. I couldn't hear through the noise.

There was a phone. He lifted the receiver like was going to make a call. I tried to hurry him up. "I've got to call in an adult," he said. "I can't leave these kids in charge." I told him to get on with it. He spoke to someone for about a minute and hung up.

"You want me, you got me," he said. We started out the door. I stopped and told Keith to go ahead, I'd be right out.

I went back behind the counter and pulled the girl aside.

"What time did you get here?"

"Five o'clock," she said.

"Has Chrisler been here the whole time?"

"The whole time," she said, then added, "unfortunately."

We loaded Chrisler into the back seat. Keith drove, I rode shotgun.

"It's hot," said Chrisler. "How 'bout turning on the air-conditioning?" Keith rolled up the windows and cranked it up.

Traffic was light. It only took two or three minutes to get back to the station. Except for the lights over the door and window, the street was dark. The town's never gotten around to putting in streetlamps. The only sounds came from the jukebox down the block at Edna's Eats.

As Keith parked in front of the station, I thought I saw something or someone move in a doorway across the street.

I turned around to get a better look, just in time to see the car's back window explode.

Along with Jim Chrisler's head.

CHAPTER 35

I was blinded and thought I'd been hit until I wiped my eyes and realized my face was covered in pieces of Jim Chrisler.

A second shot followed. It shattered the back window on the driver's side. A third flattened one of the rear tires. I pulled out my Colt .45 semi-auto and ducked down as low as I could. Keith had done the same. "You ok?" I asked.

"Yeh, I'm fine, how about you?"

"I'm pretty good," I said. That is, except for having a face full of glass and someone else's gray matter. "You see who it was?"

"Nah. You?"

I heard footsteps running down the street. "You ready to get this clown?" I said.

"Let's go, then," said Keith.

We opened our doors. I crouched behind mine to use as a shield. A figure disappeared into an alley fifty yards down the street. I started after him, then heard an engine starting up. A dark blue junker Chevy pickup skidded out of the alley onto the street and drove straight at me. For an instant I thought I'd finally found Randy Braley's truck, then realized if I didn't get out of the way real quick, it wouldn't matter who it belonged to. I dodged, but it didn't miss by much. We got off a couple of shots. One of them broke the pickup's rear window, but the driver paid no heed and sped off. It didn't take long for his taillights to become red specks in the distance.

Keith started to get back in the car, then stopped and slapped the roof with both hands. "Damn!"

"What?"

"Sumbitch shot out our rear tire."

"I know."

"How'd you know?"

"I felt the car sink after that last shot," I said. "Anyway, forget about that. Did you get his plate number?"

"No. Did you?"

"I wouldn't have asked you if I did."

The entire scene was in danger of becoming an Abbot and Costello routine, only there wasn't anything funny about it. Keith got on the radio to Bernard and told him what had happened. I ran into the station to find George crouching behind his desk. "What's going on out there?" he asked.

"Call the state troopers and an ambulance," I snapped. "Tell them there's been an officer-involved shooting, suspect driving north toward Butcherville in an old dark blue Chevy pickup. We're about to pursue."

I'm a good driver, and those Javelins can scoot, but by the time we got going, that Chevy was long gone. We drove north about five miles, turned off a couple of times on roads where we thought he might've gone, but had no luck.

We got back to the station to find the Fury parked in the street, its emergency lights flashing. Eugene gawked at Keith's cruiser like a hillbilly at his first X-rated movie. A few drunks had staggered down the street from Edna's to see what was going on. I told Eugene to keep them back. A state-issued slicktop was already on the scene and Agent Isabel Cruickshank was peering into the ruined car at what was left of Jim Chrisler.

A good look at Keith's car told me how lucky we'd been. The first shot shattered the rear window and blew apart Chrisler's head. Had he been sitting directly behind one of us, instead of in the middle, either Keith or I would've shared his fate. As it was, the bullet whizzed past both of us with inches to spare, made a football-sized hole in the windshield, and burrowed into the cinderblock wall on the outside of the station. I reckoned the second shot was likely meant to discourage us from giving chase. The third—the one that flattened a tire—was to make sure we didn't.

"My Lord," Isabel said when she saw us. "It's like a watermelon full of blood exploded in there." She took a long look at me. "You look like hell."

"I'm fine."

"Really? You could've fooled me. Have you looked in a mirror?"

I ran my hand over my face and picked out tiny pieces of greenish glass. "Well, I'll live, anyway."

"That makes you better off than this guy," she said, nodding toward the cruiser's interior. "Who is it, anyway?"

"Jim Chrisler," I said. I fought off an urge to duck.

She stood mute. "Jim Chrisler," she said after a few painful seconds. "Jim. Chrisler. What in the world were you doing with him?"

I looked at Keith and Keith looked at me. I said: "We'd better go inside."

*****

Isabel wanted to talk to Keith and me separately. She took Keith into my office and shut the door. While they talked, I filled a cup of water from the cooler and attempted to clean myself up. I looked like I'd washed my face in organ meats. I was able to remove most of the gore, but the little shards of green glass were another matter. I got most of them, but I'd need tweezers to get them all. I was just lucky they didn't get in my eyes.

After a short while, Keith came out, and I went in.

"Ok," she said, a pencil and yellow legal pad at the ready. "I've got Sheriff Belcher's version. What's yours?"

"I reckon mine's a lot more involved than his."

"I've got time."

I talked. She took notes. I began with my trip to Kingfisher, which seemed a lifetime ago, but was only seven or eight hours in the past. I told her I'd discovered Patsy Fechner was an accountant, and how I'd found a ledger that led me to suspect she'd been working for Jim Chrisler. I described how later, Keith and I thought Chrisler might suspect Shannon had informed on him. We went out to check on her and found evidence that seemed to indicate she'd been abducted.

"Since we suspected him anyway," I said, "it made sense that we confront him."

"'Confront' is not the same as getting him killed," she said.

"No, it's not, but we were worried about Shannon. We drove to his business and asked about her. He laughed in our faces. It pissed us off. We figured the best thing to do was bring him here and pressure him to cooperate." I paused. "By the way, Shannon is still missing."

She nodded. "I put someone on it," she said. "Go on."

I told her how we let him make a phone call before we led him to Keith's cruiser. "He said he needed to call in an adult to run the place while he was gone, since the only other person working was that little Glenda gal. He used the telephone behind the snack bar, so we couldn't tell who was calling or hear what he said." I swallowed hard. "That was our big mistake." I related the remaining sequence of events that led to Chrisler being shot.

"It looks like whoever he called was waiting for you when you got here."

"Looks like," I said.

She scribbled something down. "If that's the case," she said, "I'd assume Chrisler called this person to help him escape. But the shooter killed him instead. Do you think it was a mistake?"

"Eh," I said, "I'm not so sure."

"Did you get a look at him?"

"No, it was too dark. I think he had on a ski mask, too."

"But you think he was aiming at Chrisler, right?"

I nodded. "Yeh, the more I think about it, I do. He shot Chrisler in the head from a distance of at least twenty feet, through the rear window, in the dark, using a handgun. That's some pretty solid marksmanship."

She wrote some more. "How do you know it was a handgun?"

"Find the slugs. I guarantee it was a handgun. Probably that Nagant you're looking for."

"Explain the second and third shots," she asked.

"The second one went through the driver's side back window while Keith and I were ducked down. The third one flattened a tire. If he'd wanted to get us, he could've just come up and shot us point-blank. I think the second one was a warning shot, meant to keep us down so he'd have time to escape."

"Or perhaps he didn't want to give you a look at his face. Maybe he was afraid you'd recognize him."

"That could be."

"So you seem convinced he was after Chrisler and not you or Sheriff Belcher."

"Yeh, I am."

She tapped a pencil on the desk.

"Hey," I said, "did you dig anything up on that orange Trans-Am?"

"Oh, that," she said, lowering her voice. "You didn't hear this from me, but the guy driving that car is FBI or DEA. I'm not clear which. It's part of a sting those agencies were running on Chrisler."

"So I guess that means he wasn't Chrisler's silent partner."

"I don't know. It's possible he was posing as a business partner as part of the operation. But my impression was that it hadn't gotten that far. Don't let any of this get out. I'm not even supposed to know."

"I'll keep it to myself."

She stood awkwardly. I tried to lend a hand, but she brushed it away and steadied herself on the chair back. "Ok, then. Let's see if they've found those slugs."

On the way out, I asked where Agent Raksin had gone off to. "I revoked his probation," she said through tight lips.

I walked her to the door. "You're getting close, aren't you?" I asked.

"You mean the baby?" she said. "Could be any day now." I could hear in her voice how tired she was. "Believe me, I'd like nothing better than to solve this before the baby comes."

"Let's make that happen, then."

She smiled wearily. "From your mouth to God's ears."

CHAPTER 36

Outside, it looked like the circus had come to town. Emergency lights were spinning, and floodlights had been set up to illuminate the scene. The highway patrol and medical examiner were there, as well as the other sundry personnel involved in investigating a murder. A couple of state troopers had come to Eugene's aid, holding back the gawkers.

Except for Kenny and Lester, all my people were there, even Cindy, who'd come by to help in any way she could. Lester was probably in Kansas by now. Kenny lives too far out to have heard the commotion. I asked Cindy to call him and ask him to come in.

Karen was there, too. She'd just gotten out of the shower when she heard the shots. She put aside her anger long enough to fret about my condition. I assured her I was unharmed. She told me I should come home when this was over. I said I would and asked her if she was still mad at me. She didn't give me a straight answer, but she did say we'd work it out. That made me feel better than I had all day.

While I talked to Karen, Isabel conferred with the crime scene investigator who'd pried a slug out of the station wall. I went to see what was going on.

She held up an evidence bag. "You were right. It's from a Nagant."

"I figured. By the way, no one told me Randy Braley's cause of death."

"This," she said, waving the bag.

"That means Chrisler didn't commit the murders himself, then."

"Probably not. That doesn't mean he wasn't involved, however."

"If so, that would mean the guy who killed Chrisler was probably working with him."

"Or for him."

I felt a sudden wave of certainty. "If the guy in the Trans-Am isn't the silent partner, it must be Sam Carter."

"Whoa, there," she said. "There's no reason to believe that, Emmett."

"Why? Who else could it be? We've already got him delivering drugs to Chrisler ..."

She held up her hand. "We don't know that for a fact."

"Maybe you don't, but I do." I immediately regretted saying that, but she didn't seem to take offense.

"You might be right," she said, "but the fact remains, regardless of how mean and tough he looks, Sam Carter's record is clean. He's 25 years-old, has never been convicted of a crime, never been arrested, never even been a suspect. That motorcycle getup of his is an act."

"Where'd that ugly scar on his face come from, then?"

"He walked through a sliding glass door when he was twelve."

"How about that potato chip delivery? Shannon told us that's how Chrisler gets his drugs. We caught Carter red-handed."

"What did you see? Potato chips. Corn chips. Not drugs. Braley could've been lying to Shannon about that. Or Shannon could've been lying." She patted me on the chest. "C'mon, Emmett. We've got nothing on Carter. That doesn't mean we won't, but right now ..." She shook her head.

She was right about us not having evidence. But I couldn't shake the feeling Carter was involved—in the drug business, in Frankie's death, and by extension the Fechner and Ballard murders.

"How about the fact that Frankie's body was found at his movie theater?" I said, trying to break through her self-assuredness.

"We've accounted for all his movements leading up to the murder and after," she said. "Carter didn't kill Frankie."

"That doesn't mean he didn't kill Chrisler."

She rolled her eyes, her first sign of frustration. "Why would he?"

"Who knows? Maybe something went south between the two."

"The person who killed Chrisler drove an old blue Chevy pickup, the same kind as was seen at the Idabel and Kingfisher killings. Sam Carter drives a motorcycle."

"That doesn't mean he doesn't have a pickup parked somewhere. Randy Braley drove a junky old blue pickup, too. There are a lot of old blue pickups in this county."

She sighed. "Listen, Emmett, I agree Carter needs to be checked out, but I don't see him as being involved with what happened tonight." She looked at her watch. "I've got to get out there and coordinate things. If you want to go talk to Carter now, it would be a help to me. I don't think you're going to find what you *think* you're going to find, but question him, by all means."

She walked over to Keith's cruiser and exchanged a few quiet words with the forensic team and the OSHP watch commander. Keith was finishing up a conversation with one of his deputies. He came over to me when he'd finished.

"I just radioed Bernard," he said. "He was still out at Shannon's place. I told him to patrol Butcherville looking for that old blue Chevy pickup."

"With the rear window shot out," I added.

"Right," he said. "Think that was Braley's truck?"

"Stands to reason. Whoever shot at us probably killed Braley, too."

We went over and asked Isabel about it. "No, we found Braley's truck in a barn south of town this afternoon. Your blue pickup isn't his blue pickup." She went on to say she'd issued a BOLO for Shannon Gately. "I don't know how much it'll help since she's not driving, but it's worth a try." Someone else got her attention. She said we'd talk later.

Things didn't begin to calm down until after midnight. Isabel issued a second BOLO for a beat-up old blue pickup. Jim Chrisler's next of kin had yet to be tracked down, and someone needed to attend to the Family Fun Center. The ambulance carted away the body. The state troopers scattered.

As crucial as it was to find Chrisler's killer, I was more concerned about Shannon. Kenny and I were the only ones who seemed sure she'd been taken against her will. I thought it possible—maybe even likely—that the person who'd abducted her was the same person who shot Chrisler. If I was right, finding Shannon would lead us to Chrisler's killer. I had Sam Carter in my sights.

While Isabel and the other state folks combed the crime scene, I gathered my people in the station. Kenny had finally rolled in, so it was him, Karen, Cindy, Keith, George, and me. Eugene was out on patrol, but our tiny little cinderblock box was still about as jam-packed as it could get.

"There's a lot I'd like to tell you about what's going on," I said, "but right now there's no time. I'll just say that I'm close to being convinced that Sam Carter's both tonight's shooter and the person who snatched Shannon Gately. Which means I'm on my way to his place as soon as we're done here."

"Excuse me for butting in, Chief," said George, "but why are we so worried about Shannon Gately?"

"I'm afraid Chrisler might've thought she'd snitched on him and used Sam Carter to shut her up."

"Why would Chrisler think that?" he asked.

The room went quiet.

"Because she did," I said.

Karen made a gesture that included Kenny, me, and herself. "Who else besides the three of us would know that?"

"I knew," said Cindy.

Every head in the room turned to her. "How?" I asked. "Did we talk about it in front of you?"

"Actually, you talked about it with Agent Cruickshank on the phone," she said. "Remember? You used mine because yours wasn't working."

"That's right," I said. "I remember."

"All I heard was your end of the conversation," she said, "but it wasn't too hard to figure out what you were talking about."

"You didn't mention it to anyone, did you?" said Karen.

She thought for a second. "Well, Officer Filer came in after the rest of y'all cleared out. I talked about it with him."

"Maybe Lester told someone he shouldn't have," said Kenny.

"Sam Carter said Les had been a lot of help to him, clearing teenagers out of the drive-in after hours," I said. "Could Les have brought it up with him?"

"Nah," said Kenny without sounding completely convinced. "He wouldn't. Would he?"

Karen asked if anybody had seen Lester. Nobody had. I said I assumed he'd left for Kansas.

"Maybe someone could go out there and ask if he talked about Shannon to anybody else," said Keith.

I told Cindy to try calling him. She dialed, let it ring, and hung up. "No answer," she said.

"It wouldn't hurt to send someone out there," said Kenny.

"I'll go," said Red. "I'll never sleep after all this, anyway."

"I'll go with you," said Kenny.

Keith suggested we drop by the foosball place after we talked to Carter. "That's if he's not the man we're looking for," he added. I asked Cindy if we had Carter's home address. She handed me the pickle bag he'd written it on, the morning after Frankie's killing.

"Alright then, everybody, let's all do what we're supposed to do and meet back here in a couple of hours," I said. "Except you, Cindy. George is on the clock. You can go home."

"I'll never be able to sleep. I think I'll hang around."

"Suit yourself." Everyone but Cindy and George filed out the door.

There were still a few state and county cops milling about. Keith talked with one of his deputies. I walked over to where Isabel sat getting a minute's rest in an OSHP cruiser. I told her what we were up to.

"Let me know what happens with Carter," she said. "I've got some people at the foosball place now. I'm going over there myself in a little while. Maybe I'll see you."

I started to walk away, then turned around. "Make sure you search Chrisler's car," I called to her. It didn't matter as much now, but if he had something to do with Frankie's death, I wanted it known.

She looked at me warily. "What is it about that car? Do you know something I don't?"

I did my best to look innocent. I'm not sure I pulled it off.

CHAPTER 37

Kenny and Red commandeered one Javelin. Keith and I got the other. Both were blocked in by various other vehicles on the scene. I tried and failed to get someone to move them so we could get out, so I jumped the curb and drove on the sidewalk until I was clear. I didn't wait around to see how Kenny and Red managed to get out.

"There's a reason Frankie was killed at the drive-in," I said to Keith once we'd gotten under way.

"You really think it's Carter we're after?"

"In my bones."

"I don't know, Emmett. I talked to him, too. He strikes me as one of those guys who act tougher than they are."

A car cut me off. I realized I hadn't been using my emergency lights. I turned them on. The guy almost ran into a utility pole, trying to get out of my way.

"Maybe the whole Hell's Angel thing is a front, but it doesn't mean he didn't do it. Weak people kill, too. Most killers are cowards."

I pulled the pickle bag with Carter's address on it out of my shirt pocket. I couldn't read it in the dark, so I handed it to Keith. "Can you read that?"

"115 Division Street."

"115 Division?" I said. "Are you kidding?"

"That's what it says here. Why?"

"115 Division Street is the shoe house."

Keith laughed. "Ah, the shoe house. This should be fun."

We were headed in the wrong direction. I hung a U-turn a little too fast. Keith grasped the dashboard to steady himself.

"Who taught you to drive?" he said.

"Taught myself."

"Never would have guessed," he mumbled.

***

I remember back in the '60s, Oklahoma City hired a world-famous architect to develop a plan on how to rebuild itself. Urban renewal, they called it. They had the fella build a fancy model of how it would look, paid him a bunch of money, then decided they could do it better themselves. They were wrong. All they did was tear down a bunch of historic buildings and replace them with a butt-ugly convention center surrounded by the world's biggest parking lot.

But at least they started with a plan.

Burr never bothered. Starting on the day of its birth—April 19, 1892, the day the U.S. government opened the Cheyenne and Arapaho lands to white settlement—people built whatever and wherever they damn well pleased, regardless of whether it made any kind of sense.

The shoe house is a good example.

Back in the '20s, the son of some of Burr's early settlers built a house on a lot he'd inherited upon the death of his parents. No one had ever built a house on Division Street, mainly because it ran alongside the railroad tracks and was as noisy as all get out. With no town planning commission to put the brakes on it, however, this fella built it anyway, gambling he'd be able to sell or rent it. He thought a gimmick might help, so for reasons known only to himself and whatever god he prayed to, he designed it to look like a shoe. It didn't work. When he couldn't unload it, he moved in himself. He lived there for years, the only house on Division Street, until one night he sleepwalked out his back door into the path of a Santa Fe freight train.

Thereafter, the house sat unoccupied except by the occasional transient. Awhile back, I heard some hippie had moved in and fixed it up. Folks in these parts can't tell the difference between a hippie and a Hell's Angel. If a man has long hair, he's a hippie. In that respect, Sam Carter qualifies.

Carter's Harley sat on the kickstand in front of the garage. The garage door was padlocked.

"Think there's a blue Chevy pickup parked in there?" asked Keith.

"I'd bet on it," I said.

The glow of a television set shone in an upstairs window. As we got out of the car, Carter's head appeared. He saw us and tried to jerk out of sight, but realized it was too late. He nodded down at us. "We need to talk to you, Sam," I hollered.

Keith and I waited for the door to open with our hands resting on our sidearms.

The porch light came on. The globe over the bulb was painted to look like a death's head.

Carter answered the door wearing the same black T-shirt as last time, only now he was wearing a blue Cat Diesel Power baseball hat, and, instead of black jeans, a pair of red-on-white polka-dotted pajama pants.

"How's the potato chip business, Mr. Carter?" I asked.

"Great, never better," he said grumpily. "Is that why you woke me up in the middle of the night? To ask about potato chips?"

He hadn't been asleep, that much was sure.

"Nah, not that. It's a couple of things. First, we were wondering where you were earlier this evening."

He smiled. It made his scar look like a caterpillar trying to climb his face.

"You mean around the time of that shootout in front of the police station?" he said. "You don't think I had anything to do with that, do you?"

"I'd be obliged if you'd answer my question."

"Oh man," he sighed. "I was drinking at Edna's. I was there when it happened, and I left afterwards. Ask anyone who was there. Hell, ask that wimpy little cop who was working the scene. He saw me."

That put a chink in my suspicions.

"You weren't working at the theater tonight?" I asked.

"No. I didn't get my regular night off because of that murder, so I took tonight off instead."

I asked him for the name of someone who'd confirm his alibi. He gave me several. I wrote them down, feeling like I might've taken a wrong turn.

"There's something else," I said. "A friend of ours has gone missing. We were hoping you might be able to help. We were thinking she might be a friend of yours, as well."

"Who?"

"Shannon Gately."

His right eye twitched. I'm not much of a poker player, but I believe that's what the high-rollers call a "tell."

"That guy who got killed was named Gately, right?"

"The young man killed at your drive-in was Frankie Gately. Shannon Gately is his sister."

His eye twitched some more. Beads of sweat sprouted on his forehead. It wasn't even that hot.

He laughed like a hyena. The tough guy act was slipping away. "I wouldn't know Shannon Gately if I met her on the street," he said.

Keith spoke up. "Mr. Carter, would it be possible for us to come inside?" Carter looked over his shoulder. Another tell. "Well, you guys got me out of bed, and I got to get up early ..."

"That's funny," I said, "because the first thing I noticed when we got here was the light from a television in that upstairs window."

"You never heard of someone falling asleep watching TV?" he said, opening the door wide enough for us to enter.

He either didn't know or didn't care that he was within his rights to tell us to go to hell. I expect it was the former, since my nose was assaulted by the reek of marijuana as soon as we walked in the door. Maybe it was that he was nervous about—not being involved in a criminal conspiracy with Jim Chrisler. Neither Keith nor I said anything about the smell. That wasn't why we were there.

The only light was still coming from that upstairs TV. Carter led us down a dark hall into the living room and hit a switch. The room turned an unearthly blue.

"Black light," he explained. For an instant, wall posters glowed in florescent shades of red, blue, green, and pink. He turned on a regular table lamp. Those otherworldly images turned into uninteresting pictures of mushrooms and marijuana leaves and logos of rock bands I'd never heard of.

The only real furniture was the end table the lamp stood on. Where there weren't posters on the walls you could see plywood paneling. The floor was covered with brown wall-to-wall carpet that looked as old as the house.

"Sit down if you want," he said, gesturing towards any of the several large pillows and cushions scattered across the floor. I combined two cushions that looked like they'd once belonged on the same couch and folded them until they approximated a chair. Keith stood in the doorway. Carter dropped onto a giant green vinyl bag that made crunching sounds when he sat on it.

"So who got shot tonight?" he asked.

"You don't know?" I said.

"No, that little cop and those highway patrol guys wouldn't tell."

"I hate to break the news," I said, taking my time to better gauge his reaction, "but it was a friend and business partner of yours. Jim Chrisler."

He sat, frozen. "Who?" he said.

"Jim Chrisler," I repeated.

He shook his head like he was trying to clear it of cobwebs. "No, I mean, who shot him!" he said. "Did you catch him? Please tell me you caught him."

He got up and started pacing like a caged animal. Out of the corner of my eye, I saw Keith move his right hand to the butt of his pistol.

"We didn't catch him," I said. "To tell you the truth, we were thinking it was you who killed Chrisler. Also Frankie Gately and Randy Braley. Maybe even a few others while you were at it."

"You think I killed those people?" he said, leaving space between each word. "I never in my life shot a gun. Never. Not even one time."

That's not something any red-blooded Oklahoma boy was likely to admit, unless, well, someone put a gun to his head. Or maybe if he was afraid of going to the electric chair.

As much as I hate to be wrong, I was beginning to think in this instance I might be. Still, I pressed on, because that's what I do.

"Look at it from our point of view," I said. "You worked either for or with Jim Chrisler, selling drugs. So did Randy Braley. The county sheriff here was investigating Chrisler, weren't you Sheriff Belcher?"

"We were, indeed."

Carter gave Keith a jittery glance, then turned his attention back to me.

"We reckon—or shall I say, I reckon—that you were starting to feel the heat and decided the best thing was to eliminate anyone who could testify against you."

I threw that out there based on my original feeling that it had to be Carter. Who else could it be? Chrisler could've shot Frankie and the Fechners and Travis Ballard. But he didn't shoot himself.

Unfortunately, as was becoming apparent, neither did Sam Carter.

He was involved, though. Somehow, some way.

By now his hair was sweat-soaked. It stuck to his face in long, greasy strings. He shivered like a heifer licking an electric fence. His skin was so pale you could almost see through it. For a second I thought he might faint, then his fearful expression morphed into a crazy grin and he cackled, not like a hyena now, but more like the Wicked Witch of the West. I thought he'd lost what little of his mind he had left.

"You freakin' cops are unbelievable." He stopped pacing directly in front of me, bent down and put his face close to mine. "You don't know, do you?" he almost half-giggled and half-whispered. "You really don't know."

I heard the strap on Keith's holster snap open.

"Tell me," I said.

"Lester Filer. He killed 'em all."

CHAPTER 38

"You're as crazy as you look," I said. "And that's saying something." I thought Carter had to have been the guy and was fingering Lester Filer out of desperation. "Admit it, Sam. You killed all those people because Jim Chrisler told you to." It sounded wrong even as I said it.

Carter wiped his face with the collar of his T-shirt and sat back down on his beanbag. "Unless you're as dumb as you look, you'll find out I didn't kill anyone," he said. "But listen, man, I'm trying to help you. It's Lester Filer you want. He killed 'em all: Gately, Braley, that family in Kingfisher, Travis Ballard. And now Chrisler, I'll bet anything."

"Why?"

"For Chrisler," he said, then paused. "I mean, he didn't shoot Chrisler because Chrisler told him to. He shot Chrisler because he hates him."

"Why?" asked Keith.

"Chrisler has something big on him, I'm not sure what, but it was big enough to get him to do whatever Chrisler wanted him to do. And Chrisler wanted those people gone."

I wasn't surprised to hear Chrisler had those folks killed. He had connections to them all. I'd assumed he'd done it himself, but it made sense that he had someone else do it. I just couldn't believe it was Les.

"Why'd Chrisler want all those people killed?" I asked.

Carter shrugged. "They cheated him," he said. "The woman in Kingfisher embezzled from him. Ballard took money for a shipment and disappeared. I don't know what Braley did, but it must've been something." He sighed. "I'm telling you, Lester did it. And I'm next."

"Why would Lester kill you? Especially now that Chrisler's dead."

"Because I know what he did."

We heard a whistle, then the rumble of a locomotive. The walls began to shake.

"Emmett," said Keith, raising his voice to be heard.

"Yeh?"

"Karen and Kenny were going out to Lester's place."

I've been plenty afraid, plenty of times, but never more than I was at that second.

***

Keith handcuffed Carter and threw him in the back seat. I hit my emergency lights and tried to beat the train to the nearest crossing. I didn't make it. We had to stop and let it pass. It was a freight—we don't get passenger service anymore—and it crept by at a snail's pace. Those bastards can be miles long and there were no shortcuts. All we could do was wait.

After five minutes that seemed like an hour, the caboose passed and the gate rose. I floored it. We were the only car on the road, pegging the speedometer at 120 mph.

I tried to raise George or Bernard or Eugene on the radio, but no one responded. I did not hit the siren.

Never warn an SOB.

We turned onto Lester's long driveway. The house was dark, but a sodium lamp mounted on a telephone pole turned the barnyard and everything in it a sickly yellow. The other Javelin was parked between the house and the barn, facing the latter, exactly as it had been when I visited Lester days earlier. Its emergency lights were flashing, but neither Kenny nor Red were in view.

Keith said, "Let's be careful, bud."

I said, "I'm always careful." Red laughs when I say that. "You *never* are," she'll say.

We came to a stop a few yards from the other Javelin. Keith cuffed Carter to a metal bar attached to the front seat. I grabbed my flashlight. We got out.

I took a moment to survey the scene. The driver's side door was open on the other car. I motioned to Keith that I was going to take a look. He nodded and drew his gun.

A figure lay on the ground next to the cruiser. Kenny, flat on this back. His eyes were open in that sightless way folks have when you're talking to them, but their minds are somewhere else. His left arm lay out to his side, and his right arm was bent like he'd been reaching for his gun. He had wounds in his chest, but I expect it was the shot in the middle of his forehead that killed him.

I felt a stab in my chest, and for a second I thought I was having a heart attack. I thought about telling Lester that dealing with death gets easier, and how that was nothing but wishful thinking. At least it was for me. Dealing with death never gets easier. Especially when the person who dies is someone you love.

I had to push the feeling away for now. There was work to do.

I shouted Karen's name.

Inside the barn, a woman screamed. It wasn't Karen.

A moment passed, then a voice called, "We're alright, Emmett."

That was Karen.

"Is Lester there?" I asked.

There was no response. I was about to ask again when she called out, her voice failing. "He is," she said. "You can come in. It's safe."

I tried the door on the side of the barn. It was locked. We walked around to the big double door in front. Keith stopped me as I grabbed the handle. "Stand to one side, just in case. Don't give him a target."

"You heard the woman. It's safe."

"He could be making her say that."

I might've smiled under different circumstance. "No one makes Karen Hardy say anything she doesn't want to."

I pulled open the doors. In front was an old junker of a blue and white Chevy pickup with the rear window shot out.

The floor was smooth concrete. The room smelled more like an auto-repair shop than a barn. A light shined somewhere in the back. Karen called out: "We're over here, Emmett."

I switched off the flashlight. We could see well enough. In the back of the room was a workbench with a lamp mounted on it. Shannon sat on the floor against the east wall. A pair of handcuffs lay on the floor next to her. She was crying and rubbing her wrists, and her hair was caked with dried blood. But she was alive.

Karen sat against the back wall, a few feet away. As with Shannon, her wrists were red and a set of handcuffs lay on the floor nearby. She wasn't wearing her gun.

Next to Karen sat a tall, painfully thin young man. I remembered he'd once been as handsome as Marlon Brando. Now, however, he seemed an empty, wasted shell. This person wasn't just lovesick. He was physically ravaged. Why hadn't I noticed? Why hadn't I done something?

The man's head rested on my wife's shoulder. His mouth hung open. His eyes were closed, but the rims were red and his cheeks tear-stained. He might've been asleep, but his chest did not rise and fall. I recognized him, of course.

Officer Lester Filer, late of the Burr, Oklahoma Police.

Karen patted him on the leg as if comforting a small child.

His legs stretched in front of him in a V-shape. He wore his khaki uniform pants with the stripes down the legs, but no socks and no shoes. No shirt, either.

Les didn't wear those long sleeves because he was cold.

His left arm extended to his side with the palm facing up. The inner part of the arm was covered in sores from a few inches above his wrist to the crook of his elbow. Some were as small and harmless-looking as mosquito bites. Others were large and scabbed over. Some oozed pus. On the floor next to him was a strange-looking revolver—a Russian Nagant—and a needle and syringe.

Karen was in tears.

"He's gone," she said. "It's over."

CHAPTER 39

Red untangled herself from Lester, careful not to let him slump to the floor. I held out my hand and helped her up. I was relieved she was safe, but I had to wonder why she'd been giving comfort to someone who'd killed more people than I could count—one of them, a man I loved like a son.

Keith used the telephone in the barn to call in his people and the highway patrol. Before long, most of the folks who'd attended the earlier shooting were at this scene as well.

Bernard rolled in first, followed by Eugene. Isabel showed up shortly thereafter, as did the same OSHP watch commander from before. A different forensic van showed up this time. They set up their lights, put on their rubber gloves and got to work. A police photographer jogged from place to place, taking his flash pictures in a hurry, like he couldn't wait to get out of there.

I told my story to those whose job it was to know. So did Karen, Keith, and poor Shannon, who needed emergency care just to calm her nerves.

The medics also tried to help Karen. She wasn't having any of it. A cup of hot coffee was all she'd accept.

The last thing I did before I let Eugene drive me back to town was to say goodbye to Kenny.

I can't tell you how hard that was, so I won't even try.

"We left at the same time everybody else did," Karen began. "Kenny wanted to drive. On the way, he said he'd been a little worried about Lester. Something happened recently that gave him concern. He didn't have time to say what it was." She looked at me. "Did he tell you?"

"No."

"Then I guess we'll never know," she said, her eyes moist, her face red and puffy. "The lights were off when we got there. There wasn't a car or truck in the driveway, so we assumed it had been a wild goose chase, that Lester had gone to visit his girlfriend like you told him to.

"Kenny wanted to check the barn just to make sure. He knocked on the side door. When no one answered, he came back to the car. He opened the door and was about to get in when we heard what sounded like a woman trying to scream with a hand over her mouth. I expect he thought it was Shannon, so he called out her name."

She took a sip of water. Her hands were shaking.

"All of a sudden there was a scream. Loud this time. Kenny'd just started to draw his gun when Lester burst out that side door." She paused and wiped her eyes. "He shot Kenny. Didn't even say a word. It happened so fast, the poor boy didn't know what hit him." She paused to compose herself. "At least I hope he didn't."

"Do you want to take a break, Karen?" asked Isabel.

"No, let's get this over with. I'll be fine."

She's tough, that one.

"I couldn't get my own gun out in time. Lester jerked me out of the car. He made me take off my gun belt and had me throw it on the front seat. He pushed me into the barn. Shannon was sitting on the floor, handcuffed to a pipe. She was crying and shivering but didn't say anything. I told her everything was going to be all right.

"I saw that blue and white pickup with its back window shot out, and I recognized that Nagant pistol he was using from the pictures you found at the library, Emmett. I was dazed, but everything clicked. Lester was who we'd been looking for the whole time.

"He handcuffed me to another pipe, different from Shannon's. He still hadn't said a word. I saw those horrible sores all over his arm and asked where they came from. He laughed and walked over to that work bench. 'This,' he said, and held up a syringe.

"I tried, but I couldn't get him to talk about it. He just sat at that workbench with his back turned. I didn't know it at the time, but he was preparing his shot or whatever he does to get high. After a while, I asked what he was going to do with Shannon and me. He said he hadn't decided yet. I told him to keep me if he needed a hostage, to let Shannon go, but he didn't answer.

"I wanted to talk him out of hurting anyone else. I said he was sick and that we'd get him help. I didn't know what to say, so I tried everything I could think of. I asked about his family, and where he was from, and if he was sorry he decided to become a cop instead of a preacher. Sometimes he'd laugh to himself. Mostly, he was just quiet. Finally, I asked him about his girlfriend. That's when he broke."

"What do you mean by that?" asked Isabel.

"Broke down. Wailed. He threw a hammer at his truck, knocked out a headlight. He started crying and clawing at those sores on his arms and making them bleed, like he was trying to hurt himself on purpose. I was afraid I'd only made things worse, but he seemed to calm down. 'Let me tell you about my girlfriend, Mrs. Hardy,' he said, kind of laughing and crying at the same time. 'In fact, how about I tell you everything? Would you mind if I did that?' I said of course I wouldn't mind if that's what he wanted.

"So that's what he did."

CHAPTER 40

"He told me his story," said Karen. "About his girlfriend, about why he became a cop, why he decided not to become a preacher. It turns out, everything we thought we knew about him was a lie."

"Lying's the least of what he did," I said.

"Maybe. But you can't separate the lies from the rest of it." She shook her head. "You just can't."

Those of us crowded into my office—Keith, Isabel, and myself—waited for her to elaborate.

"Lester's daddy was a preacher. His folks raised Lester to follow in his footsteps. 'I never thought about doing anything else,' he said. Everybody just took for granted that's what he was going to do. This little girl, Marta went to his father's church. She and Lester knew each other all their lives. They went together all the way through high school and got engaged right before Lester went off to college. The plan was they'd get married after he graduated and got his own church.

"The trouble was, Lester loved that little girl, but he already knew he didn't want to be a preacher. Marta's folks were even more religious than his own. They didn't like Lester except for the fact he was going be a minister like his daddy. The girl wouldn't marry him without her parents' approval. Lester figured he'd have to follow through if he wanted to get the girl, so he went to bible college."

"So far I'm not hearing anything that excuses what he did," I said.

Isabel gave me an annoyed look.

"Sorry to interrupt," I said. "Go on."

"He took classes to learn how to be a Baptist minister," she continued, "but the whole time he felt like he was lying to everybody. His folks, Marta, her parents, and God. Especially God. He wanted to find a way out of being a preacher, yet still get the girl, just in case he decided one day that he couldn't go through with the original plan.

"That's when he discovered his college had a criminal justice program. He thought perhaps the girl and her parents would consider a career in law enforcement a decent substitute for being a minister. So he began criminal justice courses as a safety valve."

I'd heard some of this when he interviewed. "At least that part of what he told us was true," I said.

Red nodded. "Eventually, he changed his major, but he couldn't bring himself to tell anyone. As far as his family and Marta and her family knew, he was still on track to be a minister. He knew his decision would disappoint his folks, but he was more worried that Marta would break it off when she found out.

"He finally told her a few months before he was scheduled to graduate. She said still wanted to marry him, but it depended on what her parents had to say. They were against it, so she broke it off. And broke his heart."

She took another sip of water. Her hand was steadier than before.

"Lester fell apart. He drank heavily for a while, then a so-called friend told him he had something that'd ease his pain better than alcohol."

"Heroin," said Isabel.

Red nodded. "He tried it and got hooked. His parents disowned him when they found out he wasn't going to be a preacher, so he didn't have anywhere to go. He lived on the streets until he got disgusted with himself and got help. It took the better part of a year, but he kicked the habit. There was still that compulsion, though. He said it never went away, not completely."

That sounded familiar.

"Anyway," she went on, "he wasn't on drugs when he started with us. He kept straight for a considerable time. Then one day he caught Randy Braley pulled over to the side of a county road, shooting something into his arm. Les meant to take him in, but when he saw that heroin, something clicked inside him. He told Braley he wouldn't arrest him if he shared his stuff. From there everything went downhill in a hurry."

***

I don't know how long Karen talked. Hours, maybe. Lester had a lot to tell, and she didn't want to leave anything out. What she didn't say, I managed to piece together from what I already knew or would shortly find out.

After the traffic stop, Braley went to the fella he was working for—Jim Chrisler—and told him about what had happened. Chrisler knew having a cop on a leash could come in handy. He approached Lester and told him he knew about the transaction with Braley. He threatened to go to me about it. Lester should've known better, in my opinion. Had Chrisler followed through on his threat, he would've had to incriminate himself. But Les didn't see it that way. Not only did he feel trapped, he craved the heroin. He was hooked again. Chrisler told him if he worked for him, he'd provide him with all the junk he needed. He'd just have to do Chrisler a favor now and then. So Lester went along.

For a while, Chrisler didn't ask him to do much of anything, although he did supply him with heroin. As Lester's addiction got worse, Chrisler started holding back. He'd give Lester some, but not enough. Lester would beg for more. Chrisler told him if he wanted more, he'd have to work for it.

By that point, Lester would've done anything.

His first job for Chrisler was to break into a pawn shop and steal a specific gun, a Russian Nagant revolver. A Nagant isn't the kind of gun you just waltz into your neighborhood gun store and buy. They're rare in this country. Chrisler knew about a pawn shop in Broken Bow that had one for sale. He sent Lester to steal it. Why it had to be a Nagant ... well, I guess Chrisler took that to his grave.

After stealing the gun, Chrisler instructed Lester to check into a particular hotel in Idabel, 12 miles from Broken Bow. He was then supposed to telephone Chrisler for further instructions.

Lester drove his old blue junker pickup to Broken Bow. He broke into the pawn shop in the middle of the night and stole the Nagant, along with some ammo. He drove to Idabel, checked into the hotel, and called Chrisler. Chrisler gave him a room number. He told him to sneak in and kill the occupant using the stolen gun. The occupant was Travis Ballard. Ballard had stolen money from Chrisler, then disappeared. Chrisler tracked him down. He wasn't the forgiving type. He wanted Ballard dead.

Lester tried to argue his way out of it. It was no use. He wasn't about to kill Ballard in the motel room, however, so he snatched him at gunpoint and drove him a few miles out of town. He shot him and left him in a culvert.

Given where the body was found, it made sense that folks assumed Ballard had been hitchhiking. The fact that it was Lester also squares with what Isabel told me about a beat-up old blue pickup being seen in the vicinity the night of the murder.

That was the last "favor" Lester did for a while. Chrisler gave him the drugs he needed, and Lester kept things together. Before long, however, Chrisler started holding out on him again.

He had another job for Lester.

Patsy Fechner was Chrisler's accountant. Chrisler was her only client. She laundered his money. Don't ask me how. In fact, don't ask me how a wife and mother living in a little town like Kingfisher ends up doing the books for a drug dealer. There's probably a good story in it, but this ain't that story.

Chrisler was nothing if not paranoid. I reckon he had good reason to be. In any case, he started to suspect Patsy was embezzling from him. Whether she was or not, Lester didn't know. All he knew was, according to Chrisler, she had to be killed.

Lester drove to Kingfisher on one of his nights off, snuck into her house, and shot her in her bed. Using the Nagant, of course. Her husband was lying next to her, so he got it, too. When Les came out of their room, their little girl was standing in the hall looking up at him. Les panicked and shot her, too.

Again—as Isabel later learned—a neighbor of the Fechners remembered seeing a beat-up old blue pickup parked on their street the night of the killings.

Ballistic evidence determined that the same gun was used in both the Ballard and Fechner homicides. In fact, the Oklahoma State Bureau of Investigation narrowed it down to the one stolen from the Broken Bow pawn shop. In the beginning, there appeared to be nothing linking the two crimes except the gun and the sighting of an old blue pickup. With nothing logical tying the murders together, they were forced to speculate—the consensus being, the killer was some kind of sicko who got a kick out of killing people.

That suited Jim Chrisler just fine. In fact, it was probably part of his plan. If the cops thought the perp was a spree killer, he figured they'd be unlikely to come after some guy running a foosball parlor. Or his triggerman, who by day worked as a small-town cop.

Lester's addiction worsened and his state of mind continued to deteriorate. He managed to hide it from us, for the most part. To my everlasting shame, it wasn't until after he'd "found" Frankie Gately that I noticed something was bothering him. I thought I knew what it was. I was way off base. My renewed acquaintance with the bottle undoubtedly had something to do with that.

Chrisler was right up there with Les when it came to losing his marbles. He decided Randy Braley would be the next to go. Chrisler suspected Braley of stealing product, which he almost certainly was. He also distrusted Braley's friendship with Frankie. Frankie was close to Kenny. Kenny was a cop. What if Braley blabbed to Frankie and Frankie blabbed to Kenny?

In Chrisler's mind, both Braley and Frankie had to be dealt with. He gave Lester new marching orders.

He wanted Lester to pull over Braley and tell him Chrisler was afraid Frankie knew too much about the drug operation. Les would tell Braley to pick up Frankie that night, then meet him—Lester—at an old barn south of town. Supposedly, Les and Braley would scare the boy into keeping quiet.

The real plan was for Lester to kill them both.

Braley didn't know that, of course, nor did he sense any urgency in Lester's request. That night, when Frankie got to be too much of a handful, Braley dumped him at Chrisler's. He then kept his appointment with Lester. I'm sure getting shot took him by surprise. Lester took the body home and cut it up in his bathtub. He stuffed the pieces in a couple of large plastic garbage bags and hid them under the floorboards of that old abandoned house behind Laverne Colley's place—where, days later, her little dachshund Burt Reynolds discovered them.

Meanwhile, at Family Fun Center, Chrisler kicked out Frankie for allegedly harassing a girl. As we'd suspected (and later pieced together), he gave Frankie a head start of a couple of minutes then chased after him. He lured Frankie into his car and drove around looking for Lester, who was busy killing Braley and hiding the body. Eventually, Chrisler found Lester and gave him Frankie. He told Les there'd been a change in plan. He wanted Frankie shot at the 89er Drive In. Sam Carter needed to be sent a message.

After the movie was over and the place had cleared out, Lester drove to the back of the lot and shot Frankie in the head. Frankie knew what was about to happen and tried to run away. Les chased after him. When he got close, Frankie threw rocks. When Frankie couldn't find another rock to throw, he took out his wallet and threw that.

The little boy's wallet with the Foreman Scotty Club membership card.

That brings us to the final act of this lunatic exercise. Chrisler calls Lester, tells him Shannon's about to squeal, and needs to be killed. Lester tells him he's running out of junk. Chrisler says, kill Shannon and I'll give you some. Lester says, give me some junk and I'll kill Shannon. Chrisler says, fine, come get it. Lester says he can't drive into town because he's supposed to be in Kansas. They go back and forth. Chrisler finally agrees to make the drive and gives Lester the drugs.

Lester abducts Shannon. He takes her home and handcuffs her to a pipe in his barn. He then gives himself a shot and passes out. The telephone wakes him up hours later. It's Chrisler phoning from the foosball parlor—the call Keith and I let him make before we took him in. Chrisler tells Lester he's being arrested. Les needs to come down to the station and shoot me and Keith, or Chrisler's going to tell everyone about Lester's drug use and the people he's killed.

Lester's had enough. He drives to town in his old junker blue pickup. What happened, happened. There's no need to rehash the rest. Like Karen said: He's gone. It's over.

***

"When he finished, he said he was tired and sorry and was going to kill himself," said Karen. "My God, I'm so sorry, but I couldn't bring myself to try to talk him out of it."

She stopped. For a second I wasn't sure she'd be able to finish, but finish she did.

"He undid our handcuffs and sat on the floor beside me. He wrapped a belt around his arm and poked around until he found a place to stick the needle. He was in so much pain."

She paused again. We waited.

"It was all infected and bloody where he'd been scratching himself," she said. "It didn't take long for him to pass out." She couldn't hold back the tears any longer. "Before he did, though, Emmett ... before he did ... he called out for his mama. I'm sorry, but that broke my heart. I hugged him."

Isabel moved a box of Kleenex where Karen could reach it. She took one and dabbed at those beautiful green eyes of hers and trained them on me. "I mean, he was in so much pain," she pleaded. "Do you understand?"

"I think I do."

How could I not?

She took a huge, shuddering breath and exhaled. "I tried to give him some comfort," she said, her voice a husky whisper. "Nobody should die alone if they don't have to. Even someone like Les."

Next to me, Isabel added: "Maybe even *especially* someone like Les."

CHAPTER 41

For a couple of weeks, the eyes of the state—heck, the eyes of the whole country—were trained on us. Mass murders are big news, whether they happen in Chicago, Vietnam, or Burr, Oklahoma. All the TV networks sent people. Walter Cronkite didn't come, but I recognized a colleague of his I'd seen reporting from Memphis on the assassination of Dr. Martin Luther King back in '68.

Pretty soon, all those folks went back where they came from, and things started getting back to a version of normal. Needless to say, what was normal before and what became normal afterward were a lot different. I reckon that's what happens to a town like ours when it's dragged kicking and screaming into one of the more terrifying corners of the 20th century.

After everything that had happened, the only person left to prosecute was Sam Carter. The DA charged him as an accessory to murder in the Frankie Gately case, knowing it probably wouldn't stick, and was happy when Carter's attorney agreed to a plea deal for possession with intent to distribute. The 89er is closed and up for sale. Last I heard, there hadn't been any offers. I hear a lot of people are interested in the shoe house, though.

Shannon Gately wasn't charged with anything, although she probably could've been. Karen had a talk with her about sniffing glue. Shannon said she just tried it once, with Randy, and didn't like it. It gave her a terrible headache, she said, and promised never to do it again. She left town soon after, so I guess we'll never know if she kept her word.

Lester's body was sent home to Kansas for burial. I couldn't bring myself to talk to his parents or his ex-girlfriend. I'm pretty sure they wouldn't have cared to talk to me, either.

No one claimed Chrisler's body. I believe it's still in cold storage somewhere. The doors to the foosball place are chained shut. A lot of people think it should be torn down. I'm one of them.

I'm still doing what I can to earn back Karen's trust. A condition of her forgiveness was that I attend meetings in the basement of her church once a week. I reckon one day soon I'll be standing in front of a group of strangers struggling with the same problem as mine, saying: "Hi, my name is Emmett and I'm an alcoholic."

Agent Isabel Cruickshank gave birth to a healthy baby boy a week after the events I've described. I met her husband for the first time when I visited her in the hospital. He's a nice enough fella. Isabel tells me he wants her to quit her job, stay home, and care for the baby. She's thinking about it. I hope she stays with the Bureau. I enjoy working with her.

By the way, they named their little boy Kenneth. I didn't ask if it was in honor of our Kenny, but knowing her, I'll bet it was.

I flashed my brand-new permit to the fella guarding the town dump and heaved the Champion Jack Dupree tape as far onto the pile as my achy right arm would allow. I still listen to a lot of the other music Kenny introduced me to, but after all that's happened, I'm in no mood for songs about drugs and degradation.

Officer Kenneth Chitto Harjo's funeral was held in Muscogee, Oklahoma, his hometown, but we had a memorial service for him here. Most of the old-time Burr-ites came out. I say "old-time." Folks who moved here recently to work in the oil fields, and the Cudahy plant, and the livestock auction place never knew him and had no reason to come. A lot of those who did come were people who'd given him grief when he started with us, because he was an Indian. I'd like to think the fact they attended his memorial service meant they'd become less bigoted, and that Kenny's example had something to do with that. Lord knows, he was as fine and as honest a man as I've ever met. To know him was to love him. I only wish I'd worked harder at knowing him better.

At his funeral, I got into a conversation with one of Kenny's uncles—an elaborately wrinkled old fella who, I later learned, had worked in Pawnee

Bill's Wild West Show as a child, around the turn of the century. He told me Kenny was especially interested in the folklore of his tribe, the Creek, or, as he called them, the Muscogee. One of Kenny's favorite folktales was called The Thunder Helper. I can't tell it as well as that gentleman did, but I'll do my best:

There was a young Muscogee boy who liked to go on hikes by himself. One day, he was walking in the forest when he came upon Tie-Snake wrapped around the neck of Thunder. Tie-Snake was an evil spirit, and he intended to drag Thunder into the underworld. The boy shot Tie-Snake with a bow and arrow, and Thunder was saved. Thunder rewarded the boy by making him strong, brave, and wise. Even though he was just a boy, he became one of the most respected members of his tribe. One day, the people got word a group of marauders were on their way to destroy the village. They sent the boy out to defend them. The village was saved, but the boy never came back. He lives on, though. The tribe's elders say they can see his face in the lightning and hear his voice in the thunder.

Here in Oklahoma we get so many storms you almost don't notice. I reckon from here on out I'll have to start paying closer attention.

ABOUT THE AUTHOR

In addition to being a writer, Chris Kelsey is an accomplished jazz saxophonist, composer, and educator. The Oklahoma native currently lives in Dutchess County, New York, with his wife Lisa.

Note from the Author

Word-of-mouth is crucial for any author to succeed. If you enjoyed *Junker Blues*, please leave a review online—anywhere you are able. Even if it's just a sentence or two. It would make all the difference and would be very much appreciated.

Thanks!
Chris Kelsey

We hope you enjoyed reading this title from:

BLACK✿ROSE
writing™

www.blackrosewriting.com

Subscribe to our mailing list – *The Rosevine* – and receive **FREE** books, daily deals, and stay current with news about upcoming releases and our hottest authors.
Scan the QR code below to sign up.

Already a subscriber? Please accept a sincere thank you for being a fan of Black Rose Writing authors.

View other Black Rose Writing titles at
www.blackrosewriting.com/books and use promo code
PRINT to receive a **20% discount** when purchasing.